BEAUTIFUL TORTURE

by

C. P. MANDARA

Published by **Chimera Books**
ISBN 9781780806846

Beauty is unbearable, drives us to despair, offering us for a minute the glimpse of an eternity that we should like to stretch out over the whole of time. Albert Camus

Chapter 1 - Harper: *Two years ago*

My face whips around one-hundred-and-eighty degrees. For a moment, I am blinded. My face stings like it's on fire and the burn rises up through my eyes and down into my neck. The backhander I've just been given is brutally hard and disorientating, driving me instantly to my knees.

"Get up," he barks. I stumble back to my feet. There are punishments for disobedience, and they are much worse than the one I've just received. When he's in this mood, I need to do everything he says. It's the only way to limit the damage. If not, I'll be driven to my bed for most of next week, and the last thing I need to be is helpless before this man.

"Have you got the package ready?" He's advancing towards me again, waiting for another opportunity to strike. I'm not going to give him one. I learnt the hard way that I need to be obedient and dutiful at all times.

"Yes," I whisper. I know my role. The package was prepared almost the instant he told me about it, and I have been waiting to deliver it ever since. Nausea swims in my bloodstream at the thought of what's ahead, but barely a day goes by where I don't upend the contents of my stomach, so that's nothing new.

"Good." Alex pats my head. "If Mal wants you to sweeten the deal you know what to do, don't you darling?" His fingers tangle in my hair, and he tugs at my roots, drawing my head back until his face looms over me.

"Yes." I know exactly what to do. If I'm told to drop to my knees and am presented with his cock, I suck it. If I'm told to spread my legs wide and masturbate in front of his friends, I plaster a smile upon my face and give them a good show. If they want to watch while I'm sandwiched between half a dozen men, with fingers and cocks in every hole, I'll take that, too. My mouth is rarely used for talking, and I know exactly who is in charge of me at all times.

"Then what are you waiting for? Get that shit on the road." Alex spins me around and slaps my ass hard, making me stagger forward on my spike heels. I'm amazed I haven't managed to bust one this evening, but perhaps that will come later. I've heard Mal is an evil bastard, and I'm under no illusions that I'll come out of this transaction the same way I went in. The girls all shudder in horror whenever his name is mentioned, so I already know I'm not going to like him much. Most of the men in this business are dark and depraved, and I've come to expect that, but Mal is reputed to be the worst of the worst. I've been fortunate enough not to meet him until now, but my honeymoon period with Alex is officially over. It's time to earn my keep, or so he informs me. What he really means is that we've got to the stage where he doesn't really give a shit if someone shoots me.

Nodding, I say, "Tell him I'll be with him immediately." My voice is devoid of all expression, mostly because I'm dead inside. Where once upon a time there was a warm, beating heart, there now resides a burnt offering of cinders and ashes. The merest breath between my ribcage would blow my house of cards over. I'm living a lie, and I'm one step away from prison or something far worse at all times. Alex says prison is not a safe haven for me, anyway. He knows people on the inside. People who could kill me and make it hurt. Thugs who could drag my death out for days, or butcher everyone who's close to me. I don't disbelieve him for a second. I've met some bad people in this industry, and I've seen some scary shit. I am one step away from suicide at all times, but I don't have enough courage to take the plunge. It's going to be the death of me.

Alex picks up the phone and in lowered tones, lets Mal know I'm coming. I'm already halfway out of the door before his voice halts me.

"I haven't checked the goods yet, sweetheart." As my back is towards him I close my eyes. The last thing I need is his hands on me before I'm about to do a job, but Alex trusts no one, least of all me.

"Of course, darling. I'm sorry." Turning around with another one of my plastic smiles, I feel my face stretch so tight I fear it might break. Still, with any luck this won't take but a moment. Walking towards him once again with sharp clicks of my heels, I don't stop until our bodies are touching. My pulse is rocking wildly, and I know he'll be able to feel it, but I swear that turns him on. Alex is a sick bastard in every way that counts.

When my eyes reach his I'm sure he can almost see the panic swirling in them, but that's not what he's interested in right now. We always play this game just before I walk out of the door. He's a bit like a dog marking his territory by pissing on every street corner. He needs to mark me as his before some other fucker gets his hands on me. Just to make sure I know what the consequences of defying him are. Believe me, I know. We've been through this routine so many times before, I could almost tell him what he's about to do before he does it. Call me clairvoyant, why don't you.

Trying to control my breathing, so I'm not panting out loud in his face, I wait patiently. Alex likes to make people wait. He enjoys making them uncomfortable, and he loves seeing them sweat. I've seen this game one too many times before, though. He knows I'm on edge, but that's all he's getting from me.

When the silence feels like it's stretched out longer than all the completed seasons of Smallville, the man finally begins to roll up my dress. *Just get on with it, asshole.* The cheap red viscose that clings to my thighs is pushed up towards my hips, and Alex is uncaring of who sees me like this. In fact, this is small fry for him. He often parades me around naked in front of his friends, just because he can. Even though the asshole whores me out to whoever he chooses, his friends know better than to touch me without his permission. You do not cross Alex Wilkinson. If you do, you aren't around long enough to breathe a word of it to anyone. Still, I made my bed. While I knew dating Alex wasn't one of the smartest decisions I would make in my life, the other options at the time hadn't looked promising. Rock plus hard place equals hideous consequences.

When the whole of my lower body is on display, Alex brushes a hand up the inside of my thigh. I moan softly. This isn't because I'm aroused. It's because if I don't I'll get into more trouble than I can handle. I discovered a few months ago that Alex and I would never be equals. My job is to look pretty, spread my legs when ordered, and be his very convenient drugs mule. If I can do all of that without complaint and look fairly enthusiastic about it, the black eyes and broken ribs are kept to a minimum. Hospital stays aren't on the cards for me, so I need to keep the internal bleeding to a minimum.

"Are you wet for me, love?" Love. Now there's a word. Alex doesn't know how to love. He knows how to push people around, bully and castrate them, though. You think I'm kidding? I've seen him do it. If you're one of Alex's mules, you don't lose your cargo. If I ever lose mine, I'll have to kill myself. There's no way I'll wait for him to finish me off.

"I'm always wet for you, sweetheart," I purr. Yet another lie leaves my mouth, but thankfully I won't get called on it. The amount of lube I've thrust into my vagina to enable myself to cart his heroin about is fairly impressive, and he won't be able to tell the difference. Alex thinks I'm a walking hot mess for his cock, but nothing could be further from the truth. I might have been hot for the bastard at the beginning, but that was a long time ago. Any lust I might have felt for him has long since left, but I've found ways to cope with his madness. It's survive or die around these halls.

When his fingers thrust inside me they find a cylindrical shape wrapped in crinkly plastic - very firmly, I might add. If that stuff escapes the two freezer bag's worth of plastic I've parcelled it up in, I'm a goner. I'm not absolutely positive whether the heroin could be absorbed into my bloodstream from down there, but I do know I don't want to find out.

"Come see me when you get back, darling," he growls, his eyes lighting up with the thought of sinking his fangs into me later. That will be the absolute last thing I need after tackling Mal, so I'll just have to hope he does a 'Speedball' (a really dangerous mix of heroin and cocaine) and crashes out on the sofa. It seems to be his new 'thing', and anything that keeps him away from my body is A-OK with me.

"Will do, sweetheart," I say, pressing my lips to his. Will I ever. I'll be tiptoeing my way around our apartment with the lights out when we get back. There's only so many times you can be fucked over in a day without being committed to the nearest mental asylum - not that he'd allow it.

Grabbing my ass with a ferocious squeeze, he leers down at my boobs before pushing me away.

"Get on with it. The sooner it's done, the sooner you'll be back." He waves me away with a casual flick of his hand and walks out of the room. It's nice to see he's worried about my safety with one of the most notorious drug lords London has ever seen. I didn't even get a 'Good luck.' Let's hope I don't need one.

Mal's headquarters, if they can be called that, are located on the outskirts of town in Bexley. His building is a big, corrugated iron shed that looks like someone's dropped a bomb on it. The roof is rusting so badly that when I get inside, I'm pretty sure I'll be able to see daylight through it. It must be cold as hell in there in winter. Perhaps that's why he chose it. It's certainly a good way to keep uninvited guests at bay.

When I approach the wooden door that's falling off its hinges, I suddenly have a bad feeling about this. It's eleven pm, I'm waddling along with a packet of heroine shoved up my nether regions, and I'm about to go chat with one of the East End's most notorious villains. What could go wrong? Everything - that's what. Still, it's not as if I have a choice. I can't run, I have no money, and Alex has men everywhere. They'll find me and gut me. I have to do this.

Raising my hand up to the door, noting that the interior is dark, I pray that someone's made a mistake and he isn't here today. Who knows? Perhaps Alex can send someone else in my place tomorrow? A sliver of hope squirms in my chest as my fist bangs three times against the wood. I wait patiently for an answer but hear nothing bar the faint hum of cars in the distance. Maybe my luck is in, after all. Banging once more on the door, when I hear no response, I turn around to leave.

"Oo are ya, and what are ya doing 'ere?" The accent is a thick cockney one and comes from behind me. Spinning around with my heart in my mouth, I take a step back in shock. Holy fuck. There's a man standing behind me in a black suit and tie, and he looks like Jason Statham from Transporter. He's mostly bald, has a day's worth of stubble, and if looks could kill I'd already be in the mortuary. I can see his hand reaching underneath his jacket for what I'm guessing is a gun, and I don't want to give him a reason to use it.

"Harper. Harper Wilkinson. Alex sent me." I hope to hell Alex told him my name because if not, I'm guessing I'll shortly be buried six feet under. At least it will be quick. I hope.

"'Arper?" It's a common fact that no one this side of London can pronounce an 'H' worth a damn. He looks at me confused for a moment, as I hop from one foot to another trying to stay warm. The cheap jacket I've thrown over my dress is made of cotton, and it'd be fine anywhere nearing the equator, but is utterly useless in England. There is no point asking my husband for a replacement, though.

"That's me," I confirm, nodding for effect. His gaze darkens.

"Do you 'ave my dirt?" His eyebrows raise and his lips flatten. I can tell just by looking at him that he's one cruel motherfucker. There are certain people in this world you should never mess with, and Mal is one of them.

"I do," I say, hoping to hell that 'dirt' is slang for heroin. I've heard a lot of terms for it before, but that's a new one.

"Good." He then reaches past me to open a rusty wooden door that squeals in pain. The sound makes my teeth clench and my ears bleed, but a firm hand is pressing against my back, ushering me inside the dark interior.

Lights snap on in the form of two massive halogen strips and Mal strides off. Looking around, I figure I'm in a workshop of sorts. There's welding and cutting tools everywhere. Maybe this place is a front for car body work repairs? Who knows? Stepping over the various debris that litters the concrete floor, I stroll forward on my spike heels. I'm going to break an ankle if I'm not careful, but I realise that's the least of my worries.

Following Mal to the small room at the back, I watch as he opens the door and beckons me inside impatiently. I realise my mistake seconds later. The room is warm. We're in a bedroom. There's a single wicker chair, a bedside table, a sink, and a double bed. On the table there's a half-opened bottle of Jack and two glasses, both of which still have whisky inside them. The room smells damp and stale, and I'm guessing it doesn't get much of an airing as there are no windows. Unless I'm much mistaken, I'm trapped. There's no one around here for a mile or two, and no one will come running if they hear screams. Hell, I'm in the part of town where they're almost expected. Fuck.

"Want a drink?" Mal looks at me expectantly. I'm a done deal. My darling husband has whored me out yet again, and I'm expected to perform. This is not what I signed up for. Every time I strip and have a stranger's hands all over me all I want to do is vomit, but I've learned to control the reaction. If Alex hears I've misbehaved he takes it out on me with his fists. That can mean anything from sassing one of his colleagues, to retching upon someone's cock. I'm beaten for the tiniest infractions. Alex doesn't really need an excuse to let his hands and feet fly, but he always seems to find one. I've given up trying to avoid them and have almost accepted my place in society.

I have fewer rights than the doormat in front of our apartment, and just like the doormat, people wipe their feet all over me.

Chapter 2 - Brandt

When my alarm goes off at crazy o'clock, I rub my hands over my eyes and curse at the world in general. The last place I want to go to this morning is New York, and the last person I want to see is Helena, but no one cares what I want these days. All everyone cares about is 'saving face' or limiting the damage my disgrace might have caused them. This is doubly insulting when you consider that if my parents had thought to throw a decent lawyer at me, I might not have been sent to prison in the first place. It wasn't as if they were short of a bob or two.

Reaching over to my nightstand I grab my phone and switch it on. I'm not expecting any messages, but I want to go through the news before I get up and face the world. In prison you only get to find out about current affairs by watching the TV, and more often than not the telly is focused on sport. Darts, football, rugby, cricket, boxing, WWE, MMA, tennis and even golf have the inmates' rapt attention - but not much else. Current affairs don't seem to be a high priority when you're on the inside looking out.

When my phone bleeps at me I blink and struggle upwards. I think that's the tone for a text message, so I'd better see who's on fire. It better not be Gabriel. If it is, Harper's on her own for the next couple of days, and knowing my little princess she'll probably knock herself unconscious or do something equally as stupid the minute my head is turned.

Thankfully, it's not Gabriel. It's Simmons. Scanning through the brief message I find out I'm not going to New York after all. When my parents tried to get me a visa it was refused due to my current status as an ex-con. There is a God. Actually, scrap that, because this means Helena will have to come to the UK to visit me, and sure enough, Simmons confirms this in the next couple of sentences. I'm to go to her parents' house this evening. Her parents are inviting me to dinner, no less. This has all the hallmarks of being an epic disaster. I have to remind myself that it's just a meeting. No one is getting married - yet.

It's not all bad news, though. If I'm still in the UK I can get back to Harper ahead of schedule. Even if I can't catch a flight back home this evening, I'll be able to get a train or a hire a car. The train will probably be my best bet. At least I'll be able to get some sleep. Otherwise, I'll be driving forever and dead to the world by the time I arrive home. We wouldn't want that, would we? I'm sure Harper's anxiously awaiting my arrival and counting down the hours until I return. That reminds me, I'd better call Gabriel and tell him he's off the hook. Ringing his cell, I'm not surprised when no one answers, seeing as it's three-thirty a.m., but I leave him a message. He'll get it when he wakes up. Harper will be able to cope on her own for a day. It's too bad if she can't. If she wants to lay those little fists of hers into my chest when I get back I'm pretty sure I'll enjoy it - along with everything else I'm going to heap upon her.

Skimming towards the end of the text, I find out that I've been volunteered to pick Helena up from the airport. My lips twist. Why is nothing in my life ever easy? That is the last thing I need. Still, at least I can go back to bed for the foreseeable future. She doesn't arrive until four p.m., thank God. My head then crashes back into the pillow and within seconds, I'm once again dead to the world.

Where are you? My phone dings and vibrates with the arrival of a text message, which is just as well because the noise in Gatwick airport's arrival hall rivals that of an exploding volcano. Kids are screaming, suitcases are rushing by one after the other, and everyone around me is trying their best to yell so they can be heard above the cacophony of sound. Most of the people waiting here are excited to meet loved ones, but I'm not one of them. I just want to get this farce over with.

Waiting in the arrival hall. You'd have thought Helena could figure that out all by herself, but nothing's guaranteed where she's concerned. Honestly? Shop lifting in Harrods? The place is wired with CCTV and security guards are everywhere. It's not exactly the first port of call in the shoplifter's handbook. As to the accidental pregnancy, I have no words. I hope someone's checked her out for STD's, not that I'll need to worry on that score. There's as much chance of me sleeping with Donald Trump as there is Helena Foster-Lyle, and if I'm honest, I think I'd rather sleep with Trump.

Well, who is going to carry my suitcases?!! There are several frowning emoticons after that text, as well as a couple of exclamation marks. This is going to get tedious very quickly.

Tell you what, I'll just jump through customs and run like lightning past the security guards lining the doors. Prince Charming has nothing on me. Don't panic, babe - I'm putting on my superhero costume as we speak. What the fuck is this woman on? Can't she lift a suitcase by herself? Is she afraid she'll break a nail? I then remind myself that she's pregnant and probably shouldn't be carrying things. If this is the case then I will virtually slap myself in the face, and hope she has enough brain cells to ask a passer-by to help her out.

Would you do that for me? I get smiley faces this time and love hearts. I kid you not. Love hearts. I know what your game is, Helena, and it's not going to wash. I've seen you at work.

No. Get your ass out of there, Helena. We're on a schedule here.

I then add, *Get a luggage trolley and ask an airport official to give you a hand.* Even though she is smart enough to figure that one out all by herself, I play along with her act. Thankfully I hear nothing more, and twenty minutes later she breezes through customs looking like she's just stepped out of a glamour magazine.

What the hell? This is not the Helena Foster-Lyle I remember. Mind you, I've been inside for the past five years. A lot can change in that time, and believe me, it has. Helena has made quite the transformation. I remember her as slightly nerdy with straggly, mousy brown hair, a wardrobe full of different colour cardigans, and a pair of oversize black spectacles that took up most of her face. Her favourite pastimes were dressing her pet Chihuahua in bright pink bows and horse riding. That was then. Now she is a tanned blonde bombshell, with curves in all the right places - including some aesthetically enhanced ones, if I'm not much mistaken. She's wearing a slinky wool dress, Chanel shades, and enough red lipstick to stop traffic. My eyes blink several times as she walks towards me, waggling her manicured fingernails breezily in the air.

She recognises me immediately, which I find odd. I'm twice the size of the man she knew, and I'd be the first person to admit I've changed quite a bit. Mind you, I recognised her as well, and that's saying something.

"Darling, it's so good to see you. You look amazing," she trills at me. Her voice is a pitch too high to be comfortably heard, but I manage not to wince.

"Helena, what the fuck is going on here? The stupid act might wash on your parents, but I know better. Shoplifting? Really? You couldn't come up with anything better than that?" My eyebrows raise.

"Needs must when the devil drives, darling. Why, what's your problem? I don't see a whole queue of girls lining up to marry you. You should be thankful I took pity on your sorry ass." Helena hands the luggage trolley to me and I push it reluctantly. The thing weighs about two tonnes and is almost as reluctant to move as Michel Barnier is on Brexit. Seriously, there are four suitcases piled up high on it, and the excess baggage charge for those beasts must have equalled the UK's national debt.

"I don't need anyone to take pity on me, Helena. I'm more than capable of looking after myself." If I could get through five years' worth of prison, the real world should be a cinch in comparison.

"Without Mummy and Daddy's money? Who'd want to do that? Come now, marriage won't be so bad." Her voice is horribly patronising. She then puts her arm on my shoulder and this time I do wince, although she can't see it as she's behind me.

"If you were so worried about your parents' money it might have been an idea to stay on the right side of the law, and not get yourself knocked up," I say dryly.

"Kettle, pot, black," she responds glibly, and giggles. I see red. Fucking Harper. That woman has so much to answer for.

"While we're on the subject of misdeeds," I say, seeking retaliation, "who is the father?" Knowing Helena, she's probably got herself knocked up by some cocaine sniffing R&B star. It's certainly someone who's pissed off her parents, else she'd be marrying him right now.

"None of your business," she sing-songs in my ear, while reaching for a mirror compact and checking her reflection in it. I take a deep breath. It is going to be a very long day.

"Glad to see we're going to be upfront with each other from the get-go," I reply acidly, while negotiating the trolley through the throngs of tourists that line the airport. The walk to the car hire depot is going to feel like a three-mile hike up Everest while carrying Helena's mountain of cases. It's a good job I work out.

"Come now, Brandt, don't be like that. I'm positive we're going to have lots of fun together. Preparations for the wedding have already started, and I plan to honeymoon in Fiji. We're only allowed a small affair, but I'm sure we'll manage to enjoy ourselves." The woman then blows in my ear and plants a kiss on my cheek. I want to murder her. Scrubbing off the sticky mess of lipstick she's left behind with one hand, I stop at the car and unlock it.

"Buckle up, Barbie," I growl, as I wonder how the fuck I'm going to fit four suitcases into a Mercedes C Class saloon. Now I'm not an astrophysicist, but even I know that's going to be an impressive achievement. I get two in the boot, and the remaining two I manage to squeeze into the back seat, although there's no way I'll be able to see out of the rear-view mirror for the foreseeable future. I'm tempted to leave one behind for the bomb squad to have some fun with, but it's not worth the grief I'll get. I can do without any major theatrics on the drive into town, and I'm positive Helena could put on a show that would rival *Les Misérables*. Speaking of misery...

We hit London just as rush hour traffic clogs up every artery that leads into the city. We should have taken the train. Why didn't we take the train? Oh yeah, because Helena is a bigger diva than Madonna with her entourage of cases. Someone upstairs must really hate me. The amount of crap I've had to deal with in the past five years has been pretty phenomenal.

"So, what have you been doing with yourself lately?" Helena is filing her nails into points and trying her best to while away the hours with idle chitchat. All I can think about is Harper, and every time she opens her mouth it serves to distract my very pleasant, albeit evil thoughts of revenge.

"Funny you should ask, Helena. For the past five years I've been living the high life, babe. Clubs, bars, parties, skiing in Aspen, and the odd beach holiday to the Virgin Islands. Also witnessed the odd murder, got stabbed, and made a mental note never to bend down to pick up the soap in the showers. Had an utter blast, thank you. Now if you don't mind can you sit back, enjoy the ride, and shut the fuck up for the rest of the journey?" My fingers are tapping angrily against the leather steering wheel. My eyes feel like they should have those red rays that superhero's use to melt through metal. If they did, Helena's head would currently be several feet away from her body. If I've just pissed her off, I couldn't care less because there is no way in hell I am marrying the woman. The sound of her snotty, posh voice grates on me in a way that I cannot tolerate for more than ten seconds at a time. That has to be an omen.

"Prison has changed you, Brandt. You used to be so nice. What's up with you today?"

She stops filing her talons for a second and looks at me with a big frown on her face.

You, I want to scream. You're what's up with me today. I haven't got time for this shit.

Now I'm beginning to feel guilty for leaving Harper on her own. She looked like she was going to freak out before I left her, and I daresay she won't be in any better state by the time I arrive tomorrow morning. I hope to God she eats something while I'm away or I'm going to spank that ass red raw. Oh, fucking hell. I'm suddenly sporting an erection half a mile long and the devil incarnate is sitting right across from me. I swear the woman can read my thoughts, and the next words out of her mouth are confirmation of the fact.

"Oh, honey. Do you need me to take care of that for you?" She's almost licking her lips with excitement. What is wrong with this woman?

"You come anywhere near me and I'll snap your neck. That's a promise. I'm here under duress and I am unamused by our unseemly collaboration."

Helena snorts. "Your junk seems to disagree, but hey, I was only trying to be nice. If you want to suffer in silence for the next hour or so, be my guest." She sniffs, turns her face away to look out of the window, and pretends to be offended by my outburst. Like I care.

For the next thirty minutes we don't say a word to each other. The quiet that now surrounds me is bliss. You learn to embrace it in prison. It's noise that you have to be scared of. At least that's one thing Harper has going for her; she doesn't feel the need to fill up our space with unnecessary chatter. Helena, on the other hand, is going to pop. I can feel her rage from here. The pampered bitch is used to getting her own way. I have news for her. She's not going to get away with that shit on my watch.

Eventually the dam of silence bursts. "Baby's due in November," she whispers.

"And? We're not playing happy families, Helena. One look at you has STD written all over it." Like I can talk. I need to get tested. I hope to hell Gabriel was clean because if I find out I've come out of the clanger with a 'little present', so to speak, I'm going to flip my shit.

"I'm clean. I was tested a week ago when they checked the baby over. I've got the paperwork in my bag." Helena's voice has lost its earlier animation. I have a feeling she thought I'd just roll over and take what was coming to me. She'll learn.

"Good to know. I still don't want you anywhere near me." My lips sneer as I speak the words, and I can see her visibly recoil. Score one for me.

Helena twists in her seat, wringing her hands together. I like this new look on her.

"Why did you agree to this, if you don't want to go through with it? I thought you'd be pleased." Helena sounds puzzled. It's as if she can't believe I'd be anything but grateful for her rescuing me from the depths of social obscurity.

"You thought I'd be pleased to be forced into marriage and raise some bastard's child as my own? What planet do you live on, Helena? Are there many men you know that would be pleased with that?" There's another huff of air and once again she faces away from me. I'm hopeful that's the end of the conversation for the time being, but my optimism is premature.

"Don't you want to be happy, Brandt?" Her voice lacks the sincerity I'd need to believe that little sentence.

"Happiness is a fickle thing, Helena. It comes upon you when you are least expecting it, and it can leave just as quickly. I don't think happiness is in our future. I think this arrangement is destined for misery, and lots of it."

I finally get more of the silence I've been craving, and not a moment too soon.

Dinner is a torrid affair. The heating in the Foster-Lyle's household has been cranked up to excruciatingly unbearable, and it's almost as if they want to see me sweat, sauna-style. I'm equally as determined not to give them the satisfaction. Stripping off my blazer, I roll the sleeves of my shirt up and try to stay as still as possible.

"So, Brandt, I bet you're glad that all this nonsense is behind you now." This comes from Helena's mother, who is sitting across from me, looking supremely elegant while raising a forkful of greens to her lips.

I am unamused. "Yes. I'm very glad to be out of prison, if that's what you mean." I watch her shoulders shake as the word 'prison' is mentioned and resist the urge to smile. This is too much fun. Awkward, much?

"I suspect your parents will be very glad to see you settle down," Helena's dad interrupts, as if sensing his wife's distress. The man finally swallows the piece of steak he's been chewing for the last five minutes and we can all be thankful for that. It appears that the Foster-Lyle's are not friends with their chef, and my sympathies are wholly with the household staff.

"I have no idea. They haven't spoken to me for the last five years, so one can only speculate as to their thoughts and desires," I offer, somewhat sharply. I'm really not in the mood for pleasant chitchat. It's not as if they're doing me a favour by allowing me to marry their daughter. She's almost in as much shit as I am. At least my disaster was not of my own making.

We sit there awkwardly for a while after that, with nothing but the clinking of silverware on plates for company. I'm more than content with that, but it's apparent the Foster-Lyle's want to assure themselves that an axe-murderer is not about to marry their daughter because the conversation eventually begins again.

"What do you intend to do with yourself, after you're married?" This is from Helena's father again, Rupert, who has thankfully finished his steak.

"Well, Mr Foster-Lyle, I'm guessing we'll be quite busy raising Helena's child together. I will obviously be looking for employment when Helena feels she can cope on her own, but for an ex-convict that won't be particularly easy." I'm addressing all sorts of elephants in this room and while mine is probably the worst, Helena isn't doing too badly herself.

Steering the topic off crime and punishment, Helena's mother, Julia, turns to her daughter. "Darling, how are the preparations for the wedding going?" This is fucking laughable. I haven't even agreed to marry the girl yet, and they're talking as if it's a done deal. They assume I'm just going to bend over and take it, and to be fair, I haven't disabused them of the notion. I wonder who my replacement will be when this all falls through? What poor shmuck is going to have to deal with this clusterfuck of a family? Time will tell.

Helena is all too happy to be the centre of attention now and wastes no time sharing her one-sided excitement at our upcoming nuptials.

"Well, Mummy, I found a florist, and she does these wonderful tall-stemmed crystal vases filled with roses. I was thinking white and cream roses, with maybe some pearls in the design. What do you think?" Her eyes are shining and for all intents and purposes she looks every inch the glowing bride-to-be. Those acting skills of hers are second to none. I need to practise mine, apparently.

"Well, it will be nearly summer by the time you get married, Helena. How about pink or lemon?" Is this Julia's tactful way of saying that nothing should be ivory or white on our rather rushed special day? I think it might be. Bringing a glass of particularly good claret up to my lips, I savour the wine on my tongue as the two women talk dresses, invitations, napkin colours, and the like. They're even discussing what sort of suit I should wear, which is laughable. When, or if I get married - I will not have my clothes dictated to me. I'm prepared to compromise, but I'm not being walked over. I've had enough of that in prison.

The evening drags on, slower than a Lada full of elephants going uphill. Rupert is trying his best to discuss current affairs with me, but as I've been inside for the past five years, most of what he's talking about flies straight over my head. In the few days since I've been home, I've been mostly concerned with trying to get Harper to confess (not to mention trying to get into her pants) than catching up with the news. This becomes blatantly obvious after five minutes, when Rupert sighs and tries a different tack.

"What sports do you enjoy, Brandt? Are you a golfer?"

Not a lot of call for that in prison, Sir. The only sports available were football and snooker, although we could shoot hoops, too. He probably wants me to say something like polo or rugby, but I'm not going to humour him.

"I'm really not into much sport at the minute. I love working out, but sport will probably take a back seat for a while as I adjust to the outside world." We continue to talk pleasantries, that are anything but pleasant, for the better part of an hour, and after that time I'm exhausted. I cannot take any more of this rubbish.

When the meal finally comes to an end after a rather painful six courses, I can't wait to escape. The thought of marrying into this family fills me with horror. I'd quite honestly rather be single and celibate for the rest of my adult life.

Making my excuses, I give my future bride-to-be a chaste peck on the cheek for appearance sake and dart out of the door as fast as I can.

On the ride to the train station something occurs to me. I still haven't heard a thing from Gabriel. Has he got my message or is he down there with Harper now? The thought fills me with dread. The man has a tendency to go off the handle on occasion, and Harper has a mouth on her like a squaddie. While I trust him not to kill her, and not to whisper a word to anyone, I don't trust him with much else. The sooner I get home, the better.

Chapter 3 - Harper

When Brandt left me I cried into my duvet for a solid two hours. It is still slightly damp with my tears several hours later. I just couldn't believe he would up and leave me all on my own. No one knows I'm here bar him, and I'm locked in the basement of a house that is virtually lost to civilisation. The nearest village is miles away, so my monster tells me. I am all alone, without a single friend to my name. Oh, happy days.

My lip wobbles again, but I try my best to hold back the tears. Drowning in salty self-pity won't get me anywhere. Brandt will come back. He hasn't abandoned me. Burying my head under my duvet because the room is so cold, I want to burrow under here and fall asleep until he returns. But that would be the coward's way of dealing with things. Am I a coward any more? I hope not. I promised myself I wouldn't be once Alex died, but it's hard to stand firm in the wake of Brandt's anger. I want to break down and tell him everything, but I'm afraid that if I do he'll be in just as much danger as I am. Mal will come for me, eventually. I'm a loose cannon that needs to be silenced. He's been in Mexico these past few months, but I know his return is imminent. If I hadn't run because of Brandt, I'd certainly planned on running before Mal set foot back in the UK. My husband was evil, but Mal is in another league entirely. He's the kind of guy that needs to wear a warning label around his neck.

I stay in my little cocoon of warmth for the better part of an hour with memories swimming through my head. Unpleasant, vile memories that are better pushed to the dark recesses of my brain and left to rot. Can Brandt keep me hidden here from the outside world? If he could, it might almost be worth staying behind bars. Better the devil you know, and all that.

For Christ's sake, Harper, get up. He's given you some time to yourself. You have books to read and food to eat. Get up.

Throwing the duvet to the foot of my rock-hard mattress, I wander over to the little fridge he's left me and open the door. Inside there are packaged sandwiches, yogurt, milk, cheese, salads, olives, cuts of meat and dips. In another carrier bag beside the fridge I find crackers, soft white rolls, cornflakes, cereal bars, bananas, apples, and a packet of biscuits. It might not be fare for a princess, but to me this is manna from heaven. I barely know where to start. Figuring I could do with a pick-me-up I grab the biscuits and a bottle of water. I might as well get started now because Brandt is sure to throw a hissy fit if I haven't eaten anything by the time he returns.

I don't understand him at all. Why does he care if I eat or not? Surely it would be a bonus if I starved myself to death? Mind you, I guess he wouldn't get his confession then, and that seems to be all he's worried about. I have news for him. He's never getting that confession. If I give it to him I'll be signing his death warrant, and I can't have that on my conscience along with everything else. I've done enough damage. I'm pretty sure I've destroyed his life beyond any reasonable idea of repair, and for that alone I deserve to die a long and painful death. There's still time. It's not a cheerful thought.

When I've managed to work my way through three biscuits, wishing to hell Brandt had left me a kettle so I could dunk them in a hot cup of tea, I grab a banana and decide to while away some hours reading. The books Brandt has left me are a bit of an eclectic mix, but I settle for a spy thriller by John le Carré. The rest are a mix of drama and horror, and I've seen enough of that in my lifetime without having to read about it as well.

By the time I'm ready for bed I've managed to eat a strawberry yogurt, a ham roll, a couple of crackers and half an egg salad. I think I'm eating mostly out of boredom, but thankfully my stomach doesn't protest. At least Brandt won't be mad about my eating habits when he comes to let me out. I'm sure he'll find something else to be mad at, but it won't be that.

Settling down under my duvet, I tuck the ends snuggly around my body and let my eyes close. For some reason I'm suddenly really tired, and it's probably the stress of the past few days catching up with me. I know my life will be hell on wheels when Browning comes back, but until then it makes sense to catch up on some sleep. Maybe I'll figure a way out of this mess when I wake up, or maybe this will all seem like a really bad dream. If only.

Alex Wilkinson has a lot to answer for. When I first met him he was one of the cool guys at college. The kind that had slicked back hair and a girl hanging off every arm. He looked like something out of *Grease* because he always wore tight black jeans and a black leather jacket - even in summer. There was always this kind of mystery about him, the kind that girls love. He was obviously from the wrong side of the tracks, just like me, but for some reason he was Mr Popular, and everyone loved him. He'd excelled at every kind of sport there was, failed miserably at anything remotely academic, and all the teachers hated him because he had a smart response for everything. Unlike all the other girls, though, I chose not to hang around him. I think my bullshit meter must have sensed something was off, even from back then, because I made it a point to ignore him. While everyone else was actively vying for his attention, I would go out of my way to avoid him completely, and even when he'd try to talk to me I'd smile politely, answer in clipped sentences, and try to make my getaway as fast as possible. I'd learn later that what I was doing was pretty much like waving a pheromone-laced flag straight at him. Men adore the chase, but because Alex was so popular he could have anyone he pleased, except me. I might as well have painted *Fuck me* on my forehead, because when Alex decided he wanted something, he stopped at nothing to get it.

As you've probably already guessed, I was in love with Brandt. I spent all my time pining over the rich boy I could never have. Hell would freeze over before the Browning's would allow a girl like me into their son's life. All I could do was lust over the pretty boy from afar and get carried away in my daydreams. At least I was smart enough to know they would never be made reality.

Meanwhile, Alex was pulling every trick in the book to get my attention. He'd begun shadowing me, turning up in unexpected places so he could taunt or torment me, because he would never admit weakness. He wanted me, but he wanted me on his terms. Everywhere I went he would turn up, and my friends would flock around him, batting their eyelashes and wiping the drool off their chins. I would always be the one holding back. I knew I needed to keep my distance back then; I just didn't know why.

The first thing Alex tried in his quest to get my attention was parading a different woman in front of my face every week. I'm guessing he figured I was into him and was just playing hard to get. This was probably partly true. You couldn't fail to fall for that bad boy image, but I was too hung up on Brandt. He didn't know that back then, though. When he found out he'd have a fit of the most epic proportions, but more about that later.

So, when Alex figured he wasn't going to make me jealous, and he tested this to the max by going as far as to date one of my friends, he tried other tactics. Namely, he wanted to get me alone with him, by any means possible. I think he figured if he could get his hands on me and show me how good he was with them, I might just fall at his feet - and Alex was nothing if not determined.

The man then made it his mission in life to make mine miserable. He was everywhere. He studied every move I made, knew where I'd be at every given time of the day, and mapped out my schedule until he knew where I'd be before I did. Back then, I'd assumed this was a weird and disconcerting coincidence, but I'd later find out he'd bribed all my friends. It didn't take him long to find an opportunity to get me on my own, and when he did, boy did he get his money's worth.

It was a silly error on my part. My economics course had been cancelled, but I hadn't been intelligent enough to check my emails that day. This was because I couldn't afford the contract on my cell phone, and they'd cut me off three days earlier. I was getting around this by using the library's computer, or stealing my roommate's phone, but on this particular day I'd done neither. Turning up at class as usual I was a little surprised to find myself all on my own, but I sat down, figuring I must be early. Imagine my surprise when the first person to walk through the door was Alex.

At first my brow furrowed, as if trying to figure out what on earth he was doing there. Had my room been changed? Or had Alex changed classes? God, I hoped not. I couldn't cope with him in the same room as me. There was chemistry there, sizzling brightly between us, and the only way for me to fight it was to ignore or avoid him. But I couldn't do that if he was sitting next to me. There was only so much self-control I possessed, and it was wearing thin as it was.

"Am I in the wrong room?" I stood up quickly, hating that my voice sounded throaty and breathless. I swear Alex would be able to smell the lust pouring off my body from half a mile away. You want Brandt, I told myself sternly. The trouble was, as much as I knew I wanted the pretty, rich kid with the bright blue eyes and adorable smile, I also knew I wouldn't get him. What was I waiting for? Brandt was never going to date a deadbeat like me. His parents wouldn't allow it, and his friends would laugh at him.

"Nope. You're in the right room. You're with me, sweetheart," Alex growled. He then came to stand in front of me, pressing his body so close to mine I could feel his growing erection through his jeans. Fuck. I jumped back as if shot, but he was ready and grabbed me by the waist. He laughed as he pulled me into him.

"We can't do this," I whispered. "Someone will come in any second." Looking at the door anxiously, I remember willing it to open. I knew I needed saving, and I fully expected to be rescued. What a silly girl I was back then. I'd been cornered, and there was no escape.

"I've got news for you, girly. We are doing this." Pulling my body towards him until he virtually crushed my lungs with his hold, he put his lips on mine, and from that moment I was a goner. It was as if our bodies were made for each other and as soon as our lips crashed the circuit was complete. I think even Alex was shocked by the force of my response, although he didn't let it show. He just thrust his tongue inside me and created holy havoc with every single hormone I possessed. I couldn't think, couldn't speak, couldn't move - hell, I could barely breathe. My body was moving on autopilot, and there was no ejector seat on this plane.

When his hands moved between my legs you'd like to think I pushed him away. We were in a public place, after all. But I did no such thing. My brain had gone on holiday, my reflexes were shot, and I couldn't get enough of him. When his fingers slipped inside my panties I melted like an iceberg in Barbados - quickly, and with no thought to the devastation it would cause.

I'm ashamed to admit it was Alex who stopped me dropping everything and rutting about on the classroom floor. He pulled back when I couldn't. I remember the moment as if it were yesterday. He had the biggest, shit-eating grin on his face. He knew he'd won the battle before it had even begun. All it would take now was time, and a little clever engineering on his behalf. I was doomed, but I didn't know that then. I remember putting shaking fingertips up to my bottom lip, sucking in air, and wondering what the hell had just happened.

"See you around, Harper," Alex said as he strode away from me, giving me a cheerful wink. The door closed behind him a second later. I remember not knowing whether I wanted to claw his eyes out or run after him. On that occasion, I did neither. All of that would come later, much to my disgust.

When I wake up everything is pitch black. Stretching my arms out and yawning, I wonder how long I've slept for. It's probably only been a few hours. My body feels permanently wired and it won't relax. Eventually I succumb to exhaustion, but even then I don't get anywhere near the amount of sleep I normally need. I can't see that's about to change anytime soon, either.

Sitting up, I let my eyes adjust to the darkness for a few seconds. I can't hear anything bar the rustling of the wind outside, and I guess that's a good thing. It means I have a few more hours of solitude until my tormentor comes back. Actually, I lie. It's not a good thing. I'm going crazy on my own. What if he leaves me here to rot? It's no more than I deserve. If he gets held up in London, will he worry about leaving me alone? Doubtful. If I run out of food and water, there's no one to call, and there's no one to come to my rescue. This might have been his plan all along. Maybe he'll come back in a year or two to bury me. Holy shit, I'm going to drive myself crazy.

There's a flicker of a shadow on the back wall, and my eyes shoot forward to see where the movement is coming from. Didn't Brandt say there were rats down here? Oh my God. Oh. My. God. Am I going crazy or did I actually see something just then? My eyes scan the room from top to bottom, when all I really want to do is bury myself back in my duvet and never come up for air again. Am I seeing ghosts now? Really?

Meow. Jesus Christ. I nearly jump out of my skin at the sound, but seconds later I watch as a cat pads down into my cell. He's a fluffy black Persian by the looks of it, and he's looking for attention. How did he get in here? Did Brandt leave one of the windows open upstairs? I hope he can get out again. I've not got any food to give him, bar a few slivers of chicken, perhaps.

Squeezing through the bars of my cell he jumps neatly up onto my bed and looks at me. *Meow.* I'm going to take that as cat speak for 'give me some loving', and I'm only too happy to oblige. I cuddle up to the little beast and begin ruffling his fur. Purring appreciatively, he settles down on my lap and curls up into a little ball. Aww. Suddenly my day doesn't seem so bad. At least I've got some company.

"Were you my shadow?" I whisper affectionately, pressing my face down into his fur and giving him a little kiss.

"No," a loud voice booms out as I hear footsteps coming towards me. I nearly wet myself on the spot.

The voice is dark, menacing and dangerous, and it isn't Brandt's. There's some kind of accent there, but I'm too scared to figure it out just yet. Scooting back up against the wall I watch as the cat jumps off me with an angry hiss. My heart is pounding in my chest and my mouth is dry. Who the hell is this and what is he doing here? For a moment I can't say a thing - all I can do is huddle up in my duvet while I try my best not to hyperventilate. Is this a burglar? Did Brandt send him? Slow seconds tick past while each of us waits for the other to speak. In the end the intruder wins.

"Who are you?" I whisper.

"Your worst nightmare," he says, in a rough, gravelly voice that puts shivers up my spine.

"You'll need to wait in line for that position. Browning has top spot at the moment." My hands clap themselves over my mouth. I can't believe I just said that. Where has all this bravery come from? Perhaps it's because I'm standing behind a set of locked bars. Yes, that must be it.

"So I've heard, but you're wrong, sweetheart. I'm far more dangerous than Browning. He's a pussycat compared to me." Tall, dark and scary saunters towards me, until he reaches the bars of my prison. He rests against them lazily and examines me slowly, not that he can see much. Thankfully, it's dark in here.

"What makes you say that?" I ask softly. I know I'm going to regret that question, but now it's out there I can't take it back.

"You sure you want to know the answer to that, princess? Now I'm going out on a limb here, but I'm almost certain you won't." That confirms my worst suspicions. Excellent. I have a bad feeling Brandt has sent an ex-con to babysit me.

"I'm sure." I bite my lip. What the fuck am I saying? He's just warned me I don't want to hear this, and I'm encouraging him to continue.

"Suit yourself," he says nonchalantly, as the cat begins to rub against his leg. "So, we both know Brandt was sent inside for your crimes. We also know he's not a criminal. He hasn't got it in him." The cat is crying out for attention again, and Scary Man bends down to pet him, before picking him up and laying him across his chest. He turns towards me once more and smiles. "I, on the other hand, am a nasty piece of work. I've committed multiple crimes and I don't have a shred of remorse for any of them unless I'm talking to my parole officer."

This is exactly what I feared. Brandt is feeding me to the wolves. Is this man going to be my tormentor now? I hope not. He's the kind of mean that I've seen far too often. I don't think I can deal with this again. I've only just scraped myself together since the last big incident. *Stop it. You can't think about that now. You'll go nuts.*

"What was the worst of those crimes?" It's odd, but I can't seem to say a word when Brandt's in the room. Now I'm in chatty mode with Captain Evil. What is wrong with me?

"Murder." His tone is horribly flippant. He doesn't give a fuck if he's scaring me, and believe me, he is. I can feel my skin prickling and all I want to do is run. Fat chance of that. I'm going nowhere.

"Do you want to kill me?" I swallow tightly. I have a feeling I already know the answer to that question.

"Oh, you have no idea how much I want to kill you, Harper. The good news is, I'm going to show you, as soon as I can get myself in that cosy little cell of yours."

Chapter 4 - Brandt

By the time I make it to Euston Station the last direct train from London to Glasgow has already gone. It left at six-thirty p.m., and that was over three hours ago. I want to throw my head back and scream. I can still grab another train with a couple of stops enroute, but that will take around sixteen hours, versus the five hours that the direct route would have taken. However I look at it, I'm not arriving in Glasgow until about two p.m. tomorrow, and that's too late - especially as I still haven't heard from Gabriel. My body is working itself up into a sweat just thinking about what the man might do to her. What was I thinking when I called the bastard? He knows our sorry tale, and he told me a long time ago how he'd make her squeal if he ever got the chance - and believe me when I tell you it isn't pretty. Whatever happens, I can't leave him alone with her for too long. If he kills her I will lose my shit. Perhaps I'm worrying too much. I don't think he'd do anything too drastic without my say so, but is that a risk I'm willing to take? The answer is a resounding no.

Grabbing a large cup of black coffee at a drive-through Starbucks, I point my car northwards and prepare to settle in for a long drive. What a fucking nightmare.

I spend the first hour of the journey berating myself for ever having called Gabriel in the first place. He's a killer for Christ's sake - and one with the morals of an alley cat. Mind you, it wasn't as if I had a choice. Normal people do not kidnap women and lock them in their houses. If I'd called anyone else I'd be back inside by now. *Shit, shit, shit.*

Don't panic, I tell myself. At least Harper is under lock and key. Gabriel won't be able to get his ass inside her cell. Yeah, right. You learn all sorts of nasty tricks in prison, and one of the first ones is how to pick a lock. Jamming my finger into the stereo controls I try to figure out how the radio works by using brute force. Eventually it blares into life, and then there's a mad scramble to get the volume down. I need a distraction. I can't think about what he might be doing to her. Calm down. He might not even be there. Fat chance. He will have rushed over there the first chance he got. Gabriel is nothing if not curious. Thumping the steering wheel hard, I curse. I can't even break any speed limits; the last thing I need is to get stopped by the police.

There's no traffic on the drive home, which is one small consolation in what has otherwise been a colossally shitty day. The motorways are clear because of the late hour, and even the ever-present roadworks don't seem to slow me down. I switch radio channels, and the music is a welcome distraction as my thoughts turn to Helena. Will I be forced into marriage? Is any amount of money worth that? I don't think so, but time will tell. I still can't understand why my parents are pushing me down this route. Am I that much of an embarrassment to them that they need to hide me away? I can't understand why they abandoned me. Hell, they nearly killed me, and that's no word of a lie. When they didn't top up my bank account in prison I was left living off scraps for days. If Gabriel hadn't stepped in to help me I would have almost starved to death, and I'd have been too weak to defend myself from the likes of Micas and his gang. There are only so many broken bones you can recover from, and I've put myself in solitary more than once to avoid a good kicking. In the end, I could almost tell when it was coming because Micas would get this mean look in his eye and give me a sly grin that always spelled danger. That bastard loved to watch me squirm. So did Gabriel, for that matter, but in an entirely different way. Damn, I'm going to have to face him in a matter of hours and we didn't end on a good note. There are so many thoughts whirling around my head. It's such a chaotic mess, I don't know which way to turn.

Harper is probably the most immediate problem I need to deal with, and maybe Gabriel can help me with that. He doesn't have a soft spot for her like I do. He's cold and clinical. The word 'brutal' probably isn't too far from the truth. He doesn't play well with others. Having said that, if the man is on your side no force on earth will stop him from protecting what's his. The man means what he says, and once he gives his word, he keeps it. There's a lot to be said for that. In the past five years I've seen some dubious specimens of society, and I've learnt to trust no one. Gabriel is the only exception to that rule. He isn't without his faults, but he's never given me a reason to doubt him - with anything that isn't sexual in nature, anyway. But therein lies the problem. Don't kill her, Rodriguez. Not in the next nine hours or so, anyway.

My thoughts bounce back to Helena. What am I going to do about that little problem? If I don't go through with the marriage there's no question my parents will cut me off. If they couldn't be bothered to send me a lawyer, let alone speak to me for the past five years, they won't think twice about leaving me high and dry. I still can't understand my father. Fine, he would never have won any father-of-the-year competitions, and he was a horrible snob, but I never thought he'd disown me. If that wasn't hard enough to swallow, I couldn't believe my mother and brother had followed suit. They hadn't even tried to give me a sneaky message or phone call. That still stung. I knew they believed I'd done them a terrible injustice, but even so, I was still their own flesh and blood. Not once had they listened to my side of the story. They just assumed I was guilty. My gut still churns at the thought. I'd like to think that if it had been one of them caught with their hand in the cookie jar, I'd have given them the benefit of the doubt. What is it with me? Either I'm one of the unluckiest sods on earth, or I have a face that screams 'guilty!'. My lips curl in distaste.

I am not marrying Helena. I will not be forced into marriage to appease my parents. This not talking to each other thing works both ways. If they want to wash their hands of me, I'm happy to oblige them by travelling somewhere a few thousand miles away. But not until Harper's squawked. I need to know what happened. I deserve that much. The not knowing is driving me crazy. Harper doesn't seem like the type of person to throw someone under the bus, but she must have had her reasons. Was she afraid of going to jail? Was she covering for someone else? Her boyfriend, perhaps? He looked like a nasty piece of work if there ever was one. I remember being insanely jealous of him when he came on the scene. Once upon a time Harper only had eyes for me, but he changed all that. Not that it mattered. My parents would never have let me near her. The most I could have offered her was a summer fling, and I couldn't do it to myself. It would have hurt too much when the time came to give her up, so I did my best to stay away. Sure, I saw her eyes following me everywhere I went, but I got good at ignoring them. Having said that, I could never have been nasty to her. When she asked me for help that day, I was only too happy to rush on over. Funnily enough, that sentiment has changed. Until I get my answers I am going to be the nastiest bastard that ever existed.

I wonder what happened to Alex Wilkinson? Harper hasn't talked about him, but to be fair, she hasn't talked about much at all around me. I've barely given her the opportunity to. My rage has so far gotten the better of me every time I see her. Perhaps if I sit down with her after a couple of stiff drinks, I'll be able to leave her alone long enough to hear her side of the story. That is, if Harper was ever planning to talk to me, and I'm not convinced that she is. The girl is a shadow of what she once was, and now I've seen her up close I realise she's not in a good way. Has she been mistreated? Or was it fear that made her lose all that weight? She deserves to suffer. I can tell myself that, over and over again, but it doesn't change the fact that I care about her. Perhaps if I find out once and for all that she's the monster in all of this, I can put this sorry episode to rest and move on with my life. If there's one thing in prison I learnt, it's this: life is too short not to go after what you want. I'm going to live every day like it's my last, and no one is going to dictate my next move. No one. Having said that, I'm going to play along with the marriage charade until I get what I want out of Harper. I should be able to string them along for a few days. Hopefully this mess will all be over soon.

Chapter 5 - Harper

"Oh, you have no idea how much I want to kill you, Harper. The good news is, I'm going to show you, as soon as I can get myself in that cosy little cell of yours."

Gabriel's words echo over and over in my head as he and the cat walk back upstairs. I don't give him the satisfaction of hearing my head slam back against the wall in misery, but it's tempting. Where the fuck is Brandt? I'm guessing that's going to be a very important question shortly. If I don't figure out a way to get myself out of this mess, there's a very good chance I won't be here when he gets back.

Examining my cell from top to bottom, it doesn't take long to realise I'm not going anywhere. Unless I can pull an invisible woman trick, I'm doomed. The lock is on the other side of the cage, and even if I could pick it, I have no tools with which to do so. Is that what Captain Evil is looking for? Is he hiding Houdini-style skills beyond that dark exterior? It's more than likely; he's an ex-con after all. Or perhaps he'll just use a chainsaw. I wouldn't put it past him. I hope the previous owners of this house weren't keen on gardening or massacres. I also hope they took all their electric power tools with them when they moved.

I blink twice and then take a couple of deep breaths. I'm between a rock and a hard place, but I'm not dead - yet. If I can't break myself out of this joint, then I need to be ready for the asshole when he comes back. What do I have that I can defend myself with? A bucket? Not great, but it's a start. An iPad? If I wield it with both hands I should be able to give him a solid whack round the head, but I'm not sure I'll be able to take him down. I have a feeling that will be an important factor. If I don't manage to knock his lights out I'll just make the beast angry, and that's the last thing I need.

I go through the rest of my cell's inventory in detail. Food, books, bedding, mini fridge... Now that would make an awesome weapon, but it's too large to be stealthy, and I suspect I'll struggle to pick it up. I give it a go to confirm this, and I can barely lift it off the floor. That's another no. What does that leave? I can't even strangle him with my panties because I'm not wearing any.

If I die in this cell because Brandt got one of his psychopath prison buddies to babysit me, I swear I am going to kill him. Fine. Haunt him.

I go back to the drawing board, aware I am running out of time. What else can I use? There must be something. Hell, at this rate I'll be forced into either throwing apples or chucking the slop bucket at him, neither of which will slow him down much. I need something better.

I sit with my eyes frantically darting around my cell as if willing something to materialise of its own accord. Funnily enough, nothing does. The main thing is, I don't give up. I've learnt that the hard way. Whenever you're pressed up against the wall you focus, and then you try harder. Failure hasn't been an option for some time now. *Think. Think. Think.*

My eyes settle once more on the fridge and it's as if my subconscious is trying to tell me something. I stare at it for what seems to be an age, my eyes almost blurring with the intensity of my thoughts, and then it comes to me. I'm not exactly sure if it will work, but it is a plan, and it's better than nothing.

Hurrying to it, I unplug it from the wall and then do my best to carry it to the bed. It's bloody heavy, and I probably should have taken all the food out first, but I don't know how much time I have. Using the rough edge of the metal bedstead, I begin sawing through the rubberised wire. Thank God Brandt didn't think to file it down, else I'd be less than helpless right now. As it is, I'm not sure whether I'll be able to slice it open in time, but it's the only shot I've got, so I work the wire as fast as I can back and forth, watching as the soft rubber tears away to leave the wires beneath. They are harder to saw through, but I keep at it, all the while listening for footsteps on the stairs. A little longer and I'll have a weapon. I just need a few more minutes.

As I start to tear through the wires my body is jumpy as hell. I need to get that fridge back into place before Captain Evil comes down the stairs if I'm going to keep my plan incognito. By this time my hands are getting sore from holding the cable so tightly, but I know it won't be long before I've cut through it, and sure enough, a few seconds later I have achieved my objective. Now I just need to peel back the rubber sheathing far enough to expose the wires underneath. Thankfully, that doesn't take long.

Placing the fridge back where it was, I move the slop bucket alongside it. My plan is to chuck that at him as soon as he gets in the cell, which should give me enough time to plug in my cable and brandish it as a weapon. If he's stupid enough to come near me after that, that's his problem, not mine. I'm probably not going to kill him with a short blast of household voltage, but with any luck it will stun him enough while I give him a bash round the head with the iPad. Knowing me

I'll probably trip and drop it on him, but it's the least the bastard deserves, and I refuse to feel guilty about this. If I want to stay alive I'm going to need to toughen up, which is pretty funny considering all I want to do right now is burst into tears.

Captain Evil takes his time returning. It's just occurred to me that he's probably gone back to bed, considering it was the middle of the night when I saw him last. I've probably been rushing around like a madwoman for no reason. Oh well, at least I'll be ready for him when he wakes up. Picking up my iPad, I confirm that the time is now three-thirty a.m. Christ, is that all? I could be down here for hours yet, chewing my nails as I wait for the bastard to reappear. I wonder if my monster is a late or early riser? This could be a long night.

Grabbing a yogurt and square of cheese out of my broken fridge, I figure I may as well eat up before all the food goes to waste. I'm going to need my energy if I want to take on the bad boy upstairs.

I sit quietly, staring into space while eating my snack. As the minutes tick down I think it's a new all-time low for me. Being married to Alex was hell on wheels, but what I'm dealing with now could be even worse. I sincerely hope not, but I wouldn't like to put a bet on it.

At least the food is good. The yogurt is cold and creamy on my tongue, with a hint of lemon. It's delicious. It should put a smile on my face, but it doesn't. My mind is wrapped up in 'what if's'. What if I manage to clobber Captain Evil and escape? What if there are some clothes up there? What if I manage to find a cell-phone? Could I make it out of here on my own? There's a small sliver of hope that says I'm capable of fending for myself, and even if I'm not, dying from the elements has got to be a better way to go than being tortured by Brandt and his buddies. I've taken more crap in the last few years than anyone should have to take in a lifetime, and I'm not sure I can take much more.

It turns out Captain Evil is an early riser. At seven a.m. on the dot I hear the sound of his shoes padding down the stairs. By this time a little light has filtered into the room, and I'll be able to get a better look at him. Following his footfalls anxiously, I watch as his body comes slowly into view. When he reaches the bottom step I lose the ability to breathe. The man standing before me is tall, with jet black hair, olive skin and dark, almost black eyes. He's the type of guy that could grace the cover of GQ. He also has this air about him which says 'fuck with me at your peril'. I know that look. My husband wore it often, and Mal was a master at it. You have to have a lot of confidence in yourself to wear it well, and Captain Evil has that in spades. I can deal with that confidence in one of two ways. I can either burst into tears and shrivel up like a rotten apple, trying to make myself as small as possible while I wait for him to come and attack me, or I can fight fire with fire. Option one has a fairly predictable ending. It involves me being in intense pain, and there's a possibility the asshole might kill me in the process. Option two is a little more unpredictable. It could go either way. Either I'll end up dead, or I'll be running for my life with the possibility of still ending up dead, but at least I'm not rolling over and almost asking the bastard to kick me. I'm done with taking orders from men. Few of the men I've known have deserved my respect, and I'm fairly sure the one in front of me isn't going to be any different.

"Fancy that," Evil drawls, spearing me with his dark brown orbs, "it appears the little princess can't sleep." His movements towards my cell are slow and easy. He's in no rush because he wants to torment me first. I know how this works.

"Early riser, me." I give him a feral smile that's basically as good as shoving two fingers up at him without actually doing it, and pick up the book in my hands, giving him nothing but a bored expression. The fear is just underneath the surface of that look, but he can't see it because I've learnt to hide it well.

"Huh. The little pussycat thinks she has claws. How adorable. I don't think you'll be so cheerful when I get inside that cell in ten minutes." His lips twist in amusement as he looks me up and down. He thinks he has me all figured out. I've got news for him.

"How does it feel to be on the other side, Gabriel?" I've just figured it out. I'm pretty sure that twang he tries so hard to disguise is a Spanish accent, and those features certainly look the part. His next actions will confirm it. Sure enough, his eyes widen in surprise, and then he laughs.

"Brandt's been sharing his secrets, I see. Fancy that." He appears most entertained by this knowledge. Me? Not so much. Now I have a rough idea of what I'm facing, I can't say I'm over the moon with the knowledge. This means I'm dealing with a semi-intelligent criminal, and that can't be a good thing.

Gabriel has now reached the bars and is examining me closely - a bit like you would a bug under a microscope. Maybe he thinks I'm shortly going to be extinct, but I'm not your average victim. I know how to fight dirty, just like he does. I learnt from the best.

"Why did you set him up, princess? Why did you crap all over his life in such spectacular fashion that even his damn parents abandoned him? I'm curious." Gabriel sits down on the concrete floor and unzips his leather jacket. It's black, just like Alex's. It's obviously a warning that he's a fellow psychopath. Mal had one, too.

"Fuck you." I'm sat on top of the mini fridge which isn't the most comfortable chair in the world, but it will keep me in the right position for what I have to do. My duvet is wrapped snugly around me, but I realise I'm going to have to lose it soon, along with my modesty. Mind you, I lost that a long time ago, so it's no biggie. I'm pretty sure Gabriel will have seen it all before.

He gives me another one of his dark smiles, before tapping the bars of my cell three times. "Oh, you will be, sweetheart. Take my word for it, you will be." He proceeds to pull a leather pouch from the inside of his jacket, and unzips it in front of me. It contains all manner of metal picks, probably enough to get inside your average bank, if they didn't have everything computerised these days. No one robs banks any more. I read that somewhere. They're virtually impenetrable. Bulletproof glass, high resolution security cameras, motion sensors, window sensors, exploding dye, lower cash balances and GPS tracking devices are all a huge pain in the ass to your average bank robber. Technology has made the vault harder to crack, and the pay-out is far less appealing than it used to be. These days, the only real money to be made is in cyber-crime.

I shake my head to clear it of these errant thoughts. The only thing I need to worry about is what I'm going to do when the asshole gets through that lock, and he will. I can see it in his eyes.

Watching as Gabriel selects two picks, and slowly slides them out of the case, I summon up what's left of my courage. It's time to try a different tack. Anything that will keep him out of my cell has my vote. "Brandt will kill you if you lay a finger on me," I say. I actually believe what I'm saying because if Brandt wanted to kill me, he'd have done it by now.

"Oh, I'm sure he'll try, but unfortunately for you, Miss Wilkinson, I'm a very hard man to kill." This statement sounds like it might be true, which isn't the best news for me, but I'm going to keep throwing insults at him until I make him good and mad. If I can get him to lose his temper he's likely to be far less cautious when he bursts through that door, and hopefully rather distracted. I'll take any edge I can get at this point.

"So, when did you discover you're gay, Gabriel?" This is just to let him know that Brandt's told me everything, or at least more than he'd probably want me to know. I wait to see if it rattles him. He takes his time answering me. Meanwhile, he's bringing his pair of picks up to the metal lock in front of him. Placing them carefully, one in each corner of the lock, he begins to twist them around. My legs turn to jelly, but thankfully I'm still sitting down.

"Who told you that, princess?" Gabriel is now biting his lip in an effort not to laugh. What is so funny?

"So, you're not gay?" I raise my eyebrows in question. I'm jerking his chain, so I don't care either way. There was only one option available in prison. It's entirely possible he's heterosexual. It's interesting that he finds the conversation amusing, though.

"My, my, my, what a nosy thing you are, Miss Wilkinson. That will get you into trouble round these parts, but just this once I'll share. I'm bisexual. I like men and women. Sometimes I fuck them both at once for kicks."

His eyes watch mine as the picks do their own thing, clicking away happily in his fingers. I don't give him a reaction to that revelation, but it does make me pause. Does Brandt know this? I bet he doesn't.

"What's the point of this, Gabriel? You've been sent here to babysit. Why create all this drama? Why not wait until Brandt gets back and ask him if you can sleep with me?" It's a fair point. If they're best buddies, I'm sure Brandt would be only too happy to oblige. I'm not sure they left each other on the best of terms, though. Actually, I'm fairly certain they didn't.

"Where would the fun be in that? Brandt is far more fun to fuck when he's angry. Even you should know that by now, Harper." It's the first time he's called me by my name, and the sound of it on those sinful lips makes my skin break out in goose-bumps. I hope he sticks to sweetheart or princess in future.

"He's not even talking to me," I say, rather sourly. It's nothing short of the truth. Brandt doesn't want to hear my sorry tale just yet. He just wants to play with his food.

"That I don't doubt, but he has fucked you." Gabriel says that sentence with absolute certainty. I wonder why he thinks that? Brandt can't bear the sight of me at the moment. The only reason he's played with me is to demonstrate the misery he's suffered. I have to give it to him, too. It's been a pretty effective telling off.

"He hasn't fucked me, so that shows how much you know." I fold my arms over my chest and glare at him. I don't know why I bother because Gabriel is far too focused on the task in front of him. I can hear another series of clicks as he begins to make progress with the lock. He then begins cursing, which I guess is his way of telling me the job isn't quite as easy as it looks, and it seems that Brandt has done his homework. He's not going to be in here in a couple of seconds, the way they break into houses in the movies. By the looks of things this will take a few minutes, and for that I am thankful. It gives me time to figure out what I'm going to do as soon as he bursts through that door.

I'm clutching the cable plug in my hand under the duvet. When Gabriel finally gets in I'm losing the duvet, and if that isn't a big enough distraction my next move will be. That should give me time to plug in the cable and hurt the guy. I can feel my legs shaking already. Adrenaline is beginning to build, and my fingers are jumpy. Where was Brandt? I don't know why I'm thinking of him as my saviour. If he were here there's every chance he'd watch and laugh as Gabriel does his thing. I need to get away. That's the only option. I need to get past those bars and run as fast as my legs will carry me.

"Finally!" Gabriel's exclamation is my indication to leap to my feet. The duvet drops to the floor as I stand my ground. He pulls the door open with one heavily muscled arm, but the bucket is already in my hand.

"Don't you even think of throwing..." The rest of his sentence is drowned out by the sound of a day's worth of stale urine hitting him square in the face. His eyes look murderous as he advances towards me, but I'm already slamming the plug in the socket, careful to only hold the rubberised part of the cable. Thrusting forward with my arm I prod the wires in the centre of his chest and watch the sparks fly.

Watching someone receive an electric shock isn't a pleasant experience. Gabriel's body seems to freeze up as his muscles lock and his eyes go wide. For a moment they look like they're going to pop out of his head, and it's clear he can't believe what has just happened. I press the wires to his chest again and hold them against him for longer the second time around, hoping that I've given him enough current to stop any form of retaliation once he gets over the surprise. I'm expecting a whack around the head, but it seems the current has done its job. Gabriel takes a step backwards and his knees crumple beneath him. I utilise this momentum by whacking him round the head with the iPad as hard as I can with both hands and watch as he falls to the floor with a thud, his head cracking sharply against the concrete. I wince for him. That had to hurt.

Standing back I watch for any signs of life, but there are none. I don't think the current knocked him unconscious, I think it was the fall, but I don't stand around to find out. I have to get out of here before Brandt gets back and there's no time to lose.

Rushing up the stone steps I zoom through the house and head upstairs. I need to find Brandt's room. While there won't be any clothes around that will fit me, he'll have some jeans and a jumper stored somewhere. I'm sure of it. Hopefully there'll be a jacket too. I'll have to adjust them to fit me as best I can. Anything has got to be better than nothing. Although it's not freezing outside it's not particularly warm, and if I want to stay alive long enough to find help or shelter, I'll need to dress for the elements. My worst enemy at the moment is rain. Nearly every time I've been above ground in this infernal house it's been drizzling or raining. I'm going to cross my fingers that it isn't today. Being soaked wet through on my first day of freedom isn't my idea of fun. Mind you, I'll take it. Anything is better than being locked downstairs in that cage.

I have no idea when Gabriel will wake up, and Brandt might be just around the corner. I'm going to need a head-start to get away from those two, so time is of the essence. What do I need? Clothes and food. Everything else is surplus to requirement.

I open each door I find and begin searching through drawers and wardrobes. Most are empty. Those that aren't are filled with an odd assortment of knickknacks and memorabilia. This house hasn't been lived in for some time. It smells old, damp and musty, and there's a lingering scent of mothballs in the air. It isn't until I enter the third bedroom that I spot signs of life. The bed isn't freshly made, and there's a used mug resting on a wooden bedside table. The top draw finally reveals clothing, all of which is much too big for me, but beggars can't be choosers. I pull on a pair of jeans and roll the waist and legs up until I can walk around without tripping over them. Rummaging around, I find a T-shirt and sweatshirt, and drag these over my head. They hang off me, but there's not much I can do about it. Brandt also has an anorak, thank God, but he must have taken his coat with him. It's not going to keep me particularly warm, but at least it should be waterproof. As for shoes, there's nothing but a pair of massive trainers. I guess they're better than nothing, but they'll slow me down. Maybe if I wedge them on with a couple of pairs of thick socks they'll be almost wearable. I know I won't be able to do the entire distance bare foot. My feet are in a sorry enough state as it is. Last but not least, I spot a small duffel bag in the corner of the wardrobe, which I'm sure will come in handy.

When I've piled this lot on I feel like the Michelin man, but I'm already running downstairs. I need a few provisions, and then it's time to get the hell out of here. Racing into the kitchen, already out of breath, I dump my bag on the island and begin rummaging in the cupboards underneath. I find some fruit, a couple of cereal bars and some chocolate. Opening the fridge, I grab the remains of a chicken pie and a wedge of Edam cheese. It's enough for now. That could easily last me a week, if I rationed it out, although I'm optimistic I'll have found help by then. It might take me a day or two, but I'm sure I'll find someone before long. Stuffing all the food into my bag, I sling it over my shoulder and make my way towards the door. My hands are still shaking. This is my second attempt at escape, and I'd better make this one count.

Chapter 6 - Brandt

Rush hour traffic snarls up as I head into Glasgow. By this time I am on my knees. I didn't sleep particularly well yesterday, and I've just pulled an all-nighter. Though I have stopped for numerous coffees and some horribly caffeinated energy drinks along the way, I now feel like death warmed up. What I should do, is pull over on the motorway and take a nap for a couple of hours. That would be the sensible thing. In the back of my mind, though, the image of Gabriel fucking Harper haunts me, and I know he'll do it just to spite me. I can't let that happen. It will destroy me. I need to get back.

Turning the radio up as loud as it will go, and opening the window wide, I let a rush of cold air jolt me awake. I haven't got too far to go now. When this traffic clears up I can put my foot down and power on home. Trying Gabriel's phone one last time I swear as it heads straight to voicemail. He's there with Harper. There is no question in my mind. When I get my hands on him I'm going to plough my fist straight through his beautiful fucking face. This might be a game to him, but it isn't to me. She's the only person that knows what really happened on the day I got arrested, and if anything happens to her any hope of exonerating myself will disappear with her.

"Hallelujah!" When the traffic finally starts moving again I thump the steering wheel and sigh gratefully. There is nothing worse than having to sit still when you're tired. Now I know that I only have a few hours to go I feel a lot better about life in general. Harper will be fine. Gabriel will have behaved himself. I'm worrying about nothing. What could possibly go wrong?

When I pull up outside the house, there is no car. Is Gabriel not here, after all? Perhaps he's gotten himself into some kind of nasty mess again? Maybe he's pulled a DUI and is under lock and key for the night. Nothing would surprise me.

Pushing open the door to the house, I head straight downstairs. I'm going to make sure Harper's okay, then I'm going to bed, where I'm going to stay for at least the next ten hours. Tumbling down the steps in a sleep-deprived stupor, I unzip my jacket and pull it apart. I then stop dead in my tracks when I see her cell door wide open. What the hell is going on here? As my gaze focuses on a person laid on the floor my eyes go wide in horror.

It's not who I expect, though. Running over, I grab Gabriel by his shoulders and shake him. He stinks to high heaven, but that's the least of my worries.

"Gabriel. Gabriel!" I pray to God Harper hasn't killed him. The last thing I need is a dead body on my hands. I've got enough problems as it is. At first I get no response from him, so I check for a pulse in his neck. It's there. Jesus Christ. I don't need this kind of excitement.

"Gabriel, you bastard, wake up!" This time I slap him, hard. If he's stupid enough to have let Harper escape he deserves all this and more. His eyelashes flicker. He's coming to. I release the breath I hadn't realised I'd been holding. "What fucking happened here?" I growl. I'm so mad I could breathe fire. Did he touch her? Is that why she ran? Did he hurt her? My eyes scan their way quickly around the cell, but thankfully there's no sign of blood. They then zoom in on the broken electricity cable lying on the concrete floor. It doesn't take long for me to put two and two together. I have to give it to Harper, she's not stupid.

"God, my head hurts. I think I banged it hard," Gabriel moans.

"If you're not fucking careful it'll hurt a whole lot more in a minute," I growl. "Why the hell were you inside her cell in the first place?" All I can see is red. I want to smash his head into the concrete over and over again for doing this to me. "Actually, at the moment I don't care. Where's Harper? And where's your car?" If Harper has managed to get his car keys she could be miles away by now. This time it'll be a lot harder to catch her. She'll have no credit cards that I can use to track her with, and she'll be a damn site more cautious. The woman might have just slipped through my fingers forever. The thought freezes the blood in my veins.

"I didn't come by car," Gabriel croaks. His arm comes up to feel what I'm guessing must be a nasty lump on the underside of his head. "I caught the train, and a taxi dropped me off here. It cost a bloody fortune, too." Slowly he manages to get himself upright.

"What happened?" While I want to go tearing off into the undergrowth immediately, I need to know what I'm dealing with. If he tried to hurt her, or worse, there's no way I'm letting him come with me. I can lock the bastard up until I come back. It'll be just like old times for him.

"Nothing happened," he moans. "Sure, I wanted to play with her, see if I could get a few answers, but as soon as I walked in the cell she was ready for me. I went out like a light. You didn't tell me she's lethal." Gabriel stretches his fingers out and swears. "I've got pins and needles everywhere. What's with that? Is it the after-effects of the electricity?" He looks at me as if I have all the answers.

"I don't care what you've got, or how you got it. Get your ass in some decent clothes and get ready to go hunting. She can't escape. If she rats on us I'll go back inside, and now you probably will too. She knows who you are." Gabriel nods. He's beginning to realise how serious this situation is.

"Fuck," he swears. Getting to his feet he begins jogging up the steps, and I follow quickly after him. Zipping my jacket closed again I wonder how many hours I've been up now? Twenty-four, give or take an hour or two? I feel horrible, but there's no chance of sleep for me until Harper has been found. Racing upstairs, I open my drawer to grab a pair of gloves, only to find they've disappeared. Harper's been here. Swearing, I run back downstairs to find Gabriel already waiting for me.

"How long have you been out?" I ask. I need to know how much of a head-start Harper has on us. It'd better not be a long one.

Gabriel looks at his watch. "An hour," I think. "It can't be much more than that."

I nod. I can work with an hour or two. Much more and we would have been in real trouble.

"Shall we split up," he asks? At least he's dressed sensibly for the weather. He's got a thick waterproof jacket and trousers to match. It's more than I have.

29

"Yes. Don't bother searching to the rear of the property, there's a sheer cliff down there and she'll never be able to get down it. Out the front, the road forks in two directions, left and right. You take the left. She'll have to get on the road eventually if she wants to find help. I'm going to take the car, but you'll be on foot. Have you got a cell-phone with you?"

"No. I bust mine just after you rang. I dropped it outside in a fucking puddle. I've ordered a new one, but it'll take a few hours to arrive, and when it does it'll be in London. Maybe I should get a burner phone down here? If there is some kind of civilisation in this god-forsaken place? I didn't see a house for miles on the way down." Gabriel looks astounded that anywhere could be this desolate, but he's rarely been out of the city. Scotland and London are almost polar opposites.

"That's kind of the point, idiot." I pass him my phone. "If you get stuck call the house phone. It's already programmed in there. It won't take me long to scout the area by car. She can't have gone far. You, on the other hand, had better get a move on." I raise my eyebrows in warning.

"I'm going, I'm going. Don't worry. We'll get her back."

I give him a look. "We'd better," I say pointedly.

Gabriel nods and begins walking at breakneck speed.

I don't immediately get in the car. Scouting around outside the front door, I look for tracks. If she's taken the road I won't find anything, but if she's decided to go across country, I might. Harper, as Gabriel has just found out, is a clever girl. For starters, she managed to get me incarcerated for her wrongdoings, and secondly, she was studying with me at the Imperial College of London. I'm guessing she had a scholarship, although I don't know that for certain. If she did, it probably puts her in the top ten percent of pupils there, yet I know for a fact she failed to graduate. Was that down to Alex? It seems likely. He was a bad influence on all those around him.

I can't help but wonder where her parents are. She never talks about them, and I've never seen her with them. Are they even in the picture? I'd like to think they wouldn't have allowed her to marry Wilkinson if they were still around. Also, she wouldn't have run off to Nottingham if she had family, nor would she have starved herself half to death. I suspect they're either dead or something just as bad.

Finding no evidence of footprints as I scour both sides of the driveway on the way down, I swear. It looks like she was smart enough to take the road, at least in the beginning, anyway. It's more than likely she'll wander inland at some point, but she wants to make it difficult for us to track her. Running back to the car I start it up and reverse out of the garage. Then I power down the drive and take a right.

There's a reason I've told Gabriel to go left. The nearest village down that road is over fifty miles away. She's going nowhere fast if she takes that route. If she took a right, however, she'll start seeing signs of civilisation in thirty miles or so. My guess is she won't manage more than ten to fifteen miles on foot per day. Theoretically, I've got two days to find her. Realistically, I need to find her in the next couple of hours, or I risk becoming one of the walking dead. Thank God I didn't wait for the train.

My eyes peel left and right as I drive slowly. I'm not exactly sure what I'm looking for, but I'll know when I find it. Harper will feel too exposed on the road. Even though there's a chance a passing car might come to her rescue, she knows that's unlikely because I've already told her how remote this place is. I think she'll aim for cover at the earliest opportunity. She'll be looking to keep herself as hidden from the road as possible, while still keeping it in sight. Roads lead to places with houses and people. She knows that's her ticket out of here. That's my guess, anyway.

The first few miles are scrubland, and though my eyes are rapidly scanning left and right I don't spot a thing. She'd be too easy to spot out here. Harper probably ran this stretch as fast as her little legs would carry her. Another couple of miles in, though, there's a pine forest stretching out to my right. Now that would make an ideal hiding place. Did she veer off here or further up? My guess is here because she wouldn't know when Gabriel would wake up, and she didn't know when I'd be back either. She'd err on the side of caution.

I park up on the side of the road and start walking. My eyes are scanning for footprints, but there's more wet grass than mud and it's difficult to tell. Some of the grass nearby appears to be trodden down, so I take this as a good sign. Walking briskly towards the forest, I look for any clues that might indicate someone has been here recently. I'm assuming Harper has taken some food with her; maybe she's thrown a wrapper or apple core down somewhere? It's unlikely, but I'll take any crumb I can get at this point. Making my way through the trees as stealthily as I can, I can't spot a soul. If Harper has been through here it was some time ago.

While the trail might be cold, I have a feeling I'm on the right track. When I get to the edge of the forest there's more brush with another small forest about half a mile away in the distance. Something tells me she's there. Don't ask me what it is, but my sixth sense is rarely wrong. This means I need to be cautious. If she manages to catch me unawares and clobbers me around the head she'll be gone, and I'll never find her again.

I find the eerie silence of the outdoors oddly comforting as I make my way slowly across the clearing, keeping towards the edge of the forest. I'm guessing she'll stay more central, using the trees for cover. Too much noise tends to freak me out these days. Back in prison it was an indication that a riot was going down, or something just as nasty. To be fair, silence could be just as deadly, but I've made my peace with that. Micas is no longer out there to haunt me, and there's no one looking over my shoulder that I know of, except perhaps Gabriel, but I'll deal with that later. At the moment I have more important fish to fry.

Where has Harper gone? My eyes are drinking in the verdant landscape, but so far I've got nothing. Hoping she'll be focused on moving forward and not looking back over her shoulder, I plough on as fast as I dare. I'm exposed out here and if she catches a glimpse of me it'll either have her running or shimmying up a tree somewhere. I know I can outrun her, but if she hides and I can't find her, we're back to square one.

Keeping my footfalls soft, I comb the ground continuously for any signs of life.

In the back of my mind there's the thought that she might have headed towards the cliffs and jumped. It's a possibility. If she's dead I'll never forgive myself. I want her to pay for her sins, but I don't want her to die. That means I still care about her. I do my best to dispel that thought. I can't afford to care about her. If I have my way she'll be incarcerated for the next few years. Could I put her through that? The woman should have to pay for her crimes, I tell myself. She shouldn't be able to just walk away. It doesn't answer my question, though. Do I want her put away? I thought I did, but now I'm not so sure. What is wrong with me? I can't seem to make a decision these days. Is this what prison has done to me?

While I'm berating myself for going soft in my old age, I start to veer into the centre of the forest and I suddenly spot what I've been looking for all along. It's a footprint. It's not Harper's footprint, though, it's my footprint. One of my trainers, to be exact. She had no clothes in the house, or shoes. I burned them. I thought that would put paid to any ideas of escape, but I've been wrong twice now. Harper is far more resourceful than I gave her credit for. I can't imagine what she must look like, dressed in men's clothes that are at least twice as big as she is. I mean, how is she even walking in my shoes? They would drown her tiny feet. Anyway, the good news is that I'm on the right track. She's been through here recently.

Standing still for a minute I stop and listen. I want to hear rustling undergrowth or snapping twigs. I need a sign that somebody is still in here with me. Seconds tick by slowly. I hear nothing but the whistling of wind through leaves and the chirping of birds. Is she still here or should I keep walking? My gaze goes up into the trees. I can't see anything out of the ordinary, but that doesn't mean she's not around. I have a feeling that I'm lagging behind, though. I need to get a move on.

Picking up my pace, I follow the trail deeper into the woods. I see more footprints, often spaced quite far apart, and I wonder if she's been trying to run. It would be hard in a pair of shoes that are ten times too big for you, but not impossible. If she is, that's a bonus. It means she's not so cautious any more. She just wants to put as much distance between herself and the house as possible. Harper also knows that she'll have to cover a lot of ground before she comes across another human being, unless she's really lucky, and I hope to hell she's not. I need to get my hands on her as quickly as possible.

Breaking into a run, I do my best to push past the exhaustion that's consuming my body and start to close the gap between us. Thankfully I'm on adrenaline overload, but it won't last long. If I don't find her soon I'll be on my knees. The thought of the walk back is already making me queasy. Where is she? My eyes are once again everywhere, but I see no sign of her. When I get past the trees that have plunged the world into darkness, there's a field with nothing but rolling hills and heather in front of me. I wonder if I'll be able to spot her at the top of the next rise. It's really exposed out here, and she'll have nowhere to hide.

Hiking up the side of the hill, thankful I have my heavy-duty walking boots on, I watch a deer run off into the distance. He is utterly breath-taking with a full head of antlers, and his back legs give one hell of a kick as he sprints away from me. Has he been disturbed by someone? Sure enough, when I get to the top I spot a lone figure in the distance. It's got to be her. As I get closer I'm sure of it. She looks faintly ridiculous with my oversized clothes on her, and she's waddling about trying her best to power walk. My shoes keep slipping off her feet, and an old duffel bag of mine bangs against her hip. I'm amazed she hasn't fallen over yet, but somehow she manages to struggle on.

Breaking into a run I get within four hundred metres before her head snaps around. Her eyes immediately catch mine and she looks like I've just fired a gun at her. It makes my gut clench. She looks haunted, scared out of her mind and utterly defeated. Damn it. What did Gabriel do to her?

Putting another burst of speed on, I watch as she ditches my shoes and breaks into a sprint. But there's nowhere to hide and she's going nowhere. Harper fights until the very end, though. Her feet must be killing her on this rough terrain, but it doesn't stop her pelting off as fast as she can. I'm pushing my body to the limit as I try to keep up, but as another steep hill looms ahead I know I've got her. That sharp incline will slow her down, and as long as I keep my pace I should be able to reach her before she gets to the top. My strides are far longer than hers. Just a little further.

My lungs are screaming as I pound my shoes into the long wet grass, but I push on. Harper's feet are slipping all over the place. She's regularly stumbling and scrabbling about on the ground, and this means I'm rapidly closing the distance between us. It doesn't help that her movement is hampered by clothes that are spilling out all over the place. There is no way she'd have made it thirty miles dressed like that. She'd have ended up killing herself out here.

"Get away from me!" There's a choked sob from her as she realises the game is lost. I almost feel sorry for her. Almost.

"Stop running, Harper. You're not going to get away. It would take you days to escape from this wilderness, and there's no way you'd have ever made it."

"I'd rather die trying than stay there with him!" she spits at me. "You sent an ex-con to babysit me. He broke into my cell in seconds. I'm there naked, and he's threatening to fuck me then kill me. You're an animal." She sounds hysterical, and she's got a point.

"I didn't have a choice. I thought I was flying out to America and I could hardly invite the next-door neighbours around, could I?" I lunge savagely for her leg, but she pulls it away just in time. God damn it, I don't have the energy for this.

"He's a monster. I'm not going back. How could you do that to me?" Tears are pouring down her cheeks and damned if I don't feel guilty about them.

"You are going back, but you're going back with me. I won't let him near you." I do my best to placate her, but the reality of the situation is we need to be getting out of here before I collapse.

"I am not going back to that cell," she screeches. "Not when he can waltz in any time. I'm not a whore. You can't share me with your friends and expect me to roll over. I'd rather die." Harper seems to have got a second wind after that sentence because she tumbles over the hill almost headfirst, rolling downwards at an alarming rate. I sprint after her as if the law is on my heels, worried that she's about to kill herself or worse. She cannot die on me - not after all the crap I've been through.

"Calm down, Harper. You are not going back to that cell," I confirm. "I don't trust him either. You'll stay with me until I can get rid of him." I make another lunge, and this time I miss her jeans pant leg by a mere whisper of air. I almost scream in frustration.

"Let me go. If you want to kill me, do it. If not, let me continue to make a colossal mess of my life in peace. I was doing just fine until I met you." She stumbles again, and this time I take no chances. I leap forward, grab her butt, and tackle her into the ground.

"Get off me!" she squeals, and the woman is madder than a bulldog chewing a bumblebee. Struggling like a banshee underneath me, her nails are trying their best to gouge my eyes out. Moving higher up her body, letting my weight rest on top of her, I let her get it out of her system. I swear I could fall asleep right now, even with all the screaming and shouting, but I'd probably suffocate her in the meantime. At least the tiredness means there's no chance of me becoming aroused by this. Mind you, she doesn't know that.

"Careful, Harper, or I might have to fuck you right here in the grass." She stills immediately, like I knew she would, and the fight drains out of her.

"You're a bastard, Brandt." Her body is shaking all over, and if she's not careful there'll be nothing left of her. I'm amazed she made it as far as she did. She still looks ill. I bet she hasn't eaten half of what I left her. Maybe she's hoping she can starve herself to death.

"And you're a bitch, Harper Wilkinson. My crimes don't even compare to yours. You ruined my life. You've managed to break every little piece of it up and then spit on it." There's no anger in my voice. I haven't got the energy for anger.

"Yeah? Well, lucky you. My life was ruined a long time ago." There's an unmistakable edge of bitterness in her tone, and I know I need to find out this girl's story. Not today. I'm not going to remember much from today - but as soon as we're able, we need to sit down and get this over with.

"We'll talk tomorrow, Harper. I promise. Now will you come back with me? I can drag you kicking and screaming if you insist, but I'd rather not." I'm lying. The effort that would take would kill me. That doesn't mean I can't knock her out and sling her over my shoulder, though.

"You promise you won't put me in the cell, or leave me with him?" Her voice wobbles on the last word. I want to kill Gabriel. This whole mess is because I trusted him to do something ridiculously simple. When will I ever learn?

"You have my word. Now can you walk, or do you need to be carried?"

Harper falls into line, insisting she can walk, but after only a short way I can't bear to hear her whimpering every time she steps on something sharp. Picking her up in my arms, we march onwards. I have no idea how I'm still upright, let alone walking, but at least Harper is as a light as a feather. She weighs virtually nothing in my arms because she's all skin and bones. I want the girl I remembered back. The one with the laughing eyes and cheeky sass. The Harper I have now is a mere caricature of her former self, and she looks dreadful. If I hadn't found her when I did, I wonder if she'd have managed to last much longer. She's obviously fallen on hard times. It's probably no more than she deserved, but I can't think about her starving and feel happy about it. I know I am missing something here, but I'm too tired to join the dots together. Maybe I'll figure out this puzzle tomorrow.

I plod on in silence, listening to Harper's laboured breathing as it curls up my chest and fans into my face. It matches my own, but she's not actually doing anything now. The last few hours have really taken its toll on her. I need to get us back home as soon as possible and tucked up into bed. No one will be getting up to much for the next couple of days at the very least.

"Where are your parents?" My voice is soft and curious. When I hired someone to find her whereabouts while I was in prison, I wonder why I didn't ask them to give me the lowdown on her background. Actually, a call to any private investigator would have managed that, and those details might be important. Back then rage was consuming me, and I just needed to get my hands on her. Now I have other things to consider. Nothing about this mess is panning out the way I expected it to, and I suspect there's a reason for that.

"They're dead." Those two words let me know that Harper's guard is down. Up until now she's been careful to keep me in the dark, but she's too exhausted to think straight, and I know the feeling. Even so, she never offers any more information than absolutely necessary. It's frustrating.

"How did they die?" My footfalls are sure and even, and I wonder if the motion is lulling her to sleep. Her eyes are closing every few seconds, and although she is fighting sleep it won't take her long to succumb to it.

"A car accident." Her words are slurred now, and she sounds drunk. Has she been up for as long as I have? I can't help but wonder.

"How old were you?" Questioning Harper is like pulling teeth, but I plough on regardless. I'll take any crumb I can get.

"Seven." She sighs as if in pain. I'm not sure if it's because she's remembering that time in her life, or whether she just wants me to shut up so she can nod off. If it's the latter, there's no chance I'm giving up now.

"I'm sorry," I say, and surprise myself by meaning it. No one deserves to lose their parents that young. Mine might not like me, but at least they're alive. "Do you have any other relatives? Brothers, sisters, aunts, uncles, or grandparents maybe?" I find myself hoping she has someone to rely on. The other side of that coin is too horrifying to consider.

"No." Her voice is surly, and it's clear she wants to end the conversation. I close my eyes and sigh. This is the last thing I need to hear. Harper Wilkinson has probably been bouncing around residential treatment centres and foster care for most of her childhood. It must have been awful at best, and at worst - well, I don't want to think about that. I've read the newspapers, and I've heard the reports.

"How did you come out the other side of that?" I don't realise I've asked the question out loud until she responds brokenly, in a choked-up sob that almost destroys me.

"I didn't."

Chapter 7 - Harper

I don't remember the journey back to Brandt's house. I fell asleep in his arms shortly after he picked me up, and when I awoke I was already being carried upstairs. The house is freezing cold, and when I breathe out little clouds of condensation form in the air. My teeth begin chattering immediately, and my toes feel numb. That's what you get for walking about with no shoes on. It's probably a good thing I can't feel them. When they warm up they're going to hurt like hell.

After Brandt places me carefully on his bed I moan and curl up into a little ball. All I want to do is sleep. Then I remember that Gabriel is prowling around these halls, and I immediately sit upright.

"Gabriel..." I gasp.

Brandt shakes his head. "He won't hurt you while I'm here, but there is a price to pay for my protection - if you want to sleep with me up here. You can either be handcuffed to the bed or handcuffed to me. I haven't slept in well over twenty-four hours, and I'm not running after you again. If you don't want to do that, you can go back in your cell, and I'll sleep on the other side with you."

"I want to stay up here," I whisper. My face has gone white at the mere mention of the word 'cell' and the thought of returning there makes my stomach lurch. Besides, it will need to be cleaned up first, and I can't face that.

"Fine. Do you want to eat first?" Brandt looks at me hopefully, but I shake my head. The last thing I can think about now is eating.

He sighs but doesn't press me on the issue. "Wriggle out of those wet clothes and get under the covers, Harper."

I do as I'm told. There's no point protesting because he's seen me naked enough times that I no longer need to make a fuss. If he wants to fuck me, he will, whether I have clothes on or not, but I don't think either of us has enough energy for that. When I settle under the covers he pulls out a pair of handcuffs from his top drawer and fastens one around my wrist, while the other goes around the headboard. He doesn't trust me not to move, and I can't say I blame him.

"Give me five minutes and I'll be right back. Gabriel is not here at the moment, so you don't need to worry. Try to get some rest." I nod at him, but I can't hide the fact that I'm anxious. If Gabriel finds me again he'll probably kill me. I saw the look in his eye just before I electrocuted him, and I know what he planned on doing to me. The man has no scruples. Brandt might have lost most of his, but there's still something there. Gabriel, on the other hand, is a loose cannon. He scares me.

Brandt runs off downstairs, while I sit upright in bed thinking that I've just jumped out of the frying pan and into the mouth of an erupting volcano. Unless Brandt sends his friend away, my life expectancy around this place has suddenly taken a giant nose-dive to rival a refugee in a war-torn country. Everywhere I look death and destruction await me. Mind you, that might be a good thing. I'll take quick over slow and painful any day, and I have a feeling Gabriel is going to be just a little bit pissed with me - as in a giant fucking lot. What a lucky girl I am. I wonder how many other ladies have two beautiful hunks fighting over who gets to be the one to kill her first? Not many I'm betting.

Hunkering down into the bedcovers, as far as my cuffed arm will allow, I try to stop thinking about death, and wonder if a night in Brandt's bed will be better than a night in my cell. What am I doing? Is the small element of safety I'll feel with him beside me worth the inevitable conclusion that will happen when both of us wake up tomorrow? We'll either end up fucking or fighting, and I'm not sure which is worse.

When I hear Brandt's footfalls coming my way a few minutes later, I turn away from the door and huddle myself up into a foetal position. I'm shivering so hard I can hear my teeth banging together, and I'm not entirely sure it's from the cold. I feel like I'm falling apart at the seams - seams which were already frayed to begin with.

His weight, when he sits down, makes the bed dip, and my body rolls back towards the middle. That's the last place I want to be, but I can hardly shift back to my corner while he's watching me. I'll have to sneak back into place later, when he's asleep. Meanwhile, I do a subtle little wiggle that will at least give him some space to lie down.

"Calm down, Harper. I'm not going to eat you." Brandt's tone is dry. "Well, not today, anyway." I roll my eyes, thankful that he can't see me. Like that's supposed to reassure me. I hear him kick off his jeans and pull his shirt over his head. The next thing I know his body is flush against mine, and I nearly have a seizure.

"Do you want the handcuff to remain like that, or would you rather be cuffed to me? You'll probably sleep easier if your arm is down beside you." My eyes blink at that. A few days ago I'd have never got a concession like that out of Brandt. He must be feeling guilty. Perhaps he does have a heart, after all.

"To you, please." Trying to sleep with my arm at a right angle above me will be almost impossible, but I'm afraid the alternative might be just as bad. When Brandt releases my wrist from the headboard to reattach it to his wrist, he then wraps our cuffed hands around the front of my body and presses himself against my back. Oh God. I can't sleep like this.

"Try to relax, Harper. You'll warm up soon. Gabriel won't come anywhere near us tonight. He's sleeping down the far end of the hall, and besides, I've locked the door."

"Is that supposed to reassure me? He picked the lock to my cage, remember?" I can feel pressure building in my chest, knowing there will be a shitstorm brewing for me first thing tomorrow morning. I just hope Brandt will be on my side.

"He won't hurt you tonight. I'm right here. I won't let him touch you." Brandt's voice is already sleepy, and I can feel him relaxing into the soft mattress.

"And tomorrow?" I whisper.

"Tomorrow is another day entirely," he murmurs. That sentence makes me want to explode on the spot, but it's the last word I get out of him. I then spend the entire night tossing and turning between the comforting warmth his arms provide around me.

When I wake up the next morning, it's early. Maybe five or six o'clock, judging by the light outside. Brandt isn't beside me, and once again my arm is locked to the headboard above me. It can't have been there long. It's not sore yet. My free hand reaches out to feel the empty space in the bed beside me, and sure enough, it's still warm. I wonder if he's checking on Gabriel.

Straining my ears I listen carefully for any sounds or movement, but I hear nothing. Either they're too far away from me or the door is really thick. The Victorians certainly built their houses to last, but they didn't know a whole lot about insulation. It feels freezing outside the covers that now cocoon me. I hope Brandt doesn't put me back in my cell. All I will be able to think about is Gabriel, and when he intends to get his own back. I know his kind. He won't let my retaliation go unpunished. He will get his pound of flesh. They're probably discussing what they're going to do to me right now.

The door opens, making me gasp out loud, and in walks Brandt carrying two steaming mugs.

"Coffee," I whisper. "Oh God, how I've missed coffee." The smell is tantalising. This isn't your standard variety of instant, either. This is proper coffee. The type that is filtered through posh chrome machines with lots of whirring and giant puffs of steam.

"Coffee," Brandt confirms, "which you can have as soon as you start talking. Why did you set me up?"

Oh God, we're back to that again? I want to cry.

"I can't tell you that. They'll kill me, and they'll probably kill you, too. You don't know what you're dealing with here. Let it go." Brandt's always been clueless about what was going on right under his nose in college. He was a kid when all of this went down, though. We both were. Neither of us are now. We both had to grow up far too quickly.

"Who is they?" Brandt barks at me, placing the cup carefully on his bedside table.

"Keep your fucking coffee," I spit, turning away from him. We're back to square one and we're going around in circles. If he wants to start pulling my toenails out, he'd better get started.

Brandt sits down on the bed with a resigned sigh. "Harper, I'll get this out of you, one way or the other. I'd rather not do it the hard way, but if you don't play ball that's what will happen. I don't have much time left."

I laugh. A sad little laugh that Brandt won't understand, and that's probably for the best.

"You have plenty of time left, Brandt. I, on the other hand, have very little. They'll come for me. It won't be long now, and even up here they'll find me. You might as well kill me now." Mal has too many contacts, both inside prison and out. Nothing stays secret from him for long. He knows I'm a loose end with Alex gone, and if I'm no longer in the trade, he'll make sure I don't pose a threat to business.

"No one will find you up here. What are you talking about?"

Brandt looks exasperated, but I cannot give him what he needs. I still care about him. If I keep him in the dark, there's a chance Mal won't kill him when he finds me. Hopefully, I'll be far away from here by then. I keep trying to run, but life is not playing fair. Mind you, when did it ever?

"Just do whatever you have planned to make me feel miserable today, Brandt. I cannot talk to you. You've already been through enough, and I can't put you through any more. The rest of this sorry mess will be on me. I deserve it, and I'm ready for it."

Brandt's face darkens. He doesn't understand, and why would he? He has no idea what I've got myself into.

"Ready for what? Don't do this, Harper," he threatens. His hands curl into fists, and the look in his eyes is almost one of defeat. He thought after the last episode with Gabriel I would just cave in and do everything he says. If it was only my life at risk, I would, but I can't have anyone else's death on my conscience. I'm already weighed down with the burden of my misdeeds. I can't add any more to the list. Mal won't let me suffer for too much longer, anyway. So there's that to look forward to, I guess.

"If I talk, I put you at risk. I know you don't understand, but that's the truth of the matter. I got in with the wrong crowd back at college and there's nothing I can do to undo that. People will come for me. I don't want you to be here when they do."

"I don't believe you."

Brandt thinks I'm making all this up, and I can understand why. I have no proof. I'm not sure I could verify my sorry tale even if I wanted to. The meth labs have probably been moved by now, and along with most of the other shit. Nothing stays still for long in the drugs trade.

"Then don't believe me, but one day you will, Brandt. Take my word for it." I just hope he'll still be alive and breathing when that happens.

"I'll take you straight back down to that cell, Harper. I'll let Gabriel have some fun with you. Stop this now before something happens that we both regret." Brandt's face hardens and I can tell all his earlier friendliness has gone. Now he has me right back where he wants me, the old rules apply. All the promises of yesterday have flown out of the window. He is not my saviour. While I am under this roof we are enemies, and I have to remember that.

"Then take me back down there and watch him electrocute me." I suspect Gabriel has all that and worse planned for when he gets his hands on me. He's in another category entirely to Brandt. That man knows how to deal out pain, and lots of it. I can tell just by looking at him.

"That's not funny, Harper." He's not kidding. I'm not particularly looking forward to it, but I am resigned to the fact.

"Do what you have to do, Brandt. I'm done arguing." I am. This morning, I feel just as exhausted as yesterday, and it has nothing to do with my lack of sleep. My situation up here is about to go nuclear, and I'm pretty sure I'm not going to like it.

Brandt then stands and picks up my mug of coffee. For a moment I worry that he might throw it over me, but he simply walks around the bed and places it on the small wooden table next to me.

"I'm going to let you drink this while you think about what you're letting yourself in for today. I'm not going to protect you unless you have the decency to confess all. If not at the police station, you could at least make me understand what happened that day. You owe me that much, Harper."

I do. I owe him all that and more, but I'll put him in danger if I do so. I'm no stranger to taking pain, though. If he wants to dish it out, I'm pretty sure he can't top what Mal did to me. Gabriel is another matter entirely. I have a feeling that man could make me confess in seconds if he put his mind to it, and that terrifies me.

"Thank you for the coffee," I whisper. It's a small kindness, but it means a lot in my world right now.

Brandt gives me a dark look and shakes his head. "I suspect you won't be thanking me in an hour or so's time, Harper. Think carefully. I'll be back in twenty minutes." He turns his back to me and strides angrily out of the room, shutting the door with a sharp click behind him.

Once he's gone I almost snatch the coffee from the bedside table. It's as if I'm scared that if I don't drink it immediately someone will walk in and take it away. Alex was like that. If I took too long eating, he would just remove my plate from under my nose and dump the contents in the bin. The man had quite a temper on him, but I think it was more that he wanted to keep me stick thin and appealing, so all his friends would want to fuck me. I was a trophy wife to him, and I have no illusions otherwise. I'm not even sure the man loved me. He wanted me simply because everyone else wanted me, and he always liked to win. Dating was a competition as far as he was concerned. Could he get the girl? Well, he made sure of that, whether I liked it or not. Alex was the type of man who didn't like to lose.

Taking a sip of coffee, I swear when the mug burns my fingertips and the heat scalds my tongue. Serves me right for being so eager. It smells so good, though. I don't remember the last time I had a cup of decent coffee. All I know is that it was a very long time ago. Even so, the taste of it upon my lips is heaven. Its bittersweet aroma leaves an acid-like burn on my tongue, but it reminds me of better times. I need to savour every moment of the good stuff that comes my way because these moments are becoming few and far between. God. Since when did I get excited over coffee? How tragic. I'm a living, breathing, walking disaster. Everything I touch seems to disintegrate. Blowing on the surface of my mug to cool the molten lava within, I am once again lost in memories.

Mal bends me over the bed roughly, before hitching up my skirt. The cologne he wears is sweet and overpowering, and I can smell the whisky on his breath as he leans over me. His body is powerful and heavy, and I can feel his erection straining against his crotch.

"Have you got a little present for me, darlin,'" he asks, as his hands splayed wide over my backside. I'm not sure what I've got for him, but I wish to hell it were HIV. His fingers knead my ass with a fierce intensity that has me gasping in pain rather than pleasure, but this doesn't deter him in the slightest. He kicks my legs

40

apart with his booted feet and rests his weight upon my back as he gropes between my legs. At least the man has his priorities in order. Drugs first, then sex. I wouldn't want to think I was special. Mal wastes no time retrieving his package, and pulls it out of my pussy like his fingers are on fire. Maybe he just wants to check the merchandise is the real deal; who knows?

Sure enough, I hear the crinkle of plastic and then I can hear him sniffing, checking that the stuff is genuine. It had damn well better be, else Alex has just sold me down the river. A few painful seconds go by as I wait for his verdict. I have at least three heart-attacks while I wait for him to speak, but unfortunately I do not manage to pass out on the floor. Life is so unfair.

"Stuff's good," he grunts, before resuming his fierce manhandling of my ass. I have a bad feeling about this. This isn't going to be the normal MO. Usually I'm forced down on my knees while the fucker in front of me does his best to remove my tonsils. I'm used to this and can almost cope with it. Today, I have a nasty suspicion it will not be that easy.

"Do you like pain, 'Arper?" And those there, are words I never want to hear. It's not because I don't like pain - I do, and especially during sex. It's because I never tell the sick bastards to stop once they've started. I'll be the one on the floor begging for more, while I'm bleeding out of every major artery I own. Alex finds this incredibly amusing and has tested my powers of miraculous recuperation more than once.

"Yes," I moan. I'm going to regret those words, but I say them anyway. Besides, I know damn well that Alex has already told him everything he needs to know about me.

"That's good," Mal says, slapping my ass so hard I squeal in pain. "Are you going to be my good little slut this evening, darlin'?" he asks.

There really is only one answer to that question, so I give him the 'yes' he's looking for. The next thing I know his teeth are sinking into my ass so hard, I'm pretty sure he's just drawn blood. I squeal in horror and immediately try to get up, but there's an elbow in my back pinning me down.

"Ah, I don't think so, babe. You're 'ere for the duration," he barks. "All you've got to do is stay there like a good little whore and do every damn thing I tell you. Think you can manage that?" He's leaning over me and barking each word directly into my eardrum. My whole body trembles as flecks of spit fly across my face. I have never been so scared in my life, and I have had plenty to be scared about, trust me.

"Yes," I whimper, hoping that somehow I manage to get out of here alive. There have been others who haven't. I hear things on the grapevine. Some of the girls in the lab try to befriend me, mistakenly thinking I have some influence over Alex. They tell me all sorts of secrets, trying to gain my confidence. They're wasting their time. I don't know anything of value, and I can't help them work their way up in this industry. If they want to suck Alex's cock they're welcome to it, but otherwise there's not a lot of room for promotion around these parts.

"Good," he sneers. "I like a woman who can follow simple instructions. You might come in 'andy." Mal then positions his cock at the entrance to my pussy, wrapping both hands around my neck as he begins squeezing. Pressing tightly against my windpipe, he thrusts brutally forward, impaling me with large, monstrous thrusts that feel as if they're trying to break me apart. He pounds into me with as much force as he can muster, and I'm counting down the seconds in my head. When I get to sixty I can feel my lungs screaming for air. Is he going to let me breathe again? Or is this where I die? Panic is peeling me wide open and I have never felt so vulnerable. All sorts of crappy thoughts are reeling through my head.

There is no one around.

I'm half-naked.

He's a drug lord.

He has a gun.

He can easily overpower me.

No one will care if I end up dead in a dumpster tomorrow.

I don't want to die.

Alex, you complete and utter bastard, I think as the last of my air evaporates. He knew this would happen, and yet he sent me here anyway. I hope he rots in hell. My head lolls once as I nearly blackout, and then Mal's hands miraculously loosen their grip and I take in giant, gasping breaths of air.

"That's right, sweetheart. Breathe while you can. You've got ten seconds of air before I start over." His fingers reach for my neck again and I almost begin choking in terror at the thought of what he's about to do. This is obviously some sort of fun game for him. There's nothing like a bit of 'will-she-live' or 'won't-she' while you're messing about underneath the sheets. No wonder no one wants to have sex with this monster. He's a freaking lunatic.

Sucking in air like there's no tomorrow, I get no chance to recover before Mal's hands encircle my neck once more. It's obvious he wants to feel my fear because he lets his hands caress the soft flesh in front of my throat before he applies any pressure. This kind of foreplay is enough to send me crazy, and sure enough, I start thrashing about underneath him. I can't go through that again. My throat is still sore from the last attack and this time I'll pass out, and who knows what he'll do to me then. This guy is a loon.

He lets me thrash about on the bed for a few seconds, and I know that my struggling is turning him on because his cock is rock hard and pulsing heavily against my clit. Jesus Christ, how do I extricate myself from this mess? Pushing back against him has no effect whatsoever because the man is built like a tank, and trying to slip sideways is equally as ineffective, especially as he's decided to sheath his cock in me again, effectively pinning me to the bed.

"Please," I whimper, as his hands tighten once more. I don't manage to get another word out before his thumb is pressing against my trachea, cutting both my air supply and voice off at the same time.

"The word 'please' on a woman's lips is so fucking adorable," he says, before bending down to sink his teeth into my ear. I can't even scream, the pressure against my throat is so tight. My eyes are bulging in their sockets, and I have an awful feeling that I may not make it out of this room alive. "I think you're going to say 'please' lots this evening, 'Arper. Who knows? Maybe if you're a good girl, and you do everything I tell you to, maybe I'll even let you live through the experience. Stranger things 'ave 'appened." He thrusts into me again, over and over, brutally hard until this time I do blackout. I am revived shortly after by a slap around the face, and I find myself wheezing as I try to drag air into my chest. It hurts so much. Even breathing is painful now. Black spots dance before my eyes as my lungs burn.

"I'm going to play one 'anded now, 'Arper. That way my other 'and can play with you."

I can't tell Mal how excited I am about this prospect, because I'm still fighting for my life on the bed. He doesn't seem deterred by my lack of enthusiasm, though. Bringing one hand up in front of my legs, he finds my clit and begins circling it with his fingers. This time I have no energy left to fight him. Breathing is far too important.

"Good girl," he soothes, stroking my hair. "What a good girl you are." His fingers work me over and over, and he takes his time, alternating between sinking either his fingers or his cock deep inside me. As much as I want to, I can't fight the arousal. It comes upon me in steady, humiliating waves, and before I know what's happening I'm pressing my body back against him, eager for more.

"That's it. Give in to it. Show me how much you want my cock, 'Arper." His fingers don't stop what they're going, they just take me closer and closer towards the edge. Finally, figuring all the nastiness is behind me, I let myself relax a little, and it's easier than it should be because Mal's fingers are very talented.

He takes me nearly to the point of orgasm, but then stops just as I let out a petulant little groan. My clit pulses madly between my legs, annoyed that it has been cheated out of its reward.

"Not yet, sweets. You 'ave to earn that privilege. Now get on your knees and show me what you can do with that mouth of yours." Mal doesn't wait for me to comply. He manhandles me roughly to the threadbare carpet underneath my feet and tips my head up, so I'll be ready for him. His cock is already in his hands, and he fists it a couple of times in front of my face so I get the idea. There is no way I'm messing with the guy in front of me, so I open wide and wait for the inevitable to happen. It doesn't take long.

Thrusting forward, Mal sinks to the back of my throat and stays there, watching my eyes. He's waiting for the moment I realise he's not going to let me breathe again. I think he wants to see me lose it, but I haven't got the energy for that. Judging by his past performance he'll either let me breathe or he'll wait for me to pass out and then let me breathe. Struggling isn't going to do anything other than turn him on, and I'm in enough trouble already.

After fifteen or twenty long seconds go by he withdraws and smiles. "You're learning," he says. He thrusts in again and begins counting me down. Starting with thirty, he watches as I suck in a lungful of oxygen before sinking again to the back of my throat. Holding himself there he waits out the allotted timescale, and then begins again, adding five seconds to the clock. It looks like he's trying to work out how much time it's going to take to break me. I don't think it's going to be very much. We play this game until he gets up to a minute and ten, and then my head starts bouncing around as I begin to lose it. I get another slap across the face for my troubles, before I'm slung back over the bed.

One hand comes back to my work my clit while the other returns to my neck. At this point I want to sob my heart out, but I daren't. I don't have enough air for tears. My body is both petrified and consumed with lust within minutes of his fingers beginning again. I can tell Mal is having a whale of a time behind me with his heavy groans of enthusiasm as he thrusts inside me. The bastard then brings me to the point of orgasm and near-death a further five times, before he finally lets me come. It's the most incredible orgasm I've ever had - and the most terrifying.

You'd think after I'd taken all that I'd be allowed to go home, right? You'd think wrong.

Chapter 8 - Brandt

The walk back down the stairs is a long one. I don't know why I thought Harper and I would come to some sort of arrangement after yesterday, but it's abundantly clear that we haven't. She's taking stubbornness to a whole new level, and if I'm honest, I'm ill-equipped to deal with this shit. I want to be done with this whole sorry ordeal and I don't want to hurt her any more. I'm not sure what's happened to her exactly, since I've been put inside, but I do know it's not pleasant. She started screaming in the middle of her sleep last night. Yelling out things like 'don't touch me', or 'please don't do this again'. Now that could have been me she was dreaming about, but somehow I don't think so. The first night she was here she had nightmares, and it pains me to watch her when she's in the middle of one. Last night I thought someone was trying to kill her because she nearly screamed herself hoarse. And trying to wake her up had no effect. Once she's caught up in those dreams, they take her under.

I want to know exactly what she's got herself caught up in. What has her so spooked she daren't even talk about it?

"You're up early." Gabriel startles me, already sitting upright at the kitchen counter with a book in his hands. An unfinished plate of toast and marmalade sits beside him. Putting the book down gently, he turns to face me.

"How's the head?" I ask, draining my mug of coffee before loading it into the dishwasher. At least the kitchen is well-equipped. The rest of the house still lives in the dark ages.

"Sore, but better than it was yesterday." Gabriel rubs the back of his head, wincing a little. I don't feel sorry for him.

"What did you do to her yesterday? While I believe your answer of 'nothing', mostly because you didn't get a chance to do anything, you must have threatened her with something. She tried to kill you for fuck's sake." I have a rough idea what happened, but I want to hear it from him.

Gabriel's mouth flattens. "Fine. I threatened to fuck her. Or torture her. Maybe both. I was trying to help you out," he whines.

This is pretty much what I figured. "I can do without help like that," I say sharply. "All you created was a giant mess that I had to clean up. Did you enjoy your little walk in the forest?" I know he didn't. I saw the state of his coat this morning. It was almost covered in mud from head to toe. He must have been freezing by the time he got back here.

"Not particularly. Next time, do me a favour and rent a property in the south of Spain. It's much warmer there." Gabriel bites the corner off a round of toast and grimaces.

"I'll bear that in mind for my next kidnapping expedition," I say dryly. I'm still a little affronted I can't fly to the states due to the fact I have a criminal record on my file. Yet another thing I can thank Harper for.

"So, what are you going to do about her?" Gabriel looks up at me, takes another bite of his breakfast and waits. I have no answer for him. I can't seem to think past the next five minutes at this point, and I need to. I have Helena hanging over my head. I need to get a move on.

"I don't know. Do you have any bright ideas?" I know I'm going to regret asking that question, but I do anyway.

"Plenty but judging by your earlier reaction you won't want to hear them. Looks like you're going soft in your old age, Brandt. Have you forgotten everything you learned inside?" Gabriel sounds a little disgusted with me, which I guess I can understand. We talked about what I'd do to Harper when I got my hands on her, and at the time it seemed like a good idea. That was then, though. Now, there seem to be so many things I don't understand, I'm not sure where to begin.

"Everything isn't as black and white as I thought it would be," I say, opening the fridge door and pulling out a carton of milk. I'm having good old-fashioned Scottish porridge oats for breakfast. I need something to warm me up.

"Bullshit. You're still in love with her. I knew you were back then, and you still are. Why don't you just admit it to yourself?"

My body goes ramrod straight and the fridge door slams shut. I spin around to face him.

"What did you just say?" My face is aghast.

"You heard me. You're in love with her." Gabriel is not one to beat about the bush.

"What on earth makes you say that?" Now here's the interesting part to that answer. I should have immediately denied his statement. I didn't, and that's telling enough in itself. Am I in love with Harper? Am I kidding no one but myself here?

"I've seen her Brandt. I'm not stupid. You know, I always wondered, though I never asked. Was she pretty? Was she smart? Was she the girl you'd go to prison for? But you two weren't like that, were you? Why not, Brandt? There's something between you. What is it?"

I don't want to answer that loaded question. Besides, after all that's happened whatever was there has long since disappeared. There's no way I could ever forgive her for what she's put me through.

"Nothing's there. I need to get her to confess and then I need to get rid of her."

"And then what?" Gabriel waves his piece of toast around. "Are you going to marry some rich aristocrat and have aristocratic babies?" He smirks at me. He thinks he's joking. Gabriel has no idea how close to the truth he is.

Shoving the bowl of porridge in the microwave, I sit down wearily. "Go home, Gabriel. I can figure this out on my own. I shouldn't have dragged you into this."

"No way am I doing that. Things are just starting to get good. Want to know what I think you should do to her?"

I resist the urge to roll my eyes. The last thing I need to hear is this, but I'm going to hear him out anyway. Firstly, because he's come all this way as a favour to me, and secondly, because if anyone can make Harper squeal, it is probably Gabriel. That doesn't mean I'm going to follow his advice, but I guess there's no harm in hearing it.

"Go on then. Tell all." My breakfast pings and I pull it out of the microwave, grabbing a spoon on my way past. Taking a seat alongside him I prepare for the worst.

"Drop the girl in at the deep end. I think you should tell her you'll give her to me if she doesn't do as she's told. It'll scare her witless, take my word for it." Gabriel grabs his mug of coffee and begins waving it around. He can get very animated at times. I back my chair up a little, making sure I'm nowhere near it.

"To do what with?" This may be a stupid question, but I want to make sure we're both on the same wavelength here.

Gabriel gives me a disgusted look and I nearly laugh. "To fuck, Brandt. That thing men and women do when they don't have any clothes on. I know you've been on the other side of civilisation for the past five years or so, boyo, but you must member the fucking part. It's quite good fun. Even when there aren't any women." He gives me a coy smile. I haven't seen that look in quite some time. It does things to me that it shouldn't, and I feel my balls clench.

"I remember the fucking part, Gabe, you made damn sure of it." I don't look at him as I say that but concentrate on digging my spoon into my porridge. It's the breakfast of champions. It deserves to be studied in great detail.

"We could both fuck her together, Brandt. Just like old times, but better." Gabriel's voice darkens. Lust pools in the base of my stomach. I told myself I would never go there again, and my body is already betraying me.

"I don't fuck men any more, Gabe. I said when we were done, that would be it. I know you remember that part." If he doesn't, I certainly do. I remember the exact day I fell in love with the bastard sitting across from me, and I also remember the day he walked out on me - to shack up with someone younger and prettier. It shouldn't still hurt, but it does. Although he probably did me a favour, he still stuck the knife in, and I remember shit like that.

Gabriel shrugs his shoulders, completely unphased by my outburst. "You don't have to fuck me. You can fuck her. Stop finding problems where there are none. Threaten her with me. If that doesn't work, threaten her with us. If that doesn't work, I have one last idea, but I'm not sharing that with you yet. It's too early and you haven't got your full dose of Vitamin D. Get yourself out for a run. You'll think more clearly after that. Harper will wait. I'll keep an eye on her." He grins.

"If you go anywhere near her," I threaten, "I will play ping pong with your fucking balls."

"Well, you better get out for that run then. You'll need to practise if you want to catch me, baby." Gabriel grabs his book, buries his nose in it, and sits there smirking. I want to kill him.

"I think..."

"Run. We'll talk after that." He waves me off with one hand, and I, like the fool I am, obey him. It's an automatic reaction. I've spent too many years doing every damn thing he tells me to.

When I get back to my room I let Harper up for a bathroom break. Looking over at the table, I notice the coffee's all gone. I wonder how her thinking time went. Judging by the expression on her face when I pushed the door open wide, not well.

Pulling some shorts and a T-shirt out of my drawer, I start getting changed. I do need to run. Gabriel was right. I'm in such a foul mood I couldn't make a decision to save my life. Hopefully, I'll come back with a clearer head when I've put a good ten kilometres between me and the disaster that is my life. I'm not hoping for big things on my return, but maybe I'll figure out a way to end this once and for all.

I already know Gabriel wants to fuck Harper. She's female, and she's got a pulse. There's more to it than that, though. He wants her because I want her, and he likes to play with his toys. It doesn't hurt that she's a very attractive woman, either. I can't let him in again. My head got pretty messed up last time I let him near me, and I don't think I could cope with the fallout a second time around. I might have got over the fact that I've slept with a man, but not that I fell in love with one. That hit me hard. I'm not sure I'm over it, even now. The thought of watching him fuck Harper excites me, scares me, and horrifies me. It excites me because it would turn me on. It scares me because I don't want to face the fact I might still have feelings for Gabriel. It horrifies me because the thought of him sleeping with Harper makes me insanely jealous. See what a mess I am? If Gabriel's earlier statement about me being in love with Harper is correct, and I fear it might be, then there's a chance I might be in love with two people at the same time - neither of whom want me. It really sucks to be me.

Hearing the tap in the bathroom run while Harper washes up, I wonder what I should do with her while I'm gone. Do I put her back in the cell? I know Gabriel will be all over her as soon as I leave, but there's little I can do about that. He won't touch her without my say so, but I have a nasty feeling I might let him loose on her. She's not going to talk to me, so maybe she'll talk to him. In fact, if anyone can get her to spill the beans, it's probably him. He'll go about it in an unconventional way, but I'm not really one to talk about that.

The bathroom door opens, and Harper shuts it behind her quietly. Her face is wet from where she's just washed it, and her eyes are tired. I remember I haven't fed her yet this morning, and that's very important. I don't want to throw her out of my life half-starved. When she leaves here she needs to be in a better condition than when she arrived.

"Are you ready to talk yet?" I don't know why I ask the question. I already know the answer by the expression on her face. Sure enough, she shakes her head at me. "Fine. I'm going for a run. You're going back down to your cell where you can tidy up the mess you made yesterday." She visibly stiffens. I know why, but I wait for her objections.

"Is Gabriel still here?" The whites of her eyes are in stark contrast to the dark gloominess of the room. My little liar is not a happy liar.

"Yes." I can't see him going home before this situation is resolved, either. He seems to be on board with the 'getting Harper to talk' plan and is taking the job on as a personal challenge.

"Are you locking me inside the cell?" Harper chews her lip nervously. I wonder if she's harbouring thoughts of escape again.

"Yes." I don't want another episode like yesterday. When I get back from my run the last thing I want to do is go on a ten-mile hike.

"Gabriel can get through that lock." There's a wobble in Harper's voice, which is when I realise she's far more scared of him than she is of me. It's something to store away for future use. Maybe I should take him up on his earlier offer.

"I know he can." There's no way he'll be stupid enough to let her escape a second time around, though. I know that much.

Harper's eyes dart this way and that as she thinks of a suitable argument to prevent me from leaving her alone in the house. "Aren't you worried he'll kill me while you're gone?"

"No." I'm not worried he'll kill her. I'm worried about plenty of other things, but I know he won't kill her - not yet, anyway. But if I'm honest I think he'll wait until I come back before pressing the issue. What he really wants to do is fuck with us both at the same time. That would make his twisted little mind very happy. I know how he works.

"So you're just going to leave me at his mercy?" Harper's body sinks into the mattress as she realises the implications of what I've just said.

"Yes. You're not going to talk. You've made your own bed. Congratulations - you now get to lie in it." I hold my hand out for hers. If she gives me any trouble whatsoever she'll have my hand pounding into her ass, and I'll put her back on the damn leash.

She doesn't move off the bed. She looks at me with eyes weighed down by tears, and her lip wobbles. She's about to have a moment. I have no time for that.

"Either take my hand or get down on the floor and crawl. I don't care which." My voice again has a hard edge. She's smart, she'll get the message.

"Brandt, if I go back down there and you're gone, there's no telling what he'll do. He can be inside that cell in seconds, and you know it. You can't leave me alone with him." She makes no move to take my hand, nor does she get on her hands and knees. If she thinks she has the measure of me, she's very much mistaken.

"Get on the floor, now, Harper. Else I'll have you over my lap in a heartbeat. This is your last warning." I'm done with her cryptic comments. I'm not even sure

48

if I can believe a word she says. If she married Wilkinson, I'm pretty sure she became a very accomplished liar shortly after. He was known for it. I don't know what I'm fucking doing any more. Am I infatuated with her? I bloody hope not.

"I can't, Brandt; I had too much of that with Alex. I can't, I can't..."

She's openly sobbing now. What the hell has gotten into her?

"You can't what, Harper? What is it you can't do?" She just shakes her head at me and sobs harder. This should please me. Perhaps this means I'm getting through to her at long last. I wait patiently, but her sobs only get louder. She's not going to give me an explanation. This is yet another dead end. I swear smoke is about to come out of my ears.

I don't bother asking her to obey me a third time. The fact that she got asked a second time was a near miracle in itself. Being gentle with her has had no more effect than the rough treatment, and if I'm honest, I much prefer the latter.

Grabbing her arm I pull her towards me. She's dressed in one of my T-shirts, which is so big on her it reaches mid-thigh. I let her get away with that yesterday because I was too tired to argue, but today we're going back to basics. If I have to go down Gabriel's route to get what I want, so be it. I'm done playing Mr Nice Guy. Yanking the T-shirt up over her head I throw it to the back of the room, and watch as her eyes explode on sticks. Yep, she didn't think much of that. At least she's paying attention now. Gripping a fistful of her hair I sit on the bed and tug her body down at the waist. Yelping out loud she loses her balance and lands heavily on my legs. Hallelujah. I'm not losing my touch after all.

"If you want to sit there and sob, then we might as well give you a reason to sob, huh, Little Liar?" I don't wait for her to respond. I'm done with that. I simply let my hand fly and somewhere inside me there's a satisfied roar as it connects sharply with the soft flesh of her ass. I love that sound. The hard thwack as my palm slams into her backside, over and over again, is music to my ears. My cock suddenly revs into high gear, and the bulge in my shorts is frighteningly painful as I rain down war upon the girl. It feels good. It feels too good. If I'm not careful this will lead to something I might later regret. I can't think about that now. It's probably going to happen sooner or later, anyway. Why should I keep denying myself the pleasure of her body? The woman owes me five years of pain and misery. I intend to tear the same amount of agony out of her, one way or another.

It takes me a little while to find my rhythm, but when I find it I settle down for the ride. Harper is going to feel this for at least the next week. I'm going to make sure of it. When the first five or six spanks rain down she is too shocked to utter a sound, but it doesn't take her long to find her voice. I am spreading fire all over her pert little butt cheeks, and they're turning a very pleasant shade of red. I could look at those sweet little globes all day and not get bored, and the good news is that if I want to, I can.

"Oh God," Harper whimpers, as my hand continues its journey of ass destruction, and make no mistake, that's exactly what I'm doing. I am going to destroy them. I'm not stopping until she's a sobbing, broken mess, begging for my forgiveness. I'm not even sure I'll stop then. My anger has once again turned into rage and I'm trying to deal with the fallout.

49

"Jesus, Brandt," she yells, as my hand slams into her harder and harder. I don't care. She can yell all she likes. She knows how to put a stop to this. I'm not letting her up until I have my explanation.

"Why, Harper?" That's the question that continues to confound me. Why, why, why? I punctuate each of those 'why's with a heavy thud which makes her whole body shudder. As the third one detonates on her backside she lets out a little scream.

"Stop it, Brandt! Please stop it!"

I do no such thing. I'm just getting started. Instead my hand begins to pepper her ass with sharp swats that will let the burn intensify. I know she's feeling it. I can see her body strain to try and avoid each new and devastating blow. But while she's still wriggling and squirming I haven't done my job properly. I want her sobbing and unable to lift a single finger because she's too exhausted to do so. At that point, with any luck, she'll be ready to obey every single word I say the moment I say it. Harper needs to fear me, and I'm going to make sure she does.

She isn't an easy girl to crack, though. She fights me for the longest time, shouting all sorts of obscenities. I ignore them all, even though my eardrums are ringing, and keep swatting my hand down. I don't let up, not even for a second. She is going to remember this.

After a good half hour, when I'm beginning to wonder if she'll ever give in, the violent struggling finally stops and the wailing begins. My hand is stinging like a bastard, but even so I continue with my tirade of slaps.

She's still pleading with me, but now she can barely speak because she's sobbing hysterically. Her abused backside is a mess of angry red blotches and it looks like a raw piece of meat. She won't be able to wear any clothes for a few days, that's for certain.

Satisfied that I've made my point clear, I finally stop. I push Harper gently down my legs, so I can stand up and get the hell out because if I don't, I'm about to fuck her into next year.

"Please," she whimpers in a little voice, which reeks of despair. "Please." The woman grabs my legs as if I'm her fucking saviour. Is she looking for forgiveness? If so, she won't get it here.

I should be revelling in the sweet sound of her misery, but I'm torn. Half of me knows I need to be the abhorrent bastard I became in prison in order to fight fire with fire, and the other half of me just wants to wrap my arms around her and tell her everything will be okay. The two do not sit well with each other. I think I'm slowly losing my marbles.

"I've stopped, Harper. You can get off me now." Clearly the girl has no idea which way is up after what has just happened, and to be fair, I did go a special kind of crazy on her ass.

"No. Please let me..." Her voice dies on the last word. Please let me what? Are we back to Gabriel again? Maybe it was going to be a 'please take me with you'. There's no way she's keeping up with me on a ten-kilometre run. That's a whole different kind of pain, and she's probably suffered enough for one morning.

"Please let me what?" I say, sighing, my curiosity getting the better of me.

Harper hangs her head over my legs, and I catch the side of her face, which is scarlet. She's embarrassed? Mind you, being thrown over someone's legs and receiving a sound spanking has got to be pretty humiliating, I guess, so it figures.

"Please let me come," she whispers.

I lean back and suck in a breath. Now that, I had not been expecting. She finds being spanked that hard arousing? Holy hell, she was in tears not moments ago.

"Say that again." I need confirmation that what I'm hearing is correct because I'm pretty sure I just imagined it.

"Please let me come," she moans, squirming underneath me once more. "I'm so aroused my body's going into meltdown." Rubbing her groin against my leg she begins to hump me like an animal, and I put a stop to it by giving her another sharp spank. She lets out a whoosh of air in shock, and her body stiffens.

Now I know Harper likes pain, but the amount I dished out was extreme. I find it hard to believe anyone could find that arousing. So, I do what any red-blooded male would do given the circumstances - I check. Placing my hand gently between her legs, I run my fingers over her sex. They immediately slide into wet heat. Jesus. She is turned on. This is so fucking hot my head might explode. Placing two fingers at her entrance I slide forward carefully, but there's no need. She is absolutely soaked, and she groans out loud to confirm it. The sound makes my cock want to leap out of my pants. I need to calm myself down. This wasn't the idea of the exercise.

"Please Brandt, please," she whimpers.

In the end I can't help myself. I run two fingers up and down her clit, flicking the little nub back and forth. Her sweet whimpers do funny things to my insides. Grabbing a handful of her hair once more, I pull her face up so I can see her expression. While it's still beetroot red, her eyes are glazed and her pupils dilated. She's most definitely enjoying herself.

Dipping my fingers back inside her, I get them nice and wet before coming up to play with her again. This time I let my index finger circle her clit, feeling it swell. I know I'm going to regret this, but I can't help myself. Alternating between fingering her pussy and her clit, I bring her slowly to the edge. I know when she's close because her breathing hitches, and she makes funny little mewling noises. I'm just as close as she is. One rub in the right place and I'm pretty sure I'd embarrass myself, but that's not going to happen. This little episode was never about pleasure. It was about showing her who's boss, and I'm about to do so again. I give her clit one last little pulse with my fingertips, and then I withdraw them. Pushing Harper to the floor at my feet, I keep a firm hand on her neck to make sure she stays down. This time she has no option but to go where I put her.

Grabbing her leash from the drawer, I clip it around the D-ring in her collar and tug. She lets out a furious little shriek and stumbles forward.

"You even think of getting up on those legs and I'll get the paddle out." I mean it, too. My mood, which was bad enough to begin with, has taken a nosedive. I need a long hot shower, and plenty of fist action before I'll start to feel halfway normal, and even then I suspect I'll still be left wanting. Why don't I just give in to this attraction? Why do I keep fighting it?

"Brandt, I just want..." I cut her off immediately. Unless she's about to tell me her life story, and how it led to me spending five years of my life in the clink, I'm not interested.

"Say another word and I'll gag you. I don't think you'll want that. If I can't hear your screams when Gabriel gets inside your little cell, no one is going to come running for you." That's a horrible thing to say, and as soon as it's left my mouth I regret it. The deed is done, though, and there's no taking it back. Still, perhaps she'll be a little more pliable by the time I return. Gabriel is almost sure to spend the time winding her up. Maybe that will work in my favour. Hmm. It's an idea.

Almost dragging her down the stairs by the neck, I storm into the hallway, nearly crashing into Harper's arch enemy. Gabriel smirks, but neatly sidesteps the pair of us, openly ogling Harper's naked body. She immediately shrinks back against me, trying to stay well out of his way.

"Are you caging your little pet before you leave, Brandt?" Gabriel raises his eyebrows and grins menacingly at Harper. If I know my friend well, he'll want to get his own back after his near-death experience, and he doesn't normally play fair. He's not doing it while I'm not here, though.

"If you touch her while I'm gone I'll make what Harper did to you yesterday seem like child's play. In fact, if you touch a hair on her head you'll be kicked out of this house, and you can find your own way back..." I'm ready to blow up in his face when he interrupts me.

"I get it. I get it." He holds his hands up in surrender and smiles sweetly, but I know that is no indication that he intends to play nice. I don't think he'll fight me on this because he knows I'll do exactly what I say, and this whole situation intrigues him. I also think he's holding out for a threesome. That's the kind of thing that would set his kinky little mind into overdrive. That's one of the reasons I fell in love with him. He's just as dark and twisted as I am, if not more so. Together we'd make mincemeat of any poor girl who was stupid enough to get caught in our clutches.

"I'll play nice while you're gone. Well, I won't touch her, anyway. When you get back though, I make no promises. You're in charge of protecting your princess, so you'll just have to make sure you do a good job of it." He grins wolfishly at me. The man is feral.

"We'll discuss what you are and aren't allowed to do when I get back from my run. Until then, hands off. We clear?" He holds his hands in the air and waggles his fingertips at me. He's got the message.

Yanking at Harper's leash I make a move to walk past him, but he stops me. It's not me he wants to talk to though, it's Harper.

"I'll pop in to check on you later, sweetheart. I wouldn't want you to get lonely while Brandt's out." He pats her head and gives her a wink. She flinches visibly and crawls forward at breakneck speed, tugging me along behind her.

"Behave yourself," I yell to Gabriel over my retreating back, but he's laughing so hard he probably can't hear me. I'm going to have to get rid of him quickly, but that might not be as easy as it sounds. If I give him what he wants, then he might just leave of his own accord, but I'm not sure I can do that. Lord. Could this situation get any more complicated?

When we go down the stairs the scent of urine permeates the damp air in a very unpleasant way. I'm trying my best not to breathe it in, and I'm pretty sure Harper's trying to do the same. The fridge and its sawn-off plug have already been removed and disposed of. I don't think we need a repeat of that little episode. In future, I need to be a little more careful with my prisoner.

When we walk inside the cell Harper stops dead at the puddle on the floor. I can't say I blame her; I wouldn't want to step in it either.

"There's a bucket of soapy water over there," I say, pointing to the corner in which a large black rubber bucket resides, almost overflowing with soap bubbles. It was hot half an hour ago, but probably only lukewarm now. At least she won't be able to scald herself with it. "There's a scrubbing brush inside. While I'm gone I want you to scrub the entire floor. You made the mess, so you can clear it up. Failure to do so will be met with punishment." We stare at each other, so she knows I mean business. "Speaking of punishments," I say, "you are still owed one for not obeying me earlier."

She blinks and frowns. "But I thought the spanking..." her sentence tails off as I glower at her.

"That was only part of your punishment," I growl. "I'm removing the duvet for the course of this evening. If you get cold you'll have to jump up and down. On the plus side, it'll give you something to do because I have a feeling you won't be getting much sleep down here today." Picking up the thick wad of material in my arms, I begin walking towards the door.

"No, Brandt, please. Anything but that. I'm naked. Gabriel will be down here as soon as you leave. You can't leave me like this." Harper's voice is rising hysterically, but I'm already closing her cell door, listening for the tell-tale click of the lock.

"If you want to stop this at any time you know exactly what you have to do," I say, but my back is already turned towards her and my feet are jogging up the steps in front of me. I know she won't talk. I haven't cracked this woman yet, but I will. Maybe Gabriel is right. Maybe I should threaten to let him loose on her. I know she's scared of him, and she has every right to be. He'd fuck her up in a heartbeat. The trouble is, I can't make a threat and then not carry it out. If I threaten her with it, I have to go through with it. Could I watch those two together and somehow remain impassive? I don't think so. I think the green-eyed monster would rear its ugly head and eat me alive.

Am I in love with Harper? Is Gabriel right? He can't be. There's no way you'd want to destroy the woman you love, and I want to tear that woman to bits until she can't even utter her own name. I hate her with a passion that is all-consuming and fucking scary.

A nagging voice inside my head tells me there's a very fine line between love and hate, but I stubbornly ignore it.

Chapter 9 - Harper

When I hear the sound of the cell door clanging against metal I want to strangle Brandt, but luckily for him, he's already out of my reach. He thinks we're playing a game, but nothing could be further from the truth. I'm not even sure he believes a word I've told him so far. Yesterday I thought I might be getting through to him, but today it looks like we're back to where we started.

Actually, it's worse, because now I have his 'friend' to deal with.

With Gabriel in mind I grab the bucket and scrubbing brush and begin to wash the floor. As I get down on my knees I hiss as the tender skin on my ass stretches. Damn, that hurts. When Brandt decides to take me to task he does it properly, that's for sure. I'm still furious with myself for being aroused from his mistreatment of me. But at least I can take some of my anger out on the task, and I begin scrubbing furiously, trying my best to keep the tears at bay. I know I need to get this done as soon as possible so I can hide behind my mattress, which is the only thing in the cell that will be able to provide me with any type of cover. Gabriel will be down to gloat and start lobbing threats at me soon. He'll be telling me exactly what he's going to do to me later, and I can only imagine the things he's capable of. Anyway, the less time I'm crawling around naked, the better.

Moving as quickly as I can I get half the cell done in less than five minutes. My eyes are trained on the steps above at all times, and my ears are listening for the sound of footsteps on stone. I intend to make a run for it when that happens, but I'm worried that if I don't clean from top to bottom Brandt will come up with another punishment on his return, and I don't think I can take any more.

Thankfully I get the whole floor done in record time with no interruptions, and then make a little barricade on the steel bed, positioning the mattress in front of me. Gabriel can do what he likes now, I don't care.

Several minutes pass, and nothing happens. It's almost as if I've been worried about nothing and it's a bit of an anti-climax, if I'm honest. Don't get me wrong, I don't want to be molested, but I've psyched myself up for this for nothing. Oh well, at least my blood pressure will get a good workout.

I sit alone with my thoughts for all of twenty minutes before I become horribly bored. Now that the cell has been stripped of everything, including the iPad, iPod and books he left me before, it seems even more unwelcoming and bare. I wonder how long he intends to leave me here like this. Hopefully, only a night. Still, I'm no stranger to sleepless nights. I've had plenty of those in the last few years. Speaking of sleep, I guess I'd better get a couple of hours in where I can.

When the dreams come they are covered in black, inky despair and soul-destroying fear. I am never free of their grasp for long.

Mal has nearly strangled me to death, not once, but several times. His hands are continuously circling my throat as he watches me fight for my life. Bringing someone close to death excites him. Maybe it's because he feels he holds the ultimate power over me, or maybe he's just a sick fuck, but he clearly enjoys toying with his victims. When he's finally finished he leaves me on the bed fighting for breath while I come down from my orgasm high. But having an orgasm doesn't make up for the monstrous sex I've just endured, and my pulse is thundering through my body, wondering what the hell just happened. I can't take another one of those. My throat is so sore after all that squeezing I can barely talk - even opening my mouth hurts. My head is woozy, dizzy and disorientated. I couldn't get up off the bed, even if I wanted to.

"It's an incredible high isn't it, babe?" Mal says. He's currently pouring another couple of whiskies for us, and this time I think I might need one.

"Mmm," I croak noncommittally. While our tastes in sex might differ somewhat, there's no way I want to anger the man. What I do want to do is get the hell out of here as quickly as possible. But how do I go about that without sounding rude and getting myself killed in the process?

"Here." He hands me the glass, which someone has used prior to my being here if the lipstick stain is any indication, but I don't let that bother me. I've probably caught far worse than anything that can linger on the rim of a glass. Taking a large gulp of the amber fluid, I wince as the burn travels down my throat.

"Alex didn't want to give you to me. Did you know that?" Mal smiles and twirls the whisky around in his glass. He seems amused.

"I didn't know that," I croak. "Why did you want me?" It's probably a stupid question. Maybe he likes fucking other people's partners. Maybe he just wants to screw with Alex's head. Maybe he's a fucking axe murderer, and he's just waiting to kill me. Who knows?

"I need you to do suffin' for me." Lifting the glass of whisky up to his mouth he proceeds to drain the lot. He slowly licks his lips, as if savouring the aftertaste. I have a bad feeling about this. Anything I do for this man is going to be on the wrong side of the law, and judging by what I've just experienced, saying no isn't an option.

"What?" I whisper. I really don't want to ask that question, but I also need to know what I'm dealing with.

Mal gives me a lazy smile. "I need you to sort out a little problem for me. It ain't one that's going to arise for a few years, but when it does, I want it under control. I likes to think ahead, me."

I'm sorry I asked. He's obviously not going to tell me anything just yet. On the upside, he's not going to kill me either, because he needs me. Happy days.

"Oh," I say, as if I understand what the hell just went down. I don't. I don't understand any of it, and I don't want to. If I never come again it'll be too soon.

"Don't look at me like that, 'Arper," Mal says, tugging on a lock of my hair as he brings my face closer to his. I can smell the whisky on his breath and the cloying scent of his sweet aftershave makes me want to gag. "I need to see if I can trust you first. When you've proven yourself, then we'll talk further." Great. There goes my hope that this meeting was a one-off. I wonder if I'm going to get strangled and fucked every time I see him. I really hope not. Mind you, the alternative might be worse.

"You can trust me, Mal," I say foolishly.

"Well, I'm really glad you've said that, 'Arper," he says jovially, "because when I let you know what you've got to do you'll do it with no questions asked, won't you babe?"

He gives me a look. I know that look. I gulp and nod my head.

What Mal's just said without words is that basically, if I don't do as I'm told, I'm dead.

"Wakey, wakey, princess." I snap out of my dream world in an instant. I know that voice and I don't want it anywhere near me. Peering slowly over the top of my mattress barricade, sure enough I see Gabriel at the bars, and he's doing his best to ogle what little he can.

I'm lying on my side, because the thought of putting any pressure on my ass is abhorrent, and I peel my left leg slowly off the cold steel slab as I try to ride further up it.

"What do you want, Gabriel?" I'm not likely to get much sleep this evening, so the last thing I need is to be woken up during the little nap time I have.

"Now, now, now. That's not very polite, is it? Someone's not had their breakfast this morning." Gabriel starts walking up and down the length of my cage, trying to see if there's a better angle in which to sneak a peek. There isn't. I'm making sure of it.

Speaking of food, Brandt forgot to feed me this morning and my stomach is starting to protest rather noisily. I skipped dinner yesterday and now I'm missing another meal. Damn it. This is just like old times. I hope he remembers when he gets back.

"There's no point hiding all those lovely assets up, Harper. For starters, Brandt has cameras trained on you, so I've already enjoyed all the footage of you wagging your baboon-red ass all over the place, and secondly, I'm going to be getting a taste of them later, regardless."

My face floods with shame at his words. So that's why he hadn't bothered me earlier. He was getting his kicks by watching everything upstairs. I guess as soon as I fell asleep things got boring, which is why he's down here now.

"Brandt won't let that happen," I say, with more confidence than I feel. Yesterday, I'd have sworn Brandt was on my side. Today, not so much.

"Oh, I wouldn't be quite so cocky, Harper. In the end Brandt will do whatever he has to in order to make you talk. If he fails, I'll sort this little problem out for him. I had quite the reputation back at Larksham Grange." He sticks his tongue out slightly and runs his finger across it. Something inside me pulses, though it shouldn't. Damn Brandt for revving me up and leaving me wanting. Gabriel is a very attractive man. He could have any woman he wants, or any man for that matter. While I'm not immune to his charms, I should know better. Men like him are dangerous and should be avoided at all costs.

"I just bet you will," I purr. I'm not going to be the cowering victim in the corner. If he wants to bust in here again I might not be able to electrocute him a second time, but I'll do my best to scratch his eyes out.

"By the way, Harper, I love that collar and leash on you. I just adore it when a woman knows her place, don't you?" His eyes are twinkling. He wants to get a rise out of me, but I refuse to give him the satisfaction.

"Have you fully recovered from your brush with household voltage?" I ask sweetly. Two can play at this game. Sure enough, his eyes narrow and venom replaces his amusement.

His voice sinks two octaves lower as he says, "I still owe you for that, by the way." I get a lascivious leer, and even though I know he can't see anything, my insides shrivel up and die. Gabriel is a Spanish version of Mal. He's got no conscience, no morals, and he'll step over everything and anyone to get what he wants.

"Come and get me then," I say, with far more bravery than I feel. I hope Brandt's not decided to go out for a twenty-mile run. If he has I'm going to be in all sorts of trouble.

"You're playing with fire, little birdy," Gabriel says, waggling his very dark eyebrows at me. I ignore him. I'm well aware of what I'm doing; I just don't care. My days on this earth are already numbered. Each way I turn, there's just more misery.

"If you're coming in, get your ass in here, Gabriel." I have no idea why I'm antagonising the beast. Maybe I have a death wish, maybe I've gone mad, or maybe I just want to get this over with. It's got to be one of those three.

"My, my, my," he drawls, completely unperturbed by my forwardness. "You have so much enthusiasm for one so young." He moves closer, towards the door and the lock, seeing if it will make me nervous. It does, but I'm not about to let it show.

"You have no idea what I've got hidden behind this mattress, Gabriel. Why don't you come and find out, sweetheart?" In actual fact I have nothing hidden behind this mattress, but he doesn't know that.

"I might just do that," he says sweetly, which tells me he doesn't believe my lies for a second. It appears we can both see straight through each other. This should be an interesting standoff. Will he come in and piss his friend off, or will he wait outside and trade insults with me until he's given the go ahead to do something vile?

"Then I can't wait to watch Brandt kick your ass back to whichever hole you crawled out of," I reply, just as sweetly. We're both playing each other, and I have a feeling neither of us is completely sure which team Brandt is on. It will be interesting to find out.

"You wish, Harper, you wish." Gabriel leans his back against the bars and goes quiet on me. He's thinking. If he were a smart man, and I'm fairly sure he is, he's analysing his options and deciding what move to make next. I hope he takes his time.

We stay like that, in silence, for several minutes, until I wonder if he's gone to sleep on me, but there aren't many people I know who can sleep standing up. If he's hoping I'll relax my guard he can think again. There's no way I'm nodding off until Brandt gets his ass back here.

His next questions, when they come, shock the hell out of me. It's not because of what he's asking, it's because of how close he is to the truth.

"Why'd you do it, Harper? Did Alex make you?"

I don't answer him. I promised myself I wouldn't get Brandt into this, and anything I tell Gabriel will get straight back to him.

"If you tell him that he'll go easy on you." Gabriel's voice is almost cajoling. How interesting. Since when does Gabriel care about my fate? And then it comes to me. Gabriel doesn't want me here. He wants Brandt back. He thinks I'm a threat to him and wants to get rid of me as quickly as possible. I almost laugh. The situation couldn't get any weirder if it tried.

"You still love him, don't you?" I whisper. Two can play at the clairvoyant game. I'm only guessing, but I have a feeling I'm right. I remember Brandt telling me Gabriel became bored with him, but I'm not so sure that was the case. There's something I'm missing.

Gabriel doesn't answer, which is indication enough that I'm right. I wonder what happened between them?

"Do you love him?" Gabriel has now turned around to face me, and watching me carefully. I want to burrow myself behind my mattress, but that would be admitting defeat and I'm not prepared to do that.

"Why do you care?" I say, to deflect his original question. I'm not sure what my feelings are for Brandt, but I know I'm still attracted to him. That hasn't changed one little bit over the years, even after all that has happened.

Again he ignores me. Neither of us wants to talk to the other. We know we're enemies in all the ways that count, and probably more. Frustrated, Gabriel begins pacing up and down the length of my cell, his face deep in thought as he ponders what to do next. As long as he's not trying to force his way in here I'm perfectly content to sit and watch him.

Eventually he just stalks off up the stairs, and I wonder what's going to happen next. He's not finished with me. I have no idea what he's up to, but he'll be back. I know that much.

Sinking down lower onto the freezing cold steel slab beneath me, I try to ignore the burning pain radiating from my butt. It is driving me mad. It's not because it hurts, and let me tell you it really does, but because it's turning me on in the worst way. Alex and Mal would often spank me before they fucked me, mostly because they knew it got me wet in record time. I'm one of those weird women that don't need conventional foreplay. Just give me a few hard spanks and I'm panting in heat, ready for anything. My clit is throbbing in earnest, begging for release, but I daren't touch myself. For one, Gabriel might be watching, and two, Brandt's earlier threat is still fresh in my mind.

This room is rigged with cameras, Harper. You even think of touching yourself, and I'll be down here like a shot. I'll pin you to the wall, hands above your head, legs spread wide open, and deliver punishments, one after the other, until I think you've learned your lesson. Your pleasure is mine now, Harper, and I don't intend to be generous with you. I had to learn the hard way, and so you'll have to learn the hard way.

There's no way I'll risk being pinned to the wall where Gabriel can come and gawp at me anytime he likes.

I'm curious as to how Gabriel knows about Alex, though. Did Brandt tell him? If they shared a cell together, there's every possibility he did. I bet there was plenty of pillow talk in that relationship. It's also possible that Gabriel knew Alex before he was put inside. Depends on what sort of nastiness he was into. I'm betting a lot, but what do I know?

When I eventually get bored with waiting for the sound of Gabriel's footfalls on the stairs, I settle back and let my eyes close.

The second time Alex managed to get me on my own was far more frightening than the first. I think he thought I'd come running after the episode in the empty classroom, but that little stunt he pulled actually had the opposite effect. I was extremely careful to avoid him and did my best to hang around with a friend at all times after that. I didn't trust him, and I didn't want to enter his world. He curtailed a lot of my fun for a while, but at least I felt safe. I knew that if I started dating Alex Wilkinson my life would change, and not for the better. Don't ask me how I knew, but I knew.

As I've mentioned before, though, Alex is not someone who gives up easily. His ego can't take that kind of defeat. This time he employed all his energy into studying me and my roommate. He was most interested when I was regularly left alone for at least a few hours at a time. He knew he had to get me somewhere private for what he'd planned next, and he didn't want to be interrupted. At the time I didn't know this; he'd tell me how easy it was to outwit me later, when I had no chance of escaping him.

Anyway, back then my roommate regularly went out on a Tuesday and Thursday evening for at least two hours to attend some study group or another. She was on a scholarship, just like me, and she wasn't going to go back to her parent's empty-handed. We both knew we had one shot at this, and we weren't going to waste it. But I preferred to study on my own. So when she went out it gave me plenty of peace and quiet to do exactly that.

One day, after she'd left, I remember making myself a cup of tea and settling down in our ratty old armchair. The thing was so old it had to be propped up on wads of cardboard unless you wanted to rock about all over the place. I'd just picked up a copy of *The Principles of Economics* when I thought I heard a rattling at the lock.

"Who is it?" I called. The chances were it would be one of the girls asking to borrow something or other. It could be anything from sugar to the notes for next week's homework.

The rattling stopped. "Lianne, Rosa?" They were the two most common culprits, and I figured I'd ask what they wanted before I opened the door. It would save me running there and back twice. Waiting a full minute for a response, when the noise stopped and everything went quiet, I figured that whoever was out there must have been called away to do something else. Burying my nose back into my book, within five minutes I was once again immersed in a world of figures and facts, and anyone could hammer on the door as hard as they liked and I probably wouldn't notice. But what did shock me was a very loud slam of the door and Alex Wilkinson's booted feet coming straight for me.

I dropped the cup of tea I was holding as I looked up at him, aghast. Broken china bounced up off the floor with a splintering crash and a fountain of warm liquid splattered the bottom of my jeans. My jaw hung open wide in horror.

"How did you get in here?" I whispered. I remember squirming back against my chair as he advanced towards me, his trademark smirk firmly in place. I also remember my eyes darting towards the door, wondering if I'd make it out if I sprinted my ass off.

"Don't even think about it," Alex said, shaking his head. "You aren't outrunning me, Harper." This was coming from the captain of the football team, and he had a good point. If lucky I'd get to the door, but I wouldn't get any further.

"What do you want?" I gritted out. If I couldn't run I'd have to stay and face him, but I needed to get out of here as soon as possible. Lucy, my roommate, wasn't due back for hours, so no rescue party was coming. Mind you, there was always screaming. If I started yelling my head off there was a reasonable chance someone would come running.

"Don't even think of screaming, or I promise you, you'll regret it." He gives me a look that says 'don't fuck with me', but I ignore it. If I remain with him I know what will happen, and I don't want to go down that road. I need to stay away from the man.

Opening my mouth wide I get ready to holler to all and sundry, but before I know what's happening Alex has made a lunge for me, dragging my body close to his chest as a hand is clasped over my lips.

"Tsk, tsk, tsk," he tuts, shoving his body up close and personal with mine. It's a little too close for comfort because I can feel his erection pressing against my butt. This is not good. Not good at all. "Oh dear, Harper," he says, in a voice that is not at all disappointed, "it seems you've been a very naughty girl. Unfortunately, that means you must be punished." I have no idea what he's on about, but all sorts of horrible things are going through my head. What is he planning to do to me? Will help arrive in time before anything nasty happens? Will they find my body buried in a field somewhere twenty miles from here when this is all over? Surely I haven't navigated myself through several long years of foster care, only to end up in shallow grave somewhere? I worked hard for this. Really hard. I deserve my break.

Biting his hand as hard as I can he yells and relaxes his grip around me. This is my cue to run as fast as I can, and I do, but the beast behind me is hot on my heels. Just as my hand grips the door handle I feel myself slammed into the wall, but this time he's wrapped his right arm around my neck.

"You even think of screaming and I'll tighten this hand until you pass out." He gives me an indication of what he's capable of, tightening his grip around my throat until I choke, watching as I scrabble madly at the door that is no longer an avenue of escape. I've lost this battle, and we both know it.

"What do you want?" I repeat. My skin is crawling and I need his hands off me. Somehow I have to diffuse this situation, but I have no idea how. There's a crazy person in my dorm who's just threatened to leave me unconscious on the floor. I can't let that happen. Hell knows what he might do to me if it does. I feel my knees go weak. I know I'm overreacting, but it's difficult not to when someone's got their hands around your neck.

"I want you to go sit back down on your chair. Think you can be a good girl and do that for me?" The grip around my throat relaxes slightly. The scent of leather from his jacket surrounds me and I decide I don't like it. In a few years I'll come to hate it, but at this point we're at the dislike stage.

"Fine. I'll sit." I'll do anything if it means putting some distance between us.

Alex lets me go slowly, sliding the tips of his fingers gently against my neck before letting them tangle in my mane of hair. He then grabs a handful and yanks my head back, making me gasp out loud.

"Yes, you will. You'll sit and you'll listen to every word I have to say. When I've finished things are going to change around here. I'm sick of playing your games, Harper. Now, we're going to play my way." He gives my head another tug and I let out a small whimper, before he roughly pushes me away from him.

I walk slowly to the chair with my legs wobbling beneath me. For a moment I wonder if I'm going to make it, but they hold out. Fear has grabbed a hold of me, and it feels like someone has put my heart in a vice. What is going on here?

Grabbing hold of both arms of the chair I lower myself back down carefully. I have a feeling I'm not going to like what happens next, and sure enough, my sixth sense pulls through admirably.

"You're in love with Brandt Browning, aren't you?" Alex strolls towards me, ignoring the sofa on the other side of the lounge, preferring to stand and tower over me.

"I am not," I hotly deny, and it's mostly true. I might be infatuated with him, but I'm not in love with him - not yet.

"You're lying. I've seen you look at him. I've even talked to your friends. You're crushing on that boy bad, aren't you, Harper?" Alex raises his eyebrows, waiting for a reaction from me, but I don't give him one.

"I'm not in the market for a boyfriend, Alex. I'm here to study and get good grades. If I don't, I get kicked out. It's that simple. I don't want you and I don't want Brandt - end of discussion."

He shakes his head and gives me a nasty smile. "You're lying, Harper. Not only that, you're wasting your time on someone who will never look at you twice. He's not from our world, Harper. He's destined for great things, with a father who's probably going to rule the country one day. His family's going to pick him a well-to-do missus, and he'll be shipped off to make beautiful, posh fucking babies. Maybe he'll go into politics, too. Whatever he does, believe me when I say his future doesn't include you, babe."

"I don't want a boyfriend," I reiterate, trying not to let those home-truths hurt too much. He's not telling me anything I don't know already, but it's not nice to have them thrust in my face.

"Yet, he's standing in our way, Harper." Alex pins me with a searing look that reduces my insides to acid. "I think if I got rid of him I'd have you all to myself, wouldn't I, Harper? If I took him out of the picture there'd be no barriers left. There'd just be you and me." Alex sits down on the arm of my chair and rubs his hand against my jean-clad knee. I want to throw up all over it. I'm pretty sure I can see where this conversation is going, and I'm not going to like it much.

Alex's fingers rise up my legs, and I stare at them, completely horrified and turned on all at the same time. I'm disgusted with myself, but there's no fighting it.

"He's not," I whisper, while my eyes follow his fingertips intently. They continue their journey upwards, lightly skimming my crotch, before lingering on the top button faster of my jeans. Then, very deftly, they pop it open. "Stop," I whisper, my voice nothing more than a breathy croak. Releasing their vicelike grip of the chair arms, my hands immediately try to push his away, but button number two has already followed the same path as number one, and I'm not strong enough to get him off me.

"Stop isn't going to be a word in your vocabulary for too much longer, Harper. In fact, I never want to hear it on your lips again." The last button is released, and my jeans peel open, revealing a pair of black, lacy panties beneath. I close my eyes and hold my breath, not daring to look at him.

"No, this can't happen," I moan, but I'm not allowed to drown in my misery for long. Alex grips my chin and brings my face upwards.

"Look at me, Harper," he orders, but I can't move a muscle. "Look at me," he repeats, "or I'm going to thrust two fingers in your cunt, smear your juices on my lips, and then make you taste yourself." My eyes fly open and, unfortunately, my panties flood.

"We are going to be an item whether you like it or not. Now we can do this the easy way or the hard way. Which is it to be?" His fingers dive into the front of my jeans and grip my pussy hard. I gasp out loud, but don't answer him. Staring at his eyes, beautiful green emerald eyes that a girl could get lost in, I blink several times. My body has just gone into meltdown and talking will be nigh on impossible for a couple of seconds at least.

Alex has no patience for that. "Still undecided, huh? Well, let me tell you how it's going down if you choose the hard route." His fingers brush my panties to the side, before two of them thrust deeply inside me. I squeal in shock but can't open my mouth to say a word. I've got to get out of here.

Alex can see the panic in my eyes, and it excites him. He likes to be in control. I can tell because his face is now pressed up against me as he purrs in my ear, and I can feel the pulse in his neck. His heart rate is out of control.

"If you don't want to play ball, Harper, I'm going to do something a little unpleasant to your best buddy." I immediately think of Lucy, and now my pulse is skyrocketing. What does he intend to do to her? If he touches her, I swear I'll kill him.

"No," I wail, trying to wiggle my way out from the death-grip his fingers have on me. "No." My voice is finally back, but my head is all over the place. What do I do now?

"Yes," Alex continues, "I'm going to plant some drugs in his room, and then I'm going to call the cops. I reckon it should get him put inside for a few years. What do you think, Harper? Would you like to be responsible for ending someone's life like that?"

This is when I realise Alex is not talking about Lucy. He said 'he', and that 'he' is almost certainly Brandt. This is my first inkling that Alex Wilkinson is a very jealous man.

"Jail changes people, Harper. Job prospects virtually disappear overnight, your family give up on you, you've got no friends, no money, and plenty of enemies everywhere you look. Jail can kill, too. Make a few mistakes, and you might never see the light of day again. One phone call from me, and that will be Brandt's life." Alex's thumb begins to massage my clit, and I can't help the whimper that escapes me. "Will you be able to live with the fact that you were responsible for his downfall? Hell, he might even commit suicide while on the inside. A lot of inmates do." His thumb presses harder and harder, and my hips buck up to meet him of their own accord. I want to die of shame. How can I be enjoying this? The man is a monster.

"And the easy way?" I croak. I know I'm out of options here. I can't have that on my conscience. If Brandt gets locked away because of this it will kill something inside me, something I may never be able to recover from. There has to be another way.

Alex smiles like the predator he is. "The easy way is simple. You agree to date me until I've had enough of you. It's that simple. If you agree to that, I'll leave your precious little buddy alone, but you are never to go near him again. Do we have an understanding?"

Alex's fingers don't stop the whole time he's talking. I nod, then shake my head, then nod again. I have no idea what I'm doing. His fingers suddenly stop and his eyes narrow. Taking out his phone he speed-dials someone and barks, "You know that package I want planted? You've got the go ahead."

"Stop!" I wail. "Stop. I'll do it. Yes." My eyes are large, round, and shocked. I'm not really sure what I've just agreed to, but I know that in the next couple of days I will be. What's just gone down here is going to change my life, and not for the better.

"Change of plan," Alex says into the phone. "I'll be in touch." He hangs up. "Glad you've seen sense," he says, withdrawing his fingers slowly from my drenched pussy. He then smears them around his lips, just as he'd threatened to earlier. "Well, we'd better test this newfound change of opinion, then. Kiss me, Harper. Show me you mean what you say."

I have a split second's hesitation over what I should do. There must be a way to wriggle out of this without hurting anyone, but I don't think that answer is going to come to me anytime soon. Alex can sense my indecision because his face hardens. Picking up his phone once more his fingers prepare to dial, but I don't give them a chance to hit the button. My lips crash on his and my arms pull him to me. I know I've got to sell this. If I want to keep the man off Brandt's back for the foreseeable future I'll need to play nicely. I'm not exactly sure who Alex is yet, that he can order people around to do his dirty work, but I swear I'm going to find out. If he thinks he can trap me, then it's my job to outwit him at the earliest opportunity. Until then, we play by his rules.

The kiss isn't unpleasant. Like I've said before, I find Alex attractive and there's chemistry between us. Once I've succumbed to it, it wraps itself around my body and mind like a dark, twisted fantasy. I need this, but I know I shouldn't have it. The taste of myself on his lips is the icing on a very decadent, double chocolate gateau. When we finally pull apart, both desperate for air, he looks almost as lost as I do. We're both reeling, unsure of what that just was. I don't want to think about it; I have this awful feeling I've just tossed what's left of my life down the drain.

"So, we have a deal?" Alex looks at my lips, now swollen with the force of our kiss, and gives the bottom one a small nip. Pleasure shoots through me.

"You don't play fair," I whimper. Alex merely raises his eyebrows in response and begins fastening up the buttons of my jeans, one by one. I'd much rather he flung me on the floor and fucked me senseless, but I also know that once I go down that route there is no return.

"Just you remember that, baby. With you, I will never play fair." Standing up, he places a soft kiss on my forehead before letting himself out as silently as he came in.

The man is like Jekyll and Hyde, with a lot more emphasis on the latter. I need to get rid of him or he'll destroy me.

Chapter 10 - Gabriel

I haven't travelled all the way up to Scotland to babysit some duplicitous bitch who'll do the dirty on us the minute she sets foot out of this joint. If it was up to me, I'd kill her now. Unfortunately I can't do that. If I do, Brandt is likely to kill me.

Why am I here? It's a good question. I want my man back. I lost him in prison, for numerous reasons, not least of which is the fact that Brandt's not happy about sleeping with men - even though he enjoys it. That's my fault, by the way. I made him enjoy it. Every time we slept together I made sure the bastard came. It probably made his homophobic guilt worse, but that was half the fun of it.

It didn't take him as long to come to terms with being bisexual as I thought it would. Technically, the man isn't gay because there's no way he'd pick sleeping with me over sleeping with a woman, but I'm wondering if I can't change his mind. It's been a while since he's been with a girl, and the fact that he's resisted sleeping with Harper this long is promising. It's at least given me pause for thought.

I'm currently lying face-up in a bedroom that hasn't changed much in one hundred years, and I'm trying desperately to put my world to rights. Whichever path I seem to choose has Brandt in it, even though he doesn't want me in that way any more - or so he says.

I hurt him. I hurt him really fucking bad, and he pushed me away. Don't get me wrong, I thoroughly deserved it, but I didn't expect to be affected by it. Brandt was the first guy I've ever lost, and it was a bitter pill to swallow. I paid big time for that mistake and probably lost the love of my life in the process. I harbour no illusions that Brandt will ever come back to me, but fate has given me this opportunity to try and make it up to him, and I'd be a fool not to use it.

Running my hand through a day's worth of stubble, I wonder if I should shave. At the moment I stand more chance of sleeping with Harper than Brandt, so I'm not sure I care. Besides, girls like the rough-and-ready look, or so I've been told. It's been so long since I've been with a girl I can barely remember. I'm not sure whether I want to fuck her or bury her in cement, but that's not my call. If I want to get rid of her as soon as possible, the best way to do it is to get her to squeal like a pig - it's just a matter of finding the right buttons to press. The trouble is, Brandt is unlikely to allow that, unless he's pissed...

I have a lightbulb moment. Ka-Ching! It's time to get to work.

Running downstairs I start to prepare breakfast. It's not for me, as I've already eaten. I'm going to cook for Harper. I may even get brownie points from Brandt because he clearly forgot to feed his princess this morning, not that she's actually getting fed now, but that's beside the point. Now, what should I make her? Something messy, I think. Porridge? Brandt would probably approve. It was the prison food of champions. Then we'll need some yogurt on the side. A nice cup of tea, too. I'd better make sure it isn't too hot, or that could backfire on me later. Hmm, what else? Some diced fruit in a little honey? Oh yes. That has possibilities.

First things first, though. I've got to disable his camera upstairs. If I don't shut that off I'm going to be booted out of here faster than you can say Speedy Gonzales, and I'll have more than a slightly disgruntled coyote on my tail. I can do without the drama. If I do this right, Harper talks. She also gets kicked out, while I get plenty of cosy time with my main man. If I fuck it up I'm unlikely to set eyes on him again, so the onus is on me to get it right first time.

The camera is easily dealt with. All I have to do is unplug the receiver upstairs and then turn it on again as soon as he shows up. No, scrap that. As soon as he notices the missing footage he'll know I'm lying. I need to come up with something else. Cleo, my cat, then strolls into the room and begins to wind herself around my leg. Bending down to stroke her fluffy black fur, she looks back at me with lidded eyes and purrs happily. At least someone around these parts is easily pleased. I'm down on my haunches, rubbing the spot behind her ears that she loves, when it suddenly comes to me. I can blame it all on the damn cat. It's perfectly believable. I smile big and I smile wide. This is too perfect.

Bending down to kiss Cleo on the top of her head, I apologize to her for what I'm about to do. She is going to get in a spot of bother for this, but it's nothing she can't handle. Picking her up, I make a good deal of fuss over her before I carefully deposit her back outside the room and close the door. I then go over to Brandt's laptop, and using my arm, I sweep the thing on to the hard wooden floor with a good deal more force than necessary, but I want to make sure it's broken. When it crashes to the floor, only to bounce up and crash again, I'm confident that my work is done. The screen has also gone blank, and when I tap the on and off button nothing happens. So far, so good.

Exiting the bedroom, careful to leave the door open so my backup story holds water, I return to the kitchen to get Harper's tray ready. Looking at my watch, I note that it's been about forty minutes since Brandt left, so that means I need to get a wriggle on. Pouring the porridge into a bowl with some milk, I shove it in the microwave. Next, I set out a little pot of yogurt with a spoon beside it. I also chop up apples, bananas, strawberries and melon, and place them hurriedly on a plate before drizzling some honey on top of them. There are no points for presentation today. Last but not least, I boil the kettle for her mug of tea. Pouring a generous helping of milk into the bottom of the mug, I see that I have approximately ten minutes left until Brandt gets in. It's perfect timing, providing he doesn't decide to double his normal run. I'm pretty sure he won't. He's nervous about having me in the house with Harper. An hour will be all he's prepared to risk.

Carrying the tray carefully down the hallway, I watch my step as I begin the descent into the basement. The light down here is bad, so I take extra time and care. It wouldn't do to break anything just yet. When I finally manage to make it to the bottom, my eyes see nothing but mattress. I wait for a few seconds, listening for any sound of movement, but there is nothing. Harper is out cold, judging by the soft, even breaths I can hear. My luck really is in today. It will make what I'm about to do so much easier.

Slowly placing the tray on the floor, I get out my lock picks. It won't take as long to conquer this beast a second time around because I know what I'm doing. Sure enough, in less than two minutes I have access. Now it's time to start throwing things around and breaking them. Picking up the tray once more, I let loose a nasty grin. I wonder what Harper is going to make of this?

The first thing I let fly is the bowl of porridge. It smacks into the wall and explodes everywhere like gooey white confetti. Globs of soggy oats and milk splatter the wall and floor. It looks like someone's thrown up - which is exactly the look I was after. Perfect. Harper lets out a shocked gasp from behind the mattress and presses herself further against the wall. She'd be well advised to stay there for the next few minutes, but that's not my problem. The next thing to go is the tub of yogurt, and I hurl it at the base of her bed. It shoots out of the container in all directions, leaving strings of dripping goo slithering down the wall and bed, like I've just spunked all over it. Excellent. This just gets better and better.

"Stop it!" Harper shrieks, wondering what the hell I'm up to. She'll figure it out soon enough, though. I then throw the plate of fruit up at the ceiling, and shards of porcelain rain down, skittering across the floor as the fruit lands on top of it in sticky puddles of honey.

"What on earth are you doing?" Harper asks incredulously, cowering behind the mattress, figuring that the crazy person is coming for her next. I'm not. I'm going to wait it out until Brandt begs me to take her on. Then I'll have all the time in the world to do exactly what I want to her, and there are lots of things happily flittering through my mind at the moment. I want to tie her up, I want to throat fuck her, I want to spank her, pull her hair - hell, there isn't much I don't want to do to her. But if I start doing shit uninvited I'm going to get into trouble and that won't get me what I want. I need to play this the smart way.

Finally, picking up the mug of tea, satisfied that I've done enough damage, I pop a finger in the contents, just to make sure I'm not going to do myself an injury. The tea is warm but not scalding hot, so it looks like I put enough milk in. It's now time for the finale. Tipping the mug of tea over myself, I let the mug drop to the floor where it crashes into a thousand pieces and joins the rest of the broken debris. Looking at my watch, I figure Brandt is due back any time now. All I have to do is sit and wait for the fireworks - and there's going to be plenty of them. When Brandt gets here his temper is not only going to hit the roof, it's going to burst on through it.

"I'm getting you in trouble, girly. That's what I'm doing." Stepping out of the cell carefully, I close the door once more and place my lock picks back inside my jeans pocket.

"You're sick, you know that?" Harper whispers. Her eyes dart around the scene of devastation, her mouth still open in shock. I decide I like her mouth like that, and oh boy do I have plans for it.

I shrug my shoulders. "I'm actually doing you a favour. You don't want to be here, and I don't want you here. This is going to be one of the quickest ways to get rid of you. Once Brandt gives you to me, and he watches me fuck you, you'll be gone so fast your ass won't even touch the door on the way out. You should be thanking me, really." I nod, deep in thought, imagining all the things I'm going to do to her in a few minutes' time, and the list is long and mouth-watering.

"You are one fucked-up son of a bitch. He'll never believe you." Harper's voice is small and unconvinced, though. She knows exactly how this looks, and the likelihood of Brandt believing her is small, especially as he's already pissed with her. I have just royally screwed her over, and she knows it. The outside door chooses that moment to slam and I can hear Brandt call Harper's name, and then mine. We both stay silent, staring at each other.

"Brandt will believe every word I say, and you know it," I purr. "Brace yourself, Harper, because I'm going to press your head to the fucking floor and make you eat your breakfast off it, and not only is Brandt going to approve, he's going to sit there and watch while cheering me on. I have to confess I'm quite excited about the prospect." I lean back against the cell bars and begin humming happily.

"You bastard!" she screams, playing right into my hands. The mattress then goes flying as the naked hellcat rushes at me, wrapping her fingers around my throat.

Chapter 11 - Brandt

I've done no more than a kilometre before I realise I haven't fed Harper this morning. Shit. I was so mad with her I completely forgot. That can't happen again.

The last thing I need is for her to get sick, and she will if she doesn't start eating properly. I also need to give her another birth control pill. That's especially important if Gabriel's swanning about the place. While I don't think he'll touch her while I'm out running, I don't trust him any further than I can throw him. If I was sensible I'd get rid of him, or find somewhere else to stash Harper, but I don't have the necessary funds or the time. I suspect that when I look at my emails later there'll be all sorts of crap from Helena regarding our upcoming nuptials, and that will pose enough problems for the time being.

Just thinking about Helena makes my blood boil. If I'm not careful I'm going to find myself married with kids and I'll be treated by society at large like a leper for the rest of my life. I think I'd rather be back inside. The kid's not even mine, for crying out loud.

The next few kilometres get progressively quicker as my temper flares. Why are my parents onboard with this? Why won't they speak to me? I can't see how it's going to damage dad's political career more than it already has. Rumour has it he's set to become mayor shortly, so he can't be doing that badly. I wonder what kind of spin they had to pull to make me disappear. Or has everyone forgotten my existence? Everyone bar Helena and her family, that is.

My feet pound into the wet grass and mud, chewing up the earth as my trainer's thunder on ahead. It feels good to be out in the fresh air. I still can't get over the fact that I can come outside whenever I want to. It's a novelty you don't take for granted in prison. Hell, just being able to choose what I want to eat or read is amazing, and I am still revelling in my newfound freedom - which makes me wonder what I'm doing with Harper. If I'm not careful I'm going to end up inside again. What I did was incredibly foolish. While it was born of rage and retribution, I didn't think through the consequences very carefully. There is a very good chance I'll end up back inside after this. The only way to be sure that won't happen is to kill Harper and bury the evidence somewhere no one will ever think to look. I already know I can't do that. Gabriel probably could, but I'd never forgive him. I'm not a murderer.

So, I'm left with a problem. I can't keep her a prisoner for the rest of her life, and I can't let her go. Where do I go with that? All I want is her confession. I just want to know why she did it. There must have been a reason, surely? Hopefully I can lay the past to rest after I get the full story. I've got to let it go. This shit is toxic, and if I'm not careful I'll end up in a worse state than I am already.

My phone pings during the last kilometre of the run. Pulling it out of my pocket I scan the text message that's just arrived.

Wedding is scheduled for Saturday, a week from now. Do you want morning dress, tailcoat or tuxedo? Helena X

I nearly throw my phone through the damn window. Fuck. That is a lot quicker than I was anticipating. In no time at all they're going to want me back in London for fittings, stag parties, and all the other crap that weddings entail. My time is up. I either go down one route or another, and I'd better decide what I'm doing pretty damn quick. My temper, which had receded after my run, now begins to boil once more. I go from wanting to fuck and forget my little captive, back to wanting her severed head on a platter. Jesus.

I try to remember the last time my life was my own and therein lies the problem. My life was never my own. Even if I had completed college, I would have been forced to follow in the footsteps of my father, and the weight of his expectations would have lied heavily upon me. Perhaps I was always a disappointment to him. Maybe I just didn't realise it back then.

Pushing the door wide open, trying to clear my head of all the depressing thoughts eating away at me, I listen for signs that anything may be wrong. I've only been gone an hour or so, but a lot can happen in that time - especially when Gabriel is around. I hear nothing. The house is ominously quiet. I frown. Silence isn't always good.

"Harper," I call. There is no response, but that doesn't surprise me. I didn't exactly leave her on good terms. "Gabriel," I yell. One of them had better come running in a minute or there's going to be trouble.

I then hear Harper yell, 'You fucking bastard,' at the top of her lungs, and even though I've just run ten kilometres the shot of adrenaline that fires through my body has me sprinting like my feet are on fire.

"Gabriel if you do anything to her I swear I am going to kill you!" I scream, as I propel myself forward at the speed of light. My lungs are bursting, but I don't care. Fear is bubbling up through my veins, and for a moment I wonder if he's trying to kill her. That would be just like Gabriel. He's good at taking care of problems. He doesn't necessarily do it the right way, but he gets the job done - one way or another. That thought makes me run even faster.

When I burst into the cellar the scene that greets me is not the one I expect. It is so bizarre, in fact, that I stand there nearly gobsmacked as I take it all in. For a few seconds I do nothing but blink as I try to figure out how my little mouse has just turned into a tiger. What the hell happened here? There is broken shit all over the place, and Harper is currently trying to strangle Gabriel. It would be almost comical if he wasn't about to turn blue. I have no idea what happened, but I'm about to find out.

"Harper! Let him go. What is going on here?" My words have no effect whatsoever. Harper's face is bright red, and it's clear she's livid. I literally have to pry her fingers off Gabriel's neck, and he rushes forward clutching his throat.

"She went nuts, man," he wheezes. "That is one crazy lady. I brought her breakfast, and she started throwing things everywhere. I went to ask if she was okay, and she tries to kill me. Last time I ever try to do a good deed. I can tell you now, you're wasting your time with that one. She's a psychopath. She's never going to talk." Gabriel rubs his neck again and shoots daggers back at my prisoner. I still can't quite believe this. It's rare that I've ever see Gabriel at a loss, but it appears someone has finally got the better of him.

"Harper? What do you have to say for yourself?" My eyes linger on the mountain of mess strewn all over her cell, and I wonder if I'm going mad. She'd better have a good explanation or I'm about to lose it.

Harper just looks at me, before throwing her hands in the air and letting out a little scream. Is that temper? Irritation? Frustration? I have no idea. What I do know is that if I don't get answers soon she's going to be in the doghouse for the foreseeable future.

"One last chance, Harper," I say, in a dangerously quiet voice. My eyes hold hers, and we stare each other out. I have to admire her spunk. She's stark naked, madder than an Irishman who's been on the Guinness for a week, and totally unconcerned by my threat. That has to change, but I'm going to give her one last change. "What happened, Harper?" My voice is softer now, and has less of an edge. If she's going to talk, this is the voice she'll respond to.

I wait long, terse seconds for a reply. The urge to put her over my knee and spank the living daylights out of her is strong, but I know she can't take another session just yet, so I curb it. If she wants to play hardball, there are other ways I can get even.

"Harper," I bite out. I want to shake her, but I daren't. If I lay my hands on the woman I am almost guaranteed to do something stupid.

She's now staring straight at me, and her face is held in tight, crimped lines. I can see her lip wobble as she appears torn with indecision. The dots are not adding up here, but I can't make sense of anything at the moment. All I want to do is punch something.

"You wouldn't believe me if I told you. Do your worst, Brandt. Do your worst." She puts her hands on her waist and gives me evils. After all that has already happened this morning, this is the thing that finally sends me over the edge.

Spinning around I face Gabriel. "You," I bark. "If I go upstairs and find you've been lying to me your life will not be worth living." Gabriel holds his hands up and the expression he wears appears sincere, but the man is a good actor. This I know from experience.

"Honestly, Brandt. I haven't done anything. Go check." Harper snorts from her corner of the cell but says nothing. I don't know who to believe. Both of them have lied to me on several occasions, and Harper's even lied under oath. Actually, Gabriel probably has too, but I don't know that for certain.

"Neither of you move an inch," I hiss, before I shoot back upstairs to try and figure out who's telling me the truth. Honestly, all I want to do is have a shower and put my feet up for half an hour. Is that really too much to ask?

Stomping back up two flights of stairs, I head to my room where the door is already open. I could have sworn I shut it this morning. My eyes immediately zero in on my computer... which isn't there. What the fuck? Approaching my desk, I notice the remains of my laptop on the floor. The thing is a mess, and the screen has cracked all the way across from one side to the other. I resist the urge to howl in frustration. Did Gabriel do this?

Meow. My head spins around to find a black cat entering the room, looking for attention. She looks happy enough as she winds her way around my legs, purring. Could she have knocked over my computer? I guess it's possible if she got her legs tangled up in the wire. It seems a little too convenient, though. Closing my eyes tiredly, I run a hand across my forehead and sigh. However this happened, I have no way of knowing the culprit for sure, and now I'm going to need to order a new computer if I want to have any chance of monitoring the comings and goings of the household. Thankfully I still have my phone, so I can arrange it easily enough, but it will take at least a couple of days to get here.

Stomping back down the stairs in temper, I enter the basement where Harper and Gabriel are staring each other out.

"Did you fuck up my laptop on purpose?" I stare directly at Gabriel and wait for his response.

"No man. Why would I do that? I don't go in other people's rooms. That's just weird." There is no blinking, no eyes darting this way or that, and no trembling fingers. This means nothing, of course. Gabriel is more than capable of lying straight to my face.

I turn to Harper. "This is your very last chance. Either you talk or I'm letting him loose. My patience is wearing thin."

Harper smiles sadly. "You were always going to do that, Brandt, so let your dog loose. I can handle him." She lifts her head high and doesn't give anything away. Fuck it. I'm past trying to save her. Besides, she's here to be punished. Gabriel was always far more creative than me in that department. Maybe I should let him have a turn. Hell, maybe if I watch her suck his cock I won't want her any more. Then I can just let this thing go and get rid of her.

"Fine. Gabriel, you can do what you want with her. I'm past caring. First though, she needs to clean that mess up, and then she needs to eat." I press the key to the cell into his hands, not that he needs it, but it should make things easier.

He nods. "Agreed. Why don't you go take a shower and then meet me down here when we're ready to begin? I think I can safely promise I'll get your pretty little princess to talk by the end of the day." He gives me a wolfish grin, which tells me he's going to enjoy this. I'm not sure I am. I have a bad feeling he's orchestrated this whole mess, and I'm going to end up with egg on my face. I also don't know if I can bear to see him ripping into Harper. Good God, the woman put me in jail; I should hate her. But that's easier said than done. Mind you, after this little episode that might be taken care of.

Taking a deep breath, I resign myself to letting things play out down here. Harper can stop this anytime she wants. All she has to do is start talking. She knows that. Maybe having another man's cock down her throat will encourage her to play nicely for a change. Who knows? Somewhere though, at the back of my mind, I know things aren't going to be that easy. Things are going to get worse before they get better, and I'm probably going to regret this.

To make matters worse, my phone chooses that moment to ping again. Ripping it out of my pocket, it's to find another text from my darling betrothed.

If you don't answer me, I'll choose your outfit for you.

There's an angry face next to the text. Fuck you, Helena. Like I don't have enough problems at the moment. Shoving the phone back into my pocket, I swear.

However I look at things, I'm running out of time. If there's one thing I want before I run away from the hellhole my life has recently become, it's the truth. After five years of hard time, I need that in order to get on with the rest of my life.

Harper Wilkinson will talk whether she wants to or not. With Gabriel in charge, there is no other option. She has no idea what she's just let herself in for, but I'm damned if I'll feel sorry for her.

Chapter 12 - Gabriel

"Happy?" Harper spits at me, after Brandt's footsteps have long since receded.

As it happens, I am, and I don't see why I shouldn't mention the fact. "Yep. That went pretty well, in my opinion. I'm curious, though. Why didn't you at least try to sell your side of the story?" While Brandt might not have believed her, it would have at least been worth a try. Why isn't she trying to save her own skin? I can't work this woman out.

"There's no point. We were always heading this way, and I've learnt not to beg the hard way." Harper is no longer concerned about her nakedness. She's facing me from just behind the bars, and I can see everything. I guess she figures there's no point now. I'm about to get an eyeful of the goodies in a few minutes' time, and I'm quite looking forward to tapping it, too.

"You haven't won." Harper gives me a look and shakes her head. It would almost be intimidating, if she weren't stark naked and standing behind reinforced steel bars.

"Oh, contraire, sweetheart. I think I have." My voice is a touch unpleasant, with a whole lot of sarcasm thrown in.

She has the cheek to raise her eyebrows at me. "He'll figure it out soon enough, and then he'll kick your sorry ass all the way back to where it came from." Turning her back towards me, she walks to the bed. I've already decided we're not having sex on that because it looks far too uncomfortable. I'll either bend her over or fuck her up against the wall.

"Oh, and how's he going to do that, sweetheart?" I keep my voice low, just in case he's within earshot, even though we'd hear him if he were anywhere nearby.

"I don't know, but he will. He's not stupid."

"Well, that was a pointless, empty threat," I say, with mock horror. "Consider me duly warned. Now I believe you have some cleaning duties to attend to before I get in there and show you who's boss. I'd better get you a brush and dustpan, and a couple of bin bags so you can clear up all that mess you've made, hadn't I?" My grin is wicked as her face darkens. My bad? There's nothing I like better than fucking a girl - or bloke for that matter - who's raging mad. There's something about angry sex that turns me the fuck on. Brandt's well aware of this, of course, but Harper isn't. I'm going to have some fun with the girl.

In response Harper sticks two fingers up at me, presses them to her lips, and then blows me a kiss. We're going to get on splendidly - I just know it.

Five minutes later I'm back with all the cleaning supplies a girl could ever hope for. Opening the cell door with the key Brandt left me, I dump them all on the floor before closing and locking it once more. No way is this girl pulling one over on me again. This time she's going to do as she's told and take her punishment like the good little whore she is.

Harper is unamused by my antics, as expected, and looks at me with disgust. Like I give a fuck.

Pointing at the supplies, I say, "I'd get on with it if I were you. If Brandt gets down here after his shower and sees you lounging about he's liable to throw a fit. And I'm going to make you eat your breakfast off that floor in a minute, so it's in your best interests to do a good job." I give her two thumbs up for encouragement and an outrageous, cheeky grin.

In response she lets out a little scream of vexation and describes, with vivid hand signals, how she'd like to kill me. I grin harder. I've seen it all before, sweetheart.

"Bigger men than you have tried and failed to gut me, Princess. I wish you the best of luck, though." I blow her a kiss in return and add in a few lewd gestures of my own. Amusingly, her face goes bright pink and she snatches the brush and dustpan off the floor as if she's about to murder someone with them.

She doesn't look at me again, which is sensible. Instead, she concentrates on sweeping up my mess and carefully placing the contents in one of the empty bin liners provided. She takes her time, working from one side to the other methodically, obviously taking my earlier threat seriously. I absolutely am going to make her eat breakfast off the floor, and I'm going to rub her face in it, making sure she enjoys the experience. It's nothing I haven't done before.

"I think you missed a spot back there," I call, just to wind her up. She doesn't even raise her head to acknowledge the comment. She's no stranger to control, either. If I'd done this to Brandt he'd have gone apeshit on me. Harper, on the other hand, is reigning herself in. That usually takes practise. Hmm.

When she's swept up she leaves the bin bag at the door to her cell and gets the fresh bucket of warm soapy water I've left her. This may be a good time to exit the room, but I don't. If she throws it at me I'll have even more ammunition when Brandt gets back, and I'll take all I can get. The more annoyed he is the more leeway he'll give me, and let's just say I want plenty. I'm going to make the girl my bitch.

Surprisingly Harper doesn't throw anything at me. For the time being she seems resigned to her task and her eyes look flat and dead as they stare at the floor. They won't stay that way. As soon as I get my ass back in that cell those eyes will be trying to throw knives at me, and that's just the way I like it.

When Brandt comes back down around half an hour later Harper doesn't look at him, either. He's carrying a chair in his arms, so it looks like our little session is still on. I wondered if he'd have second thoughts, but the opposite appears to be the case. He's anxious to get the job done. That makes two of us.

"She's nearly finished. I guess I'd better go and get her some breakfast for round two. We'd better keep her energy levels topped up for what I have planned."

Brandt's face tightens, but he nods, setting the chair down on the floor and flopping onto it. Looking straight ahead as Harper concentrates on scrubbing the floor, he runs a hand over his eyes and clenches his jaw. He's not happy about this.

"I don't have to do this, Brandt. You just have to say the word." I do have to do this and get rid of the little bitch as fast as I can, but I don't want to come over as a callous bastard. That was one of the reasons we split. My moral compass can be rather warped at times.

Brandt sighs. "Get the breakfast. I'm running out of time. Helena's just emailed me again, and she wants me back in London for a fitting in two days' time. If that wasn't bad enough, I'm to be married in just over a week. According to my parents' lawyer, if I don't comply with her demands my allowance will be cut and they'll send the police over here. I have no idea if that's true or not, but I have to assume the worst. Unless I have a burning desire to rush back to prison, I need to finish this."

I nod. "I'll get her talking," I say, and give Brandt a reassuring slap on the back. I'm very confident I'll have Harper screaming her life's secrets from the rooftops in less than a couple of hours. I am pretty sure Brandt won't like my methods, but they usually produce results.

When I bring back the second breakfast tray, Harper has finished tidying her cell and is lying back on her bed. This time the mattress is where it should be. She's given up hiding from me, probably because she knows she has far more important things to worry about. She appears to be resigned to her fate and is simply waiting it out.

Brandt, on the other hand, is in brooding mode. While I've been in the kitchen I've heard him try to talk to Harper several times, seeing if she'll tell him her side of the story. Luckily, she isn't saying a word. She seems to have clammed up tighter than a pair of leather pants on a generously proportioned ass. Why? Hell if I know. Maybe we'll find out shortly.

Setting the tray down on the floor, I pull the key out of my pocket. Inserting it in the lock I move to twist it, but Brandt stops me.

"Wait. I'm not sure this is the right thing to do. Maybe we can—"

I cut him off. "Do you honestly have the time to go easy on this girl?" I knew Brandt would chicken out, but I'm ready for that.

"No, but I'm not sure I can..." Brandt's voice tails off. He can't get the rest out, but it doesn't take a genius to figure out what he's trying to say.

"Do you want to marry Helena?" Yes, I'm being an asshole, but that's the long and short of it. Besides, Harper has got to go.

"No, but I'm not sure I can watch you do this." Brandt puts his heads in his hands, which should be where I back down, but I don't. If I can't get rid of Harper I'll almost certainly lose him, and losing him to a woman is going to sting.

"Then don't watch. As soon as I find out anything I'll come and get you." Brandt's eyes are miserable as they look up at mine. I know that look well. It was the one he wore when I first took his virginity, and it was a regular feature for the first three months we shared a cell together. It turns me the fuck on. I know it shouldn't, but I've already mentioned I'm one sick individual, right?

Brandt shakes his head. "I'm not going anywhere." He closes his eyes, and his breath hisses out through his teeth. "Fine. You go in there and do your thing. Go quick before I change my mind."

I take Brandt at his word. Twisting the key the cell door swings open, and I pick up the tray behind me. Harper looks at me warily. She's wondering what happens next, although I think she has a rough idea. I'm surprised she's not lost it by now. I was rather counting on her going berserk at the thought of fucking me, but it doesn't look like she's going to put up a fight, which is a shame because I was looking forward to it. I do hope she isn't going to spoil my fun.

The first thing I do is move all the bin bags and cleaning items out of the cell. If she starts biting, kicking and scratching, the last thing we need is a load of broken crockery all over the place. When they're safely out of harm's way, I pull the cell door closed and toss the key to Brandt. That should ensure Harper doesn't bash me over the head with something in another of her vain escape attempts.

"Breakfast time," I say sweetly. I know she'll have remembered what I said before about making her eat it off the floor, and sure enough, that's exactly what's going to happen. Picking up the bowl of fresh porridge I tip it upside down and let the contents drop a few feet away from me. I then give her a very long look and smile.

"Eat up, girlie. Don't make me come over there and manhandle you." I wait patiently for a reaction. I want her eyes to light up with anger, but no such thing happens. Instead she shoots Brandt the look I want, which says something along the lines of 'I want to kill you', before getting down on the floor and obediently crawling towards me. This is not what I expected. Something's not right here.

If I thought that was weird enough, she then stops just before the mountain of porridge and buries her face in it. She then laps it up, every last drop, dragging her face around the floor as if it's the tastiest meal she's ever eaten. When she's finished she raises her face to mine, licks a line of porridge from around her lips and smiles. Oh. My. Fucking. God. She has no idea who she's dealing with here.

"What's next?" she purrs. The sound is a low throaty rumble, and it reverberates somewhere around my groin. My cock instantly hardens and all I want to do is fling her against the wall and grind into her until the rafters above us shake. There's a slight tick in my jaw as I watch her eyes bore into mine. The breakfast thing is backfiring on me, but Brandt isn't going to be happy unless I get her to eat a reasonably decent meal, so I'm going to finish this quickly. Then I can get on with the good stuff.

Picking up the tub of yogurt, I dump it on the floor, and then tip the bowl of fruit on top. I then grab the mug of lukewarm tea and pour it all over the mess. My smile is a lot less smug this time round, but she hasn't won the war yet.

"Now you can drink your tea, princess." Harper looks a little less enthusiastic about her task this time, but she doesn't fight me on the issue. I'd expected resistance, and a lot of it, but instead I'm getting instant obedience. What game is this little temptress playing? It's going to be interesting to try and figure her out.

She moves her head down towards the splattered mess and begins to lap it up. Her arms are rigid as her head bobs up and down. It's clear this type of treatment isn't going to break her, but to be honest, I'd be surprised if it did. The more shit I heap upon her, however, the more likely it is that she'll run screaming - except there's nowhere for her to go. It's talk or suffer, and it's her choice. Actually, it isn't. It's my choice and it will happen. There is no room for failure.

Gripping a handful of her hair I yank it up sharply.

"You're not going fast enough, princess. If you don't want me to spank that ass again, I suggest you put a little more enthusiasm into the job." I then push her face into the floor to make sure she gets my message. I can see Brandt squirm on the other side of the bars, but at least he doesn't say anything to stop me.

Harper takes me at my word and begins moving faster. This could be because she's afraid of me, and I know she is, but it might be because her ass is so sore she can't tolerate the thought of another spanking. I've got news for her. She's getting one whether she wants it or not, but I'm not going to tell her that just yet.

When she's finally done a tolerable job of cleaning up the mess I pull my T-shirt up over my head with one arm and step towards her. She gasps out loud. I'm not sure whether that's because she's frightened of what's about to happen next, or because she's seen the state of my torso, but it's one of those two, maybe both. I don't ask, nor do I care.

Clicking my fingers, I bark, "Come here!" I point to the floor beneath my feet. Now this is a move guaranteed to piss off any normal female, but Harper's already proven she's not one of those, so I'm going to wait and see what happens. If she decides to spring at me I'm ready for her, and there's no way she's besting me in a brawl.

She crawls forward and kneels in front of me. Fuck. Has she done this shit before? Hang on, how long has Brandt had her up here? Maybe he's been training her. That would explain a few things.

Using my T-shirt to wipe her face, I bend down to squat in front of her. Handing her the last item on the tray, which is a small glass of water, I watch as she eyes me warily. She thinks I'm about to throw it at her. The thought has crossed my mind, but for the next ten seconds I'm going to play nice.

"Drink. You can use your hands this time, but don't make me regret my decision. Things are going to get really nasty round these parts if you throw it at me." Handing her the glass, I watch as she accepts it with trembling fingers. This means she's more scared than she looks. That's a start.

Harper drinks the water quickly, as if worried I'll snatch it away. That would be against my best interests, but she doesn't need to know that. I want to use that mouth shortly, and I want it clean.

When she's finished with the glass she hands it back to me, and risks a glance at Brandt. I know what she's thinking. She's hoping he'll rescue her from this. That ship has already sailed. Grabbing her head, I focus her attention on me.

"Look at me, and only me," I say in a dangerously soft tone. "If I catch you looking at him again you'll be over my knee, and I won't go gentle on you like he did." Her eyes widen, but she doesn't look away. Instead, she gives me a small nod of acknowledgement. She knows the rules of this game, if nothing else. That's a start.

"What do you want?" she whispers.

"You know exactly what I want," I say. "The big guy and I work as a team." Brandt is taller than me by a good four inches, which may have something to do with my Spanish heritage, but where our wits are concerned we're pretty evenly matched, unfortunately. I can usually run rings around most inmates, but with Brandt things got a little more interesting. Perhaps that's why I like him so much.

"You're not getting that." Her voice sounds defeated, but her posture indicates she is anything but. This girl is a melting pot of contradictions.

"I am. I always get what I want. You'll figure that out soon enough." I give her a pitying look, and some small part of me, the one where morals once lived, does feel sorry for her. I suspect she's got a tale of woe to share with us, and this story is nowhere near as clear cut as Brandt thinks it is. Rage is colouring his vision, but it doesn't colour mine. Even though I know she's probably a broken little thing inside, I still want to unravel her piece by piece. I like knowing what makes people tick. More than that, I like knowing how to control them.

"You're not, but feel free to try your best. I've seen it all before and then some." Harper bites her lip. I don't think she knows she's doing it, but it's sexy as hell. I want to take that lip in my mouth and bite it so hard it bleeds. I won't, though. She's not earned that privilege yet.

"Challenge accepted." The confidence I have in myself is not misplaced. She'll crumple like all the rest of them when the time is right. All I have to do is find out what her triggers are. Everyone has them. It didn't take me long to uncover Brandt's and I don't see why this little thing should be any different. Actually, I know she won't. Right now, she's currently staring at my abs and the array of twisted tattoos that define them. They are a little breath-taking, if I do say so myself. When I got them I went for an *El Dia Des Los Muertos* theme, and I have to confess, I was quite pleased with the results. I'm a living, breathing skeleton of flesh and inked bone. Everywhere you look there's death and destruction. She hasn't seen my back yet, either. It looks like someone has peeled my skin apart and torn me inside out. It does wonders for my bad boy image. I had the benefit of being inside when we had a decent tattoo artist several years ago. What he did to my body borders on nothing short of magnificent, depending on whether you're easily squeamish or not.

Placing a hand on either side of her face, I gently rub her delicate skin. "You're so soft and breakable, princess." She is. Harper is a fragile little thing. A bird with clipped wings. The woman looks like she's been stumbling along for a while, and now she's met me there's no chance of her ever flying again.

She places her hands on my knees, palms up. "So break me. That's what you're here to do, isn't it, Gabriel? I'm used to being broken. Have fun."

Tipping her face up so I can examine those sable eyes carefully, I try to figure out what she means by that sentence. It would have been sensible to have got some more background info from Brandt before I began, but my impatience got the better of me. Let's hope I don't come to regret that later.

"Oh, I intend to, sweetheart. I intend to," I purr, and toss her face away from me. I've seen enough. It's time to get down to business.

Chapter 13 - Harper

Gabriel is a cross between a piece of the most dark and decadent chocolate cake you have ever dared to put in your mouth, mixed with a generous sprinkling of arsenic. Yep. You want to eat it, but at the same time you're afraid it might kill you. He's as irresistible as candy, and as dangerous as toxic waste. It saddens me to say that I'm not immune to his charms. I suspect there would be few women who were. At least I'm aware that I'm dealing with a monster before we begin, though. I'm already retreating into my protective shell, and it looks like I'll have to stay there for a while.

When Mal left the country, I never kidded myself that this was over. Even back then I knew the day that Brandt was released would come, and if he didn't kill me, then Mal would make sure the job was done on his return. I know now that it won't be Brandt who ends me. Our connection is too strong. Gabriel, on the other hand? He's more than capable of it, and perhaps I'll even enjoy myself as he extinguishes what little light is left within me. I'm not even sure I care any more. I've been waiting for this for so long, it's almost a relief that it's finally here. I just want this over with. I don't want to live in fear any longer. I don't want to be hungry. I don't want to be poor. Most of all, I don't want to be in love with someone who will never look at me the way I look at them. All other pain dulls in comparison to that one.

"Stand up." Gabriel's voice is hard, and I obey it instantly. I'm used to being told what to do. His eyes then devour my body, like a starving man who's been lost out to sea for a week. They are hungry, and they are mean.

His hands reach up slowly to caress my breasts and I shudder. His touch is soft and light, and my nipples pucker instantly. I can feel Brandt's burning stare from here. I can't believe he is going to let this happen. How can he just sit there and watch his friend fuck me? Does he hate me that much?

Gabriel then bends his head down to suckle on me, and I let him, desperately wanting to beg Brandt to stop this. I can't be passed around again. I thought that part of my life was over. I seem to be going around in circles, lost in a perpetual loop of nastiness. I have Alex to thank for this mess. Alex and his fucking insane jealousy.

When Gabriel bites down on my teat and yanks it backward I let out a little whimper of pain. It's only the appetiser, though. His hands then come around my back and rest on the top of my ass, before his fingernails drag a path through the bruised and reddened flesh. Hissing out a sharp breath, I can feel tears begin to form in the corners of my eyes. What is he going to do to me? His hands move between my legs, as if to show me. Putting two fingers inside my already soaking wet pussy, he sighs happily.

"You're so wet for me, aren't you, sweetheart? Does Brandt realise what a dirty little whore you are? I bet you spread those legs for any fucker who asks. Isn't that right, Harper?" He begins to pump his fingers inside me, and while anger is rising up through my body, desire is lacing my bloodstream causing me to lose focus. I need to pay attention. I need to stop this.

"If I ask you to drop to your knees and open that mouth wide, I'd bet you'd do it without a moment's hesitation. You're gagging for a big, thick cock to fill all those juicy holes, aren't you, Harper?" I let out a grunt of frustration and push him away from me. While he may be right, that doesn't mean I have to play into his hands.

"Brandt!" I scream, twisting my face towards him. "Stop this. I'm not some plaything that can be tossed around. This is between you and me. Please don't do this." I am slightly hysterical as I back away from Gabriel, towards the bed. When my legs touch cool, rough metal, I know there's nowhere else to go. With one eye I watch Brandt on the chair, his posture rigid and tight, while he chews on his bottom lip. From the other, I can see Gabriel advancing towards me with a big smile on his face. Oh shit. That's when I realise I've made my first mistake. I've defied the monster.

"Oh, Harper, what a naughty girl you are," he purrs, as his fingers reach behind him to pull something out of his jeans pocket. I stare at the mass of inked bones and abs before me, my eyes swimming in defeat. Brandt hasn't said a word. He isn't going to rescue me. He's going to watch as his friend fucks me in every hole I possess, and he won't move a muscle to save me. I will never forgive him for this - never.

"Don't do this," I choke, watching as he pulls a set of black cable ties out of his pocket. That's when my limbs go liquid and I fall heavily against the thin, plastic mattress beneath me.

"It's too late for that, Harper. Even if you spilled every thought in your vicious little head right now, I'd still go through with this part. The part where you talk comes later, much later, and only after you've seen what I'm capable of. That's how this works. It's called intimidation, and I'm very good at it." Gabriel takes one of the thick plastic ties, and begins to form it into a loop. I freak out. His legs are either side of me now, narrowing my escape route, but I still make an attempt to rush between them. Normally I'd have made it, too, but I'm sluggish and weak after the intense exercise of yesterday and I've only had one decent meal in the last two days. Gabriel easily manages to catch a handful of my hair, immediately stopping me in my tracks, before placing his legs tightly around either side of my head.

"This kind of behaviour just won't do, Harper," he says mockingly, tightening the grip he has around my head so I can't move an inch. "We're going to have to stop all this running about, I'm afraid. It's interfering with my plans of domination. I'm going to make you beg me to fuck you every damn which-way, Harper, and Brandt will be watching every second of it. How does that make you feel, sweetheart?" It's another sarcastic jibe designed to get a rise out of me, and it does, but I can't do anything about it. He's just grabbed my two arms from under me and fastened them behind my back with one sharp tug. Now I'm held up by nothing more than my head between his legs. If he moves I'll be lucky not to fall flat on my face.

I swear the bastard can read my mind because that's exactly what he does. Releasing the grip his legs have around my head, I fall face first because I have no hands to stop it. Bracing myself for a sharp and painful jolt, I close my eyes. But Gabriel doesn't let me fall. Shoving one booted foot underneath my chin, he manages to prevent my face getting a rather unpleasant hello from some particularly unforgiving concrete, with less than three inches to spare. He then lowers me slowly to the floor, so my chin is resting there and my ass is pointing up in the air. It's not a particularly dignified position, but I guess that was the idea.

He gently removes his foot from under me. "Lick my boots," he orders.

Oh, how I've missed these games. Alex and I used to play them lots. In the beginning it was fun; not so much near the end.

"Fuck you," I grunt. It's also what I told Alex the first time he tried it. I didn't make the same mistake again, and I'm guessing I won't this time. My pride is misplaced in here.

Gabriel bends down and wraps his hands around my chestnut curls, using them as rope to pull my head upward. He gets his face right up into mine, so close that I can almost feel his long, feathery eyelashes as they blink. His high cheekbones are sharply angled, and his wishbone lips are dangerously close to mine. When he's sure he's got my attention, he says, "As I've said before, you will be. So don't go getting impatient. Now I'm going to tell you one more time. Lick my boots."

There will be consequences to my disobedience. The question is: will I be able to handle them? I don't have the measure of him yet, but I'm sure I will have in the next hour or so. That's usually all it takes. Normally I'd just obey, but I want Brandt to see what this asshole is capable of. If he does something really stupid, there's a chance that Brandt will get rid of him.

Gabriel lowers my face to the floor again, his shoes just in front of my nose, all polished and shiny. The scent of leather makes me want to throw up all over them, but I sit there quietly and stare at them, standing my ground. The ball is in his court, and I want to see what he's made of.

He doesn't give me more than three seconds to obey before he steps back from me.

"Excellent. You and I are going to have a whole heap of fun together," he says, not deterred by my disobedience in the slightest. He then moves behind me and I can hear him playing with the cable ties once more. Soft clicking hums in my ears as he forms them into loops. I can feel one loop go around one ankle, and then he threads the next cable tie through that one to cuff both my ankles together. It doesn't look like I'm going anywhere in a hurry.

"Want to know what happens next?" He pats my head like I'm a dog. If that hand comes anywhere near my mouth I'm biting it off.

"Not particularly," I reply, as sweetly as I can.

Gabriel lavishes me with an arrogant smile. "Well, Miss Bullets and Nails, I look forward to doing this the hard way. You two have a lot in common, you know." He flicks his thumb over to where Brandt is sitting, giving me pause to wonder what went on between those two. I'm not sure I want to know. I feel guilty enough about that as it is. Brandt merely grunts in response. Now they have me intrigued, damn it. My eyes must drift off into the distance because the next thing I know Gabriel is clapping his hands together in front of my face.

"OK, Harper, here's how it's going to go. I'm going to drag you across this concrete floor by your hair, and as soon as you think you're up to the challenge of boot licking, all you have to do is yell. We clear?" Gabriel doesn't give me a chance to respond because he's already carrying out his threat. My knees are being scraped across the abrasive floor, and my skin melts from my body almost instantly. This is not the kind of pain I can sustain for any length of time, but it takes me a few moments for my mouth to figure out how to get a word out. Having your skin almost sandpapered off by concrete makes any speech kind of tricky, in my humble opinion. This kind of torture is crippling.

"Stop. Give her a second." This comes from Brandt. He can see that I can't catch my breath.

Unfortunately, either Gabriel doesn't hear him or he doesn't want to. He continues to drag me around in a circle, and I cannot say a word to save my life. The pain is excruciating. Yes, I've had worse, but it's still impressive enough to rob me of the power of speech.

But Brandt, my hero, isn't taking this lying down. Getting to his feet, he stomps to the bars and shouts, "Stop!" Thankfully this captures Gabriel's attention, and he stops mid-stride.

"Give her a moment," he says warningly, but the two share a look.

"Fine," says Gabriel, his lips thinning. "Anything you want to say to me, Harper?"

I open my mouth to speak, but no sound comes out. I try again and am rewarded with a small squeak that is nothing near what he wants to hear.

"See? We're not there yet," Gabriel says to Brandt. "This is no time to be squeamish. Get a cup of coffee and take a breather. She'll still be alive when you get back downstairs." Brandt glares at his ex-lover and waits.

"I promise," says Gabriel exasperatedly.

"Give her a moment. Let her speak." Brandt bends down so he can examine the damage through the bars. I have no idea how bad it is, but it feels like someone's taken a really sharp vegetable peeler to my knees. Now I like pain, but this one was a little too much even for me, even though it doesn't change the fact that I'm hornier than hell right now. Oh, woe is me.

"Last chance. Have you got anything to say?" Gabriel looks at me as if I'm something unpleasant he's just wiped off his shoe. He can't stand me, and I have to say, the feeling is mutual.

Still, I don't make the mistake of defying him again. Having been given a second chance I don't intend to abuse it.

"I'm sorry," I croak. "I'll lick your boots. I'll do every damn thing you tell me to the instant you say it, just please don't drag me any further." I already know there'll be no more disobedience. If this was what he went with for starters, the main course is looking exceedingly unappetising.

Gabriel is not amused. "Damn it, Brandt. You're spoiling all my fun. Do we want her to talk or not?"

"Not like this. I can't watch this. Play fair, Gabe." He taps one of the bars with his index finger in agitation. A high, tinny noise rings through the cell.

"I never play fair, you know that." Gabriel's tone is dark.

"And wasn't that always the problem?"

I can't help but notice there are sour grapes between the pair. The tension in the room is ratcheting up at a rate of knots.

"You didn't want me anyway. You made that very clear from the start." Gabriel turns his back to Brandt. Interesting. That means he doesn't want him to see his face. I can still see it though, and from the corner of my eyes I note that it's drawn and pinched.

"I did, didn't I? Maybe that was because I saw you for what you are, even back then."

Brandt turns away and I hear the chair legs scrape as he settles himself back down, but it takes a few more seconds for Gabriel to compose himself. When he does, he looks at me with fury. Great. He's about to take his anger out on me. This is just what I need.

"So, what are you waiting for, little bird? Isn't there something you should be doing right now?" His voice is downright lethal, and my head drops instantly, not that it has any choice because his hand is now circling my neck and pushing me down as far as I'll go.

When my chin hits his boots I begin licking them, thankful that they're already reasonably clean. The taste of leather is unpleasant in my mouth, and brings back memories of Alex. I want to gag, but I daren't. I'm in enough trouble already.

"Make sure you give them a good clean, and don't rush the job. When you've finished, you're going over my knee. Don't think I missed the look you gave Brandt earlier. Disobedience around these parts will not be tolerated. Your eyes are for me and me only." He uses his hand around my neck to make me bob my head up and down like a puppet. One minute my nose is being ground into his shoe and in the next he's trying to pull my neck off its hinges.

He lets me lick his shoes for the better part of five minutes before he becomes bored. Actually, I suspect he was bored after the first ten seconds but has decided to let the threat of his spanking loom over me. He's achieved his intended result. I am now quivering like a leaf.

"Move over to the bed." Gabriel walks three paces and sits himself down on my paper-thin mattress. It almost disintegrates under his weight. He's in for an uncomfortable afternoon, but nowhere near as uncomfortable as mine, I suspect.

When I don't move an inch, mostly because I'm tied hand and foot, he looks at me with irritation.

"Don't make me come over there and drag you, Harper. Once I start again I might not stop." The sound of that voice, completely devoid of emotion, makes me want to throw up. This man is a killer. What's he going to do to me when he's got what he wants? Mind you, if he did kill me, wouldn't that actually be a blessing in disguise? My life is so fucked up right now, I'm not sure I can figure out who the bigger asshole is. Do I want to take on Mal or Gabriel? I definitely know the answer to that question - neither.

Shuffling on my knees I let out a mewl of pain every time I connect with the floor. Gabriel laps it all up, and I swear he's almost rubbing his hands together in glee. When I finally reach his feet I lift my head defiantly to look at him. Show me what you're capable of, you bastard.

He does. Picking me up as easily as if I were a two-pound bag of sugar, he slings me over his legs with my ass up in the air. This is just like old times. If they think they're going to get me to talk by spanking me, they're much mistaken. I can take far more than that.

"Anything you want to say to me before we begin?" Gabriel's voice has dropped an octave; now soft and seductive. It doesn't impress me. If he wants me to talk he's going to have to try harder.

"No," I reply, already braced for the worst. I know he's not going to take it easy on me, but I also know Brandt is watching. Brandt won't let anything too dreadful happen. I don't know how I know that, but I do.

Gabriel runs his hand over my already reddened ass and squeezes it, making me gasp out loud. Oh God. This is going to hurt so bad.

"Good. I'd hate for you to spill your secrets at the first hurdle," he says. "It takes all the fun out of things." He digs his fingernails into my ass again and scrapes a long path downwards, towards the top of my thighs. I bite my lip to keep from yelling. I am not giving him what he wants.

His fingers repeat the action several times, but when he receives no reaction he moves on. This time he begins kneading my flesh heavily, literally pulling large chunks of my ass cheek into his hands, and it's just as bad as the fingernails, if not worse. I honestly wish he'd just get on with the spanking. At least I know what I'm dealing with there.

My body remains still, and my lips don't utter a sound as he continues to work my ass. I concentrate on staring at the wall in front of me and count back slowly from five thousand. It gives me something to do. I need to keep my mind busy or I will go crazy. When Gabriel's hands finally stop, there is a long pause as I wait for the inevitable spank to come crashing down. It doesn't. Instead, Gabriel leans back and there's a soft jingle of metal. *Four thousand and twenty-two.* I can't figure out what it is. Is he tapping something against the bed? Then I hear a very distinct sound. One I've heard several times before, and my stomach drops. My mouth opens on a silent wail of horror as he lifts his hips in order to remove the leather belt that encircles them.

He shuffles a little as he tugs the belt around his waist free, and there's a soft slap as the end flops on his thigh. Silence follows, but I know exactly what he's doing. He's looping the belt carefully around his hand so he can swing it at me. So much for the warm-up; the man is going straight for the jugular.

Painful seconds tick by as I wait for the slice of that belt to cut into my flesh. I already know how much it's going to hurt, and I would have given nearly anything to stop it - anything bar Brandt's life. I've already taken far too much from him. I can't take anything else. This much I have promised myself, and it's a promise I intend to keep.

"Are you ready, Harper?" Gabriel purrs in my ear.

I turn my face so I can get one last glance at Brandt, though my ass will probably suffer for it.

Raising my voice, I say, "When this is all over, I want you to remember that I did this to protect you. I've watched too many people die, and it has to stop." I know he won't believe me, but in time he will. I just hope that after I'm long gone and buried, he remembers that I tried to do the right thing.

Brandt stands up and walks to my cell. "I don't need protecting, Harper. I just want the truth." My lips thin. He does need protecting, he just doesn't know it yet.

"You don't understand. Neither of you understand. Every time I try to tell you, you automatically think I'm lying, and I get it. I get it, Brandt. You don't trust me, and you have no reason to. But I never meant to hurt you." I turn my head away. I've got nothing more to say to him. His hands slam on the bars in front of him in frustration, but I don't turn back to see the disappointment in his eyes.

"I don't understand because you won't talk to me. Talk to me, Harper. That's all I'm asking. You took five years away from me. All I want to know is why?" Brandt is nearing his own breaking point. He doesn't want to watch this, but he needs answers. I understand that. I just hope he doesn't let his friend go too far. It took eight weeks for me to recover from my last session with Mal. If anything like that goes down again, I'm not sure I'll be able to come back. Brandt begins to pace, but the silence between us drags on. I have nothing more to say.

"Sit down, Brandt," Gabriel eventually says. "We're doing this the hard way and you need to toughen up. That was always your problem, by the way." He runs the loop of the belt over my exposed ass and I shudder. I hear the sound of a chair being thrown across the room, before Brandt swears.

"Do what you want to her, Gabriel. I'm done playing nice." He then storms from the room.

"Oh dear," Gabriel says slowly, his voice dripping with sarcasm, "it's just you and me now. Don't worry, though; I'm pretty sure we're going to have lots of fun together."

That is exactly what I'm afraid of.

When the first crack of the belt explodes on my ass cheeks my insides begin to splinter. I'm already broken. Nothing can change that. I just hope these two will leave enough pieces so that I can glue myself back together again. Then again, maybe it's better if they don't.

Chapter 14 - Gabriel

When Brandt flies out of the room like a tornado, I silently celebrate. I now have free rein to do whatever I want to the girl, and there's lots of unpleasant shit going through my head right now. That's the one good thing about prison. If you have a dark side, there's plenty of opportunity to use it on the inside. When you're on the outside looking in, you have to be slightly more careful. I'm not worried about Harper telling tales on us once she's released, though. This is mostly because I'm going to kill her shortly after. If I'm trying to get back with Brandt, the last thing I need are loose ends hanging around. I'll make sure Brandt never knows. All I need is a big hole and whole lot of mud, or a bathtub and some lye, or failing that, a few pigs. There's more than one way to get rid of an annoying body.

The belt in my hand is currently tanning Harper's ass to within an inch of its life, and so far she's not made a murmur. This is strange. Most girls I know would be howling after a couple of minutes of this kind of treatment, and probably several blokes, too. That could mean one of several things. Either Harper is used to pain, it turns her on, or she has a higher than average tolerance for it. There are no cutting marks on her body, and trust me, I've checked it out, but there are plenty of scars. She could be a former self-harmer. She doesn't look the type, but it's possible. There are other explanations. I have a feeling she's into kink, and if that's the case, I'll find out soon enough. If she's had experience with the lifestyle, there's a good chance she's seen all this before. The other side of the coin is that she's been abused, but that had better not be the case. If it is, I'm going to feel shitty once I've found out, and it will piss me off. She seems far too defiant to have been some man's plaything, though. If she had been abused, she'd do everything I said as soon I said it for fear of the reprisals. There's a little voice inside my head that says she did exactly that when I asked her to eat breakfast off the floor. It doesn't make me pause while I'm busy hammering her ass, but it does confuse me. Most people would have more issues with eating food off the floor than with licking a pair of clean shoes. There is something at play here that I don't understand.

When we get to the five minute mark, and the point where her ass is redder than a watermelon, I give her a break. The object of this exercise is to get her to talk, after all, and she won't be able to do that while I'm whacking her with the belt. I just want to see if she's a little more pliant after pain.

"Ready to chat yet?" I listen carefully for a response, but I'm not expecting big things. Harper has already proved she's stubborn, and to be quite honest, it turns me the fuck on. I hope she keeps this shit up for hours. It will provide me with lots of exciting entertainment.

As I suspect, there is no response to my question, which is absolutely fine by me. Before I begin again, however, there's something I need to find out. My left hand strays between her legs. As soon as she realises what I'm doing she clamps them tight together, but it won't stop me from finding out what I need to know.

"Does this turn you on, Harper? Are you holding those legs together because you're embarrassed that your cunt is currently begging me to fuck it? Hmm. Let's see, shall we?" My fingers burrow between her tightly clamped thighs, and she lets out a ragged squeak of annoyance.

"Don't do this," she grits out. She sounds adorably cute when she's angry.

"Why? You do realise that if you don't talk we're going to be fucking later. There's no two ways about it. If you have any objections, I'd seriously consider using that mouth of yours to do good rather than evil. Although personally, I much prefer evil."

My fingers have found what they're looking for, and sure enough, it's a sticky, wet little honeypot that is practically crying out for attention. I can't believe Brandt hasn't tapped this yet. What is wrong with that boy? Is he still suffering from the tormented woes of whether he's gay or not? I wonder if he's had a woman since he's been out? I resolve myself to go ask him. It'll be an interesting question at the dinner table later, that's for sure.

"Oh dear," I say, bending down so that my voice gently resonates in her ear. "It seems that being thrashed turns you on. It's a good job there's going to be a lot more of that in your future then, isn't it?" Delving a little deeper inside her, I curl my fingers against her G-spot and listen to her sharp intake of breath.

"Don't do this," she moans again, with considerably less enthusiasm than the last time. If there's one thing I know how to do well, it's play a woman's body.

"You're as bad as Brandt," I say, a wry smile forming on my lips. "It's one thing to have a stranger fuck you, it's another entirely if you're made to enjoy the experience." Brandt was almost suicidal when he came to crave my cock. He knew I could make him take it, but he never expected to get to the point where he wanted it or would even be so desperate as to beg for it. I knew we'd get there. It just took time.

Harper's body stiffens, and I know I've hit the nail on the head.

"I shouldn't enjoy this," she whimpers, and I wonder if she's talking to me or just voicing her thoughts out loud. Anyway, however we look at it, I was right; Brandt and Harper are a match made in heaven, which is exactly why I have to get rid of her.

"Don't worry, you're not going to for long." I'm going to give her just enough to get excited, so I can do what I want to her, but not enough that she gets any real pleasure from the ordeal. This is about crime and punishment, after all.

The belt comes back down again, with my right hand, while the fingers of my left work her cunt. I'm going to taste that later. It's been a while, and though I'm reasonably sure I prefer men now, it wouldn't hurt to test the theory.

"Oh, God," Harper moans.

"Nah, I'm not God," I say, amused. "I'm an angel. A fallen one. You'd do well to remember that, princess."

I take her to the edge, over and over again, but the belt on her ass won't let her come. There's an art to this kind of torment, and I'm good at it. Too good at it, in fact. Harper has taken two brutal spankings in the last day, and her ass will be on fire by now. That's what I'm aiming for. I need to be able to control her, and this is the first step towards that. Now, if she won't do what I say instantly, all I have to do is grab it and she'll immediately fall into line. When that stops working, I'll devise new and ingenious punishments, but for now it should be good enough. A few more strikes with the belt, and she'll do every damn thing I tell her to, almost before I've said it.

I don't need to mete out too many more strokes before the girl starts sobbing, and that's the first sign that I'm getting through to her. I don't kid myself that she's about to talk, though. That will probably take a day or so's work, but we're on the right track. When the sobs turn to hysterics and writhing, I know we're ready for stage two.

When I eventually stop, more to rest my hand than to give her a break, she is wailing so loudly it's a wonder Brandt hasn't marched down the stairs and given me what for. Whatever he's doing, he's decided to do it far enough away that he can't hear us - and for that I'm thankful.

Pushing her off me, I stand up to stretch my legs. I'm assuming a position of power again. I'm standing, she's lying. When I'm around she'll always be lying or crawling, or there'll be trouble. She'll discover that soon enough. As I walk from one side of the cell to the other her sniffles are slowly dying down, and I wait patiently until she's caught her breath. I am a monster, but she needs to be able to breathe for what I'm about to do next. Now, do I just push her to the floor and shove it in, or do I torment her by telling her what I'm about to do first? Hmm. That's a no-brainer.

"Are you ready to suck my cock, Harper?" The soft little hiccups turn into a shocked gasp as her head swivels round to look at me. Her eyes are red-rimmed and swollen from crying, and her face looks as if it's dissolving in tears. Is it wrong I find that look sexy as hell? Probably, but who the hell cares?

"Did you spank Brandt?" Interestingly, Harper has ignored my question and gone for one of her own. Prevarication isn't going to work here, but I'm happy to lengthen the anticipation if she is.

"Yes." I did a whole lot of things to Brandt, and spanking was just one of them. He used to hate it, which is probably why I enjoyed it so much.

"Do you think you'll get him back?" she chokes, through the snot and tears that are clogging up her airways.

Actually, I've decided I'm not going to play this game any more. I have better things to do.

"Get on your knees, Harper. Tip that head up and open your mouth as wide as you can. If you're not going to tell me anything of interest, I might as well keep it busy for the time being." I advance towards her menacingly. There is no smile on my face now. There is just cold, calculated intent. Now it's up to her. She can either obey or face the consequences. Whatever happens, it's going to be lots of fun my end.

Harper, to my disappointment, gets off the bed and lowers herself to her knees. They have stopped bleeding, but they need a good clean up. If she's a good girl, maybe I'll attend to her later. I like doing stuff like that. It keeps them off balance. They never know what they're going to get with me.

Watching her carefully, I wait to see if she'll obey me to the letter. Her brown eyes are almost shooting sparks as she levels her gaze upon me. They tell me that while she's being a good girl, she's doing it under duress, and that's just the way I like it. She's tense, angry, and she'd rather chew me up and spit me out than talk to me, let alone fuck me. That's too bad. I've got plans for her.

Just as I'm about to get nasty because she isn't doing what I asked, she suddenly tips her head high and opens that pretty little mouth wide. My jaw snaps shut. It is an incredible sight, and it's rendered me speechless for a moment. My cock jumps in my pants and all the blood in my body is suddenly and very quickly redirected. Maybe I don't prefer men, after all.

When I regain the power of speech, I start walking towards her. Hell, my whole body is gravitating in her general direction and there's a good reason for that.

"You have no idea what I'm about to do to that pretty little mouth of yours, Harper, but I intend to show you, slowly at first, and I daresay we'll get a little quicker as time wears on. I'm very particular about how I like to be blowed, so listen up good, princess. If you fail in any part of the instructions I am about to give you, you will be punished, and it will make the earlier punishment look like a tap on the wrist. Nod if you understand."

She nods with her head still high, which has to be a little awkward, so it looks like the girl is trying. Too bad she's persona non grata around these parts, else I'm sure Brandt and I could have had a lot of fun with her.

"So, the rules go like this. You will not use your teeth. If your teeth come anywhere near my cock, I will break them. Now let's talk about tongues. You can use that. Pay particular attention to the spot at the top of the head and show it some love. I'd like to mention at this point that you will not be able to take a break while in the middle of sucking. If you lose enthusiasm for the job, I'll just grab your hair and finish it off my way and trust me when I say you won't like it. While we're on that note, make sure you use as much saliva as possible. I like messy. I also like noise. Even if you aren't enjoying yourself, you will make it sound like you are having the best time of your life. Oh, and when the time comes, you swallow like I'm feeding you fucking chocolate. Failure to do so will result in punishment. Finally, I generally like having my balls tickled or fondled at the same time, but that's going to be tricky for you at the moment, so just this once I'll let you off. Do you need me to repeat the rules?"

I'm pretty sure she will. She'll be so scared of doing something wrong that her heart rate has probably doubled. Watching her for a response, I raise my eyebrows in surprise when she gives me a short shake of her head. Huh. Maybe she's got a photographic memory. We'll wait and see. Whatever happens, I see more punishments in her immediate future, whether she's behaved herself or not.

Slowly undoing the fly of my jeans, I slip my cock out of my boxers and fist it. The beast is visibly pulsing in my hand, and looks magnificent, if I do say so myself. Harper can't see it yet because her head is still pointing upwards, but she'll get an eyeful in a minute. Giving myself a couple of strokes with my right hand, I use my left to lower her head so she can get a good view of what she's about to deal with.

"Holy fuck," she whispers.

Yes, I might not be as tall as some people, but my body has compensated for that in other areas. "That is an excellent response. Score one for enthusiasm, Miss Wilkinson," I say as her eyes bulge out of her head. Yes, I know that wasn't enthusiasm, and more of a 'what the hell am I going to do with that' kind of look, but that's not my problem, it's hers. I'm very interested in how she's going to solve it, too.

Bringing the tip to her lips, I trace a gentle pattern all the way around them. I'm waiting to see if she'll sneer her nose in revulsion, and if she does she's getting another five minutes with the belt. But no such thing happens. Her tongue even peeks out to give me a quick lick which has me twitching in delight.

Hmm. The girl is an absolute enigma. I can't figure her out for the life of me. Why is she not screaming the house down, or at the very least looking like she wants to kill me? Either she's totally into me and seriously aroused, or she's a very good actress. Now I know for a fact she's not into me, and while the arousal side of things might be true, that's probably down to the kink or pain. The actress part? I haven't decided yet, but I'll figure it out before the day is through.

I feel her lips against my flesh and hiss through my teeth. I'm going to enjoy this so much. The anticipation is killing me. Perhaps that's why I'm dragging it out to the nth degree. "Tell me how much you want to suck this monster, Harper. Make me want to bang that throat, princess." The odds are ten to one the bitch can't talk dirty. That takes practise and lots of it.

Her beautiful chocolate eyes focus on mine, tears still swimming in their depths, but they are now also filled with heat. She's taking to this like a duck to water, or maybe she's just doing her best to save her hide, I don't really care which. I'm having fun and that's all that counts.

"Please let me suck you, Gabriel." That first sentence isn't awe-inspiring, and I roll my eyes. Maybe it's best if I shut her up before she kills the moment with a load of drivel. I decide to give her a bit longer. Maybe she needs time to get into the swing of things. One can hope.

"Please, Gabriel, let me take that great big monster down my throat until you make me gag so hard I can barely breathe. I want to feel you slamming into me so hard, you nearly tear me apart. Cram that fucker into my throat, Gabriel. Make me..."

OK, so the last part was definitely an improvement and I'm getting a little carried away. There wasn't a lot of blood left swirling around my brain as soon as I saw her kneeling on the floor with her gob open, but after that... well.

"Shut up." I don't wait for her to obey, I simply thrust - hard. Now when I normally do this, girls either try to cough up a lung or their eyes almost shoot out of their head in horror. Harper does neither. In fact, she does the complete opposite. Just as I've instructed her to, she makes a groaning sound of approval. This nearly makes me laugh; she is no stranger to this type of treatment. Could it be that Brandt's sweet little princess is actually a whore in disguise? Oh, how entertaining would that be? If only he were down here to watch this. I have a feeling he would be less than amused.

As if on cue I hear the pad of feet behind me. He is coming back down to watch because he doesn't trust me with his little pet. This is too perfect. I am going to have some fun with this. If there's one thing I enjoy it's performing to an audience - especially if there's a chance I might make them jealous. It's time to show Brandt just what a little slut the girl is. I'm ninety-nine percent certain that as soon as he watches her deep throating me she'll be on the next bus out of this place. Brandt always was a stickler for fidelity.

Grabbing a handful of hair I tip it back, and compliment her on her performance so far. This isn't to boost her ego, it's to piss off Brandt.

"Yes," I purr, "just like that. Keep that tongue flat and open that jaw wide." Hammering into the back of her throat I pretend not to notice Brandt, who's standing midway down the stairs, probably wondering if he should run straight back up them again. I know he won't, though. Now he's seen what I'm doing he won't be able to walk away. He'll either come over and punch my lights out, or he'll continue to watch with sick fascination as I pound the hell out of his best buddy's throat. Is he imagining himself in my place right now? Is he jealous of my dick sliding down into the sweet heat of Harper's mouth? Maybe he'd rather it was him on his knees, taking a pounding for me. It will be interesting to find out.

To distract me from my thoughts, Harper's tongue comes into play, flicking and licking in all the right places. As I slowly withdraw from the whole length of her hot little mouth and let my cock come to rest on her lips, she lets her tongue circle the head, over and over, wrapping her saliva around me like a soft, warm blanket. I cannot lie. It feels amazing. Even if I wanted to stop I couldn't, so I hope Brandt isn't about to storm the fortress and go crazy on me. All I'm asking for is at least another three minutes. That isn't too much to ask, is it?

Placing one hand on each of Harper's shoulders, I begin pistoning in and out of her. It's a lot more fun now I know I have a second pair of eyes watching. My hands creep to the back of her neck, so I can pull her head forward on the upstroke, crushing my cock against her throat. This is when I get the gagging noises I've been craving. Harper looks an absolute picture. There's a line of sloppy saliva dribbling down her chin as I continue to work her over. She's struggling to breathe as I up my pace and her face is a tormented wash of emotions. I know she's spotted Brandt on the stairs because I saw her eyes flare in recognition a few seconds ago. Judging by the red splodges of colour that have now infused her face, it's clear she doesn't want him to see this. Too bad, because I do. I want to torment her until she screams, just to see what it does to him. I need to know how invested he is in the girl, and I hope it's nowhere near as much as I think he is.

Pulling back again, I allow her to catch her breath. I hope she uses the opportunity wisely to fill her lungs to the max because she won't be breathing very much for the next couple of minutes.

My hand grips the hair on top of her head again as I raise her eyes to mine. "Are you ready to deep throat me, Harper?" I nod her head for her as a tear dribbles out of her left eye. "Take a big gulp of air, princess, because it's the last you're getting for a while."

"No, please, no. I..." These aren't words I want to hear, so I drive my cock home inside her. While her eyes fill with fear, turning me on even more, I plunge back and forth with insane speed, feeling the first stirrings of an orgasm begin to tighten my balls.

"Let's see how talented you are, Harper," I say, playing to my audience. "Let's see just how much you can take." Grabbing each side of her head in my hands I plunge hard, counting as I go. One, two, three, four, five, six, seven, eight, nine, ten. This is a little game, and she'll figure it out soon enough. Giving her a chance to breathe I then repeat the game, but this time I double the number. When I release her she splutters like mad, and begins to tremble all over. That's odd. Perhaps she's played this before, or maybe she can already see what's coming just around the corner.

The next time I fuck her throat to the count of forty, without letting her come up for air. By the time I've pulled out her face is ashen. She knows what's coming next.

"Think you can hold your breath for a minute and twenty?" She's not got much of a choice, but hey, that's not my problem.

"Please don't do this," she stutters miserably. Fear has taken hold and damned if it doesn't look good on her.

"You know how to get yourself out of this mess. Anytime you want to press the escape button, all you have to do is say." My voice is mocking. We both know she won't pull the escape cord.

She shakes her head. We are doing this. Praise the lord. Hallelujah. I give her one last chance to talk, for Brandt's sake, but she doesn't say another word. She's concentrating on taking in as much oxygen as she can, and I can't say I blame her. This next part is going to be tough - for her. I, on the other hand, am going to enjoy it immensely.

"No last words then?" I taunt her, with my cock tracing a wet, sticky path around her lips. This is purely for Brandt. I suspect he's jealous as hell watching this play out, and I don't know what I'm hoping to achieve, but I know it's something dramatic. I want a reaction. I either want his lips on mine, trying to take my face off, or I want his hands around my throat trying to kill me. Either will do because it means that he still cares. It's his general indifference that I can't stand.

Twisting Harper's hair sideways, so Brandt can get a better view of us, I cup her face in my hands. I then kiss the top of her head gently, purely to put fire inside the loins of the bloke on the stairs, and then I shove my cock home where it belongs.

Attempting to count while you're trying your hardest not to come is quite a challenging experience. I'm not sure I'm going to make it to eighty, but I'm going to try my best. I'm enjoying myself far too much to just let go and shoot at the earliest opportunity. I need to drag this out and get Brandt's attention. If I don't get it this time, I'll almost certainly get it on my next turn.

Poor Harper is looking almost green by the time I reach sixty. I'm slamming my slug home as fast as I can, and she's taking it like a trooper. There's no question she's done this before. This little slut knows exactly what she's doing, and if I'm not careful I'm going to blow. Thankfully, just like her, I've had a little practise too. I know how to drag this out, and even though in this instance I don't want to, I will, even if it is just to torment Brandt.

When we get to eighty I pull back and Harper sways forward, gasping painfully for breath. I catch her before she falls, knowing she is light-headed because of the lack of oxygen in her system. She's not going to make the next one, and we both know it.

Holding her against my waist, while I wait for her to recover, I wink at Brandt.

I think we have this one in the bag.

"Want to talk yet, Harper?" My voice is once again mocking. It isn't really a question. It's a statement. She can't take another round, and unless the girl is completely stupid she'll call a halt to this now. I can feel Brandt's eyes on us from the side-lines. He's been waiting for this speech for five years, so I suspect he's quite anxious to hear what she's got to say.

She doesn't say anything for a moment, and I wonder if she's still trying to catch her breath. When I bend down to peel her head away from my body, the look on her face is one of abject misery.

"Do you have something to say?" I ask again. All eyes are on her as we wait for her answer.

Her head then dips towards the floor as she says, "No." I can barely hear it, but I know damn well it isn't a 'yes'.

"No?" I repeat, astounded. I want to make damn sure I heard that right. Tilting her face upwards with my finger, I watch her expression carefully.

"No," she says a little louder. There is no defiance there. She's not angry, she's just resigned to her fate. I can't believe this.

"You're willing to risk your life to keep hold of the secret?" I want to make sure I understand her reasoning.

"Yes. I'm willing to risk my life. I'm not willing to risk yours. If you want to kill me, you might as well get it over with." That's my cue to see red. Who does she think she's playing with here?

"We're both criminals, Harper. Brandt more by association, but you're protecting no one. We can handle ourselves. You can't. No one is coming to save you, sweetheart. Why don't you just get this over with?"

"No." Now there's defiance. Her head is held high as she keeps my gaze, and her posture is rigid. Fine. Once I've made a threat I always make sure to carry it out, so if she wants to do this the hard way, I'm on board. Brandt might not be, though. I wonder if, by any chance, he's left the key to her cell upstairs. If so, this just might work.

Chapter 15 - Harper

When Gabriel's cock enters my mouth for the last time, I try to figure out how much time one-hundred-and-sixty seconds is. It takes me longer than it should. Nothing is working as I would like, and there's probably a reason for that. I eventually work out that if I want to live through this, I'll need to hold my breath for three minutes, or somehow manage a gasp of air in between his lunges into my throat. I already know neither's going to happen, so either Brandt saves me, or they can try to revive me because I'm pretty sure I won't be conscious at the end of it.

It's one thing to think it, and another entirely to accept it. I don't want to die. I know I haven't got any choice in the matter, but that's the long and short of it.

Still, at least this death is preferable to the one Mal would deliver. Perhaps I should thank my lucky stars that these guys are getting me ahead of the game.

Gabriel's voice sounds in my head as he begins his countdown. I don't want to listen. I know that when he gets past eighty my lungs will feel like they're on fire, and the lights in my head will start to go out. Everything will go fuzzy and grey, and then gradually darker as the pounding continues. Eventually the darkness will win, which is when things won't hurt any more.

But there is no blocking the sound out. Forty, forty-one, forty-two. The burn has already begun in my chest and is spreading through my body. Radiating outwards from my stomach, the trapped air feels like an inflated balloon in my chest. Fifty, fifty-one, fifty-two. How is it that the bastard is as twisted as Mal? They could be fucking brothers. What's the chances of me finding two of the same? Ten to one? One hundred to one? I have no idea, and I don't really give a fuck because I have more important things to worry about.

There's yelling and banging now, but I can't make sense of it. My vision is clouding over and my head is swimming with dizziness. Gabriel must be holding me up because I'd be in a heap on the floor otherwise. I'm not even going to make it as far as I did last time. The stress of this whole ordeal has finally crept up with me.

Sixty-one, sixty-two, sixty-three. My head flops forward, but Gabriel slaps it and I have no choice but to spring back into the land of the living. It won't be for long, though. I. Can't. Breathe.

"Get off her now, you animal!"

All of a sudden my mouth is freed with a sucking pop and I crumple to the floor. For a moment I can't make sense of anything happening around me. All sound is muffled and my vision is blurred. I lay there, on the floor, gasping for air as my lungs take their time to re-inflate. It's a painful business, and it takes a while before I can concentrate on anything else. When I do manage to get myself firmly back into the land of the living, all sorts of nastiness is going on.

"If you kill her I'll kill you!" This comes from Brandt. When I flip my head over to the side to watch what's happening I can see he's got his hands around Gabriel's neck and he's about ten centimetres up in the air, being shaking from side to side. I'd like to say I felt sorry for him, but that would be a big fat lie.

"If you're serious about learning the truth," Gabriel croaks, "you'll need to fight fire with fire. Otherwise you may as well just let her go now. Since when have you gone soft? You never used to be such a pussy. You've only been out a week, and already you're forgetting everything you learnt." Gabriel doesn't appear to be worried about Brandt killing him, judging by the insults being flung around.

"I'm not letting you do that to her. No matter what she's done, she doesn't deserve that. You'll have to think of another way." Brandt lowers Gabriel to the floor, but doesn't release him. The body language between the pair is insane. It's almost as if Brandt doesn't want to let go. It's almost as if...

Gabriel moves his head forward a quarter of an inch and licks his lips. I think he's hoping Brandt will close the distance and kiss him. There's an awkward pause where I wonder the same. Do these two still care for each other? I can't decide.

Even though Brandt's got Gabriel by the scruff of the neck there is no fear in his eyes. He's not worried that a fist is going to come his way, like any other man in his position would be. Brandt then pulls his own head back and drops him like a hot potato.

"You still care about me. Admit it," Gabriel says, and I swear the man almost pouts.

Brandt looks ready to kill him. "Fuck you," he snaps. There's definitely bad blood between them. I wonder who's been cheating on who? Actually, I don't. I know who's been cheating, and it isn't Brandt. I wonder where this is going. Brandt's face is now completely devoid of emotion. Gabriel is wasting his time. Brandt's moved on, and the train has long since left the station.

"Everybody's allowed to make one mistake, Brandt," Gabriel whines petulantly.

"Yep, I agree, but nobody has to stand around while they go make mistakes two, three, and four."

Oh great. I've just had a near death experience and now I'm about to witness a male catfight. Can my life get any better? Yay. I wonder if they left the cell door open?

"That's unfair. I only made the one mistake."

I begin inching towards the door. There's no way they're paying any attention to me at the moment. I should be able to slip away relatively easily while they're taking more shots at each other than an average bottle of tequila holds.

"Don't even think of going for that door, Harper, or I swear I'll throw you to the wolves, and by that I mean Gabriel."

I let out a huff of air. Brandt must have eyes in the back of his head. Mind you, where am I going to go? We've been down that avenue before.

Feeling a long line of drool and god knows what else drop off my chin, I examine the puddle on the floor in disgust. I must look an absolute state. Shaking my head, I sigh; who cares what I look like? It's not as if I'm trying to impress these idiots. But I still need to get away. They can't be here when Mal comes looking. I can't have any more collateral damage in my life.

Brandt must be able to read my mind because he walks to the door and slams it shut. I hear it click into place, so I know it's locked. I'm not getting out unless I intend to go through his pockets searching for the key, and that isn't an option.

"Why don't you throw her this way, Brandt? Why are you protecting her? Don't you want to find out the truth?" Gabriel is once again up close and personal in Brandt's space, and the two are facing off like wild animals - the big scary kind.

"You know I do, but I don't want to kill her." Brandt places both hands against his chest and pushes him away. It's obvious he wants to keep his distance, yet Gabriel keeps up the pressure.

"You are becoming a pussy. I'd wager you'd rather I hurt you, than lay a finger on your precious little princess. Isn't that right? You're the only one who's allowed to touch, Harper. Tell me I'm wrong." Brandt doesn't answer but I can see his gaze drawn down to those beautiful abs, his mouth as he bites his bottom lip, and the swift shake of his head as he tries to get rid of the spell that surrounds him. I know, because I've been there. Even now, after the monstrous blowjob, I'm not entirely averse to the idea of sleeping with the prick which just goes to show how fucked up my hormones are.

"You want me, Brandt. I know you want me. Why won't you just admit it? Why does this always have to go down the hard way?" Gabriel's voice is deadly in its hushed undertones, and Brandt's back instantly stiffens.

"Don't you even think about it," he hisses. While I have no idea what they're talking about, I have a feeling that something unpleasant is about to happen. Hopefully it won't be to me this time, but there are no guarantees.

Sure enough, the pair begin to circle each other like the predators they are, and Brandt flexes his fingers in preparation for a fight. Oh Jesus. This is the last thing I need. If Brandt somehow gets knocked out, I'm dead.

Shuffling back against the wall I try to figure out who's the more experienced fighter between them. My face drops. It's got to be Gabriel. Brandt's not a street rat. His parents would have coddled him in every aspect of his life. While he might have learned a thing or two in prison, he's not a seasoned pro. I'll bet Gabriel's been doing this shit for most of his life. He reminds me of Mal. He's quick, sneaky, ruthless and unpredictable. That pretty much means he's a wild card.

"Unghh." The first person to throw a punch is Gabriel, and he hits Brandt square in the stomach. I know it hurts because the look on Brandt's face is pained but he doesn't double over. Instead he retaliates with an uppercut, but he's not fast enough as Gabriel simply ducks to the side. Gabriel then unleashes a volley of kicks and punches that look carefully orchestrated and placed to do maximum damage. This guy has to be trained in martial arts. I know I'm not an expert, but he's too neat and far too precise. When they keep coming, and Brandt hasn't gotten a fist or foot to connect with anything in ages, I start saying my prayers. If I wasn't doomed before, I am now.

"You know you can't win, Browning. Why don't you just give up now, pretty boy?"

Brandt, who's looking slightly worse for wear with a split lip and bleeding nose, does no such thing.

"I'm not letting you kill her. If you do that you'll be dead to me. Do you understand? I know an eye for an eye works in your world, but that's not how we do things in mine. Promise me, Gabriel. Promise me you won't touch her."

Gabriel takes to the air with his feet in response, and I can hear them connect with Brandt's bones in sickening thuds and cracks. As they move towards me, having almost forgotten I'm here, my eyes widen and I shuffle sideways towards the bed. The last thing I want to do is get in their way. I've been a punching bag for Alex too many times in my life. I can't go through that again.

Cowering against the metal frame, getting ready to dive underneath it, I watch the sickening display of testosterone with barely disguised horror. There's no way Brandt can win this fight. That's abundantly clear from the amount of damage he's taking.

"Stop. Stop!" I scream. No one hears me. They're too focused on trying to take chunks out of each other. I can't bear it any longer. Diving under the bedframe I begin rocking back and forth. Both Brandt and Gabriel are lost in their little world, and I am lost in mine.

The surrounding violence triggers memories. This time I'm back in Mal's little apartment at the back of his warehouse and we are not alone. Waiting for Mal to finish 'his business', as it were, I'm dressed in nothing more than a skimpy basque and thigh-high stockings. Now when I get summoned, I get requests. Today I've been asked to come in this get up and I can't help but wonder what kind of mess Alex has got himself into.

I know Alex doesn't like this arrangement. He doesn't mind sharing me, mostly because it seriously messes with my head, but he doesn't like long-term sharing; the kind where relationships can form. Alex is a very jealous man and the current arrangement I have with Mal, where I visit him every weekend, is tearing him apart. I can see it in his eyes, I can hear it in his voice, and most importantly, I can feel it in his fists when he takes out his anger on me. We are sleeping together less, and while that's a good thing, it's also a bad thing because he has no way to let off steam. He's constantly imagining what Mal and I are doing in bed, and this is made worse by the requests for sexy lingerie, amongst other things, that come directly via his phone. Mal is marking his territory and rubbing Alex's face in it, mostly because he knows there's no way Alex can retaliate. They're rival dealers, but Mal's empire is far bigger than Alex's and he has a lot more manpower behind him. Alex isn't stupid. He can't kill Mal, and even if he could, he'd be dead shortly after. He's got no choice but to watch me follow instructions, while we both hope Mal will get bored with the pairing very shortly. Actually, I'm not sure who's more anxious for it to be over, me or Alex, and that's saying something.

There are sounds of screaming coming from the warehouse, and they've been going on for quite a while. I don't open the door to watch what's unfolding. I got more than my fair share of that when I had to walk the short distance to this tiny apartment. By the looks of things, some bloke has really pissed Mal off because he was tied naked to a chair in the middle of the warehouse floor. That was enough to tell me to walk quickly, but I didn't walk quickly enough.

Mal was waving some kind of small tube about, his eyes sparkling with glee. An educated guess says it was superglue. This is because the naked man had one eye which appeared to be glued shut, while Mal had begun to work on the other.

"Not my eyes man, anything but my eyes!" was being screamed at the top of the naked man's lungs as Mal layered his eyelashes with copious amount of glue. That was the first time I decided there was no way I could ever cross Mal. The second came about ten seconds afterwards with his next sentence.

"It's better this way," Mal rasps, "because you really don't want to know when I'm about to smash your testicles in two with a sledgehammer."

Understandably the screaming increased after that, and I hastily made my exit, hoping Mal was careful to wash his hands before coming my way.

I listened to the sound of that poor man's suffering for half an hour, before the distinctive sound of splintering wood could be heard. After that, the screaming stopped. Hopefully the poor bastard had passed out. I couldn't imagine how much pain he was going through, but it sounded ghastly. A few seconds went by before there was the distinctive sound of a gunshot. My back jerked back in shock on the bed. *Holy shit.*

Mal breezed in a few minutes later as if nothing had happened. Yep, the man didn't appear to have a care in the world. Absolutely nothing out of the ordinary happened back there. Nope. He even has a smile on his face. I don't think it's a smile that says, 'I'm really looking forward to having sex with you, Harper'. I think it's a smile that says, 'I had a lot of fun torturing that bloke back there'. I'm not going to ask him to clarify, though.

"'Arper, you're a sight for sore eyes," Mal comments, as he begins to unbutton his shirt. It's spattered with blood, which is a little off-putting, but I pretend not to notice.

"How are you, Mal?" I ask, trying to fill in the accompanying silence. I can't ask him how his day went because I honestly don't want to know the response.

"Never been better, 'Arper, never better," he replies, and starts whistling to himself as he concentrates on getting naked. My thoughts stray to the now dead naked man outside, and I repress the shudder that wants to rip through me.

"Alex said you wanted to see me about something?" He always wants to see me at the weekend, it's kind of a standing order these days, but today he specifically told Alex he wanted to see me about running a little errand for him. I haven't forgotten what he said months earlier about this, so my blood runs a little colder. I want to know what I'm expected to do. I know I can't refuse, so I just have to hope it's not too bad.

Mal just smiles. I think he wants to drag this out. It's how he normally works. He likes to prolong the agony, and he loves to watch people squirm.

"Yep. I need you to do suffin' for me, but we'll talk about it later, 'Arper. At the moment I'm a starvin' man, darlin'. I haven't seen you for a week. I need a taste of my little girl. Come 'ere." He pats his legs with both hands.

That's my cue to go sit on his lap while he carefully examines my shaven pussy with one hand and squeezes my boobs with the other. He's so heavy-handed I fear they're going to fall off after a couple of minutes, but I know better than to argue. If he knows it hurts me, he does it all the more. Life with Alex is scary enough, but life with Mal, well. Let's just say it's never boring, in a life and death kind of way.

"Can I suck you off, Mal?" I whisper, with a breathy little voice that I hope is more lust than fear. The earlier shot is still ringing in my head, and screwing with me. The quicker I get Mal off, the quicker I can relax, but I'm pretty sure it's not going to be that easy.

"What's the rush? Let's have some fun." This is the point at which my insides turn to mush. My idea of fun and Mal's differ considerably, and I never know what's in store for me. Generally, I can bet that it's likely to scare the living daylights out of me, because that's what turns him on.

"Absolutely." The enthusiasm in my voice is forced, but if he notices it doesn't bother him in the slightest. Currently my clit is between his fingers, and he's squeezing it hard. My eyes begin to water.

After a few minutes of Mal inspecting the goods, making sure everything is how it should be, which mainly means nice and wet, he says, "I want to test out something new tonight, baby." I stiffen. New is not normally good.

"What's that, Mal?" I still can't call him anything remotely sexy. It's Mal or nothing. The thought of calling him darling or baby makes me feel physically ill.

"It's a hood. A nice big, black leather hood. It covers everyfing. You just get a mouth hole for when I feel horny. You won't be able to hear or see anything. The anticipation of waiting to see what will happen next will drive you wild, hun." It'll drive me something, but wild wouldn't have been the first word on my lips. The dead guy outside springs to mind once again. I'm going to be blind, just like him, wondering what this sick fucker has planned for me next. If that wasn't enough, I'm still waiting to hear what my later errand is going to be. Before this evening's out I'll need a hospital's store of Valium.

Now that Mal has let me in on the big reveal, he wastes no time getting the hood out to show me. It's made of thick black leather, and features padding around the eyes and ears to make sure I'm closed off from the outside world. There's a buckle which will be fastened around my forehead, and another which will circle my neck. It also has a black ball-gag attached to it, for when he wants to muffle my screams. I feel sick. The thought of being even more helpless than usual around this madman is not a pleasant one. I will be entirely at his mercy. This is bad. This is really fucking bad.

My shoulders tense. "I'm not sure if I like the—"

"Come now, 'Arper," Mal interrupts. "You know you don't really have a choice, right?"

I inhale deeply. No, I didn't know that for sure, but at least I do now. "Why don't I have a choice?" I whisper quietly. I think I already know the answer, but I want to make sure.

Mal sits down on the bed and pulls his shoes and socks off. His boxer shorts follow shortly after, revealing his very erect cock. I think I'm going to hyperventilate. The hood has him far more excited than my feeble offer of a blowjob. I'd better think up some new tricks, else he might hit me with a medieval torture device next time.

Mal sighs when he sees my face. "OK, I'm going to be nice. Do you want to know what your task is before we begin? I wouldn't usually do this, but you're not just anyone, 'Arper. I'm gettin' very fond of you." The last thing I need is for this monster to get attached to me, but I do want to know what he's got in store for me, so I nod my head.

"You've got to dump a gun and a little package of blow around someone's dorm for me. Shouldn't be too hard. He's a bloke. You're a girl. I'm pretty sure you'll think of something. See? That's not too bad, is it?" Mal smiles at me, as if he's asking me to do no more than key the poor fucker's car. This isn't going to be a random act of vandalism. If it were a petty crime that the man might get no more than a slap on the wrist for, I could probably live with that, but drugs and a gun? That's some serious shit.

"You want me to put someone in prison?" I whisper.

There's more. I know there's more. This isn't some random person I'm being asked to destroy. This has Alex Wilkinson stamped all over it. I can feel the walls closing in, to the point where they're squeezing the life out of me. Even the surrounding air has the weight of impending doom riding upon it. I can't do this. I can't put some poor fucker in jail for a crime he didn't commit.

"Yes. That's exactly what I want you to do." Mal nods. "You do know what happens to people who don't follow orders around these parts, don't you?"

And that's when it hits me. Ka-Ching. Today has been staged right from the very beginning. All this has been carefully planned to scare the crap out of me, and it's bloody well worked.

"Who?" I ask timidly. If I'm condemning my soul to hell, I might as well know who's going down with me, although I have a horrible feeling I already know.

"What does it matter? Are you really going to refuse me?" Mal looks amused.

"What happens if I say no?" It's a stupid question. I know exactly what happens.

"You end up the same way that guy out there did." Mal's thumb points towards the door. "The guy in question will still get totalled. I'll just get someone else to do it. Your choice, though. As much as I don't want to kill you, 'Arper, I'm sure I'd have plenty of fun doing so."

I don't doubt it.

"Who?" I repeat. I need to hear this.

Mal shrugs. "Some guy called Brandt Browning, and that's all you need to worry your pretty little head about." The black hood is then pulled swiftly over my head, and Mal buckles the thing up tightly. The hood instantly feels like it's suffocating me because it's too tight, and when the darkness comes down over my eyes, I have a moment. Am I going mad? I'm not sure, but I have a feeling I'm very close to it.

"You look gorgeous, darlin'." Mal thrusts his fingers between my legs and pumps them back and forth. I have no idea if I'm wet. I'm too fucking scared to care. The last words he says to me before I completely lose the plot are, "Now open wide, or you'll regret it."

A black ball-gag is then pressed hard against my lips and forced between my teeth. I decide I'm going to save the scream that's building in the back of my throat for later. I have a feeling there'll be plenty more to join it.

A heel slammed against my thigh, brings me back into the real world with a thud. Jesus. My eyes water with pain as I shriek and take a dive under the bed. These two are still at it. When my eyes can focus worth a damn, I see that Brandt's taken a lot of damage. He's stumbling about the place half drunk, lurching and staggering as he tries to aim his next punch. His coordination is now shot to hell, due to one too many hits to the face, and if he's not careful he'll go down shortly. He's no match for Gabriel, and he knows it.

"I mean it," Brandt slurs. "If you touch her, that'll be the end of us. You'll have to kill me too, because I will hunt you down and I will end you."

"You mean you'll try," Gabriel snorts. His next kick sends Brandt reeling, and he has to grasp one of the cell bars to stop himself from falling over. There's then the clang of metal against metal, and I wonder if he's slammed his head into them.

My face whips round to see what has happened, and my mouth opens in shock.

Brandt is trapped. Gabriel must have had a pair of cuffs in his pocket, because one of Brandt's hands is now securely attached to one of the metal bars of my cell.

Holy hell. Aren't those two supposed to be on the same team? What is going on here?

Chapter 16 - Gabriel

"Take this off!" Brandt roars, tugging frantically at the metal bracelet that encircles his wrist. He looks adorable when he's mad.

"No." I cross my arms over my chest. This is going down my way, and he'd better brace himself.

"Now Gabriel. I'm not fucking joking." Brandt is slurring slightly, which has me feeling guilty. Sometimes I forget my own strength. If I really hurt the guy I'd never forgive myself. But everything has been building up to this point, and I want to play the hand I've been dealt. If I can't get Harper to talk by messing with her, I wonder if she'll talk if I mess with Brandt? It seems a rather backward idea, but these two feel something for each other. I've seen it. What if she is protecting him? If so, if I threaten to hurt him then maybe she'll crack. I think it's worth a try. Anyway, it'll be fun to find out.

Turning to Harper, I say, "Go sit on the bed, princess." She's currently cowering underneath it, and I think I may have hit her accidentally. My bad? If I had my way I'd decimate every single sweet hole in her entire body, but I need to be careful. I can't piss Brandt off too much. If I crack the girl open wide he'll go cray cray on me, and it's not a pleasant sight. That's one of the reasons he's got cuffs on. I'm going to be demonstrating the other later, but for that, I'll need another set.

"The bed, Harper," I repeat loudly, after she's made no move to obey me. "Or are we back to laps around the cell floor?" This, funnily enough, spurs her into motion.

Now I could put the other cuff around Brandt's hand now, when he's not really paying attention, but that would defeat the object of the exercise. I want him to watch everything I'm about to do to her, and if he has to twist his head awkwardly round to see anything, the chances are he'll miss some of the good parts. This way, he can settle in for the cinematic version in relative comfort. I'll find some other way to distract him later, when we get down to the next chapter. I'm still going to torment the poor bastard, though, because that's what I'm good at.

Digging my hand in the front pocket of his jeans, I let my hand brush against his cock as I search for the key. I find it with little effort. I made sure to keep my eye on him when I gave it to him, just in case I'd need it later. Always plan ahead. That's what I say.

Now I'm here, though, it seems wrong not to have a little fun. Giving his flaccid cock a tight squeeze, I smile when it hardens under my hand. He's not completely impervious to my advances, then. When a left fist comes whizzing my way I hastily take a step back, then waving the key in the air triumphantly, I smile nastily when Brandt realises what's just happened.

"Right girls and boys, I just need to get a few things before we continue here. I will say one thing before I go, though. No one is leaving this room until Harper talks. Quite frankly, I'm bored of all this nonsense. One way or another I will get what I want this evening, and I'm not just referring to the talking part. You're both going to get it, so I'd brace yourselves if I were you. Now play nicely while I'm gone, or you'll be in all sorts of trouble when I get back. *Adios, mis amigos.*"

Chapter 17 - Brandt

Gabriel's fingers on my body are an aberration and a violation. I want to say I hate every second of his brief caress, but that would be a blatant lie. I hate him for what he did to me back in prison and I hate him for hurting me, but I can't hate his touch. My body won't let me. The awful thing is that Gabriel knows this. He's always known how intense the attraction is between us. He also knows that no matter what I say, he can override my brain with little more than a touch of his lips or a soft caress. I resent the power he holds over me so fucking much it hurts.

"Are you okay?" I position my body so it's facing Harper, who is now sitting on the bed as ordered. She's still tied up, and her knees are an angry shade of a bloody mess. By the way she keeps hopping from one ass cheek to another, I'd guess that he did a number on her, too.

"I'll live," she whispers. "Are you okay?" Those eyes tell me she knows what I'm feeling. The woman is far too perceptive for her own good. I look away before she can discover any more of my secrets.

Grabbing the bars in frustration I say, "You can't fight him. He thinks this is a game, and he'll stop at nothing to win. Just give in before we both get hurt. The other option doesn't bear thinking about." When my eyes reconnect with hers, they try their best to relay the precarious predicament she is in. I don't think she realises how dangerous Gabriel is.

Harper's gaze falls into her lap. "I'm not going to fight him. I don't need to win. All I need to do is endure this mess for a couple more days. Then it will all be over, and I'll be dead." Her voice cracks. She needs water. I hope Gabriel takes care of her. I want to slap myself for letting him get the better of me. Now she is vulnerable. I've walked right into his hands. I need to learn to control my rage. If prison has taught me anything, it should have taught me that.

"Don't talk nonsense. He'll see sense. Gabriel might be a monster, but he's my monster. He won't do anything really stupid. He knows he'll lose me if that happens." Harper thinks Gabriel is going to kill her, and while that may be the case, he wouldn't dare do it while I'm watching. He's a sneaky bastard, and he's probably already planning a way to dispose of Harper once this is all over, but I'll make sure he's disabused of that notion pretty damn fast. He forgets that I know how he thinks. Sharing a cell with a guy like Gabriel is a very intimate experience, and it taught me a lot. While Gabriel is very sexual in nature, he's also cunning, quick-witted, and intelligent. He remembers every word he reads. While most of his reading time might have been in prison, it's taught him a lot. It takes time to completely change a con artist, but there are cracks in Gabriel's armour these days. He's not the man he used to be. Elements of a conscience are peeking through the thick veneer he wears. No man is an island, and Gabriel is just beginning to figure that out.

"What will he do to us?" Harper half hiccups, half sobs. I think she's had just about as much as she can take. I'm worried about her, which is rich coming from me.

"I don't know. He'll either torment us, or fuck us, or both. I wouldn't like to put money on which." Wiping away a trail of blood from my nose, I grimace. If Gabriel plans to take me by force, there'll be trouble. A whole lot of trouble. We had an agreement.

Harper snuffles a bit more and looks down at her tied feet. "Do you think you can stop him?" Now I look a bit harder, I can see she's trembling all over. Gabriel had better be careful. If he pushes her too hard she'll go into shock.

I pull my right arm up sharply to the resounding clang of metal. Swearing, I shake my head. "I don't think so. Not until he releases me. He'll probably just make me watch while he fucks you." I don't add the reason why, although Harper can probably figure that out for herself. He wants to make it clear who's alpha dog in this bizarre threesome, and so far, he's not doing a bad job of it.

"That's not so terrible," she whispers, "I can cope with that."

My head snaps back. Surely I didn't hear that right. "What did you just say?" The earlier fuzziness that had taken over my brain from having ten tonnes of shit knocked out of it clears instantly. Something is very wrong here.

Harper waves her hand in the air, as if to brush off her last sentence. "Doesn't matter."

It fucking does matter. Then it hits me like a lightning bolt. She suffers from the same disease I do.

"You find him attractive, don't you?" I realise I'm insanely jealous. Gabriel has already had more of her than I have, and now it's being thrust in my face I've decided I want my share. When I get out of the cuffs I'm bending her over the nearest flat surface I can find, and I'm going to make her see stars. I shake my head. For God's sake, I'm just as bad as he is. This is the testosterone talking. That's not why she's here. I just want to hear her version of events, and then I can get rid of her.

"Everyone finds him attractive."

That is not the answer I want to hear, which is why the next question springs instantly to my lips. "Do you find me attractive?"

Harper looks at me exasperatedly and shakes her head. "I've always found you attractive, Brandt. You know that. You were the stuff of my high school fantasies. Too bad they turned to nightmares, huh?" She stares off into space. She seems to be lost inside her head, and I know that feeling. I've been lost for the last five years.

"Why can't I hate you?" I whisper. I want to. I want to so badly, my fingers clench into fists. "You seem to be the root of all my problems. Way back in college I knew I couldn't have you, so I didn't touch you - but you touched me - in all the wrong ways. After you put me inside, when everyone was picking on the poor little rich kid, I really wanted to hate you, but even then I kept telling myself that there was a reason all this happened. You wouldn't just throw me under the bus. You weren't that kind of person. But then I told myself that anyone who can stand up in court and lie under oath deserves all the contempt I can throw at them, but even now, the emotion comes and goes. My parents have me marrying another woman in less than a week's time as a direct result of your actions. Neither of them can bear the sight of me. They want me tied up and placed neatly out of the way, where I will not impact upon my father's political career. He looks set to become the Mayor of London, by the way, in case you were interested. That should also make me want to hate you so much, I'd be tempted to shoot you. I have a feeling Gabriel hates you far more than I do, though, and that doesn't make any sense at all." I have no idea why I'm telling her this. Am I sorry for kidnapping her? Yes and no. I still want to know what happened, but not at the expense of her life.

Harper lifts her backside from the mattress for a couple of seconds, sighing in relief as she does so. I hate to think what it looks like after Gabriel's had his fun, but I daresay it isn't pretty.

"I couldn't hate Alex, either. I wanted to, so bad. Especially after what he did, but I couldn't." She lowers herself slowly back down, shifting awkwardly from side to side, trying to ease the pressure on her ass, before sniffling again.

"What did he do to you?" I know it was bad. "Did he starve you?" I have an inkling he did that and a whole lot more, but I need to start somewhere.

She looks at me, wondering if she should say anything. Even now, after he's dead, I can see she still doesn't want to talk about what happened. What did that bastard do to her?

"Answer me, Harper. I need to know." My voice is pleading. We're finally in a position where we've been flung together without sex on the menu. The only thing we can do is talk, and I intend to make good use of the opportunity.

It takes her a while, but eventually she summons up enough courage to speak. "Yes. I was never allowed to weigh more than one hundred pounds. If I tipped those scales by one pound or more, he had several ways of dealing with the problem. He'd chain me up in a room for a couple of days with nothing but a jug of water for company, or he'd knock me around and spank me until the scales were back in the black." Her fingernails push into the plastic mattress as if they want to slice it in two. These memories are painful for her.

"Jesus Christ, Harper. Why didn't you leave him?"

"I couldn't leave him. He would have hunted me down, and when he found me, he would have made my life even worse than it was already. You have no idea how bad life with Alex was." Her voice shakes and her hands look like she's got Parkinson's. If we're not careful she won't make it. The woman is falling apart.

"Why did you get with him in the first place? Why didn't you leave him at the first sign of trouble? I can't understand why you would be with someone like that. You're an intelligent woman. What went wrong?"

Her lips thin and she shakes her head at me. We're back to radio silence. Why does she keep clamming up on me?

"Once Gabriel's finished, I want you to promise me something, Brandt."

Great. Now she's changing the subject. Slamming my head against the bars again for good measure, I take a deep breath. "What?"

She gets to her feet and shuffles towards me. She can only take the tiniest of footsteps due to the cable ties circling her ankles, but she's persistent and before long she's standing inches from my face.

"I want you to promise me that as soon as Gabriel's finished with me, you get yourself as far away from this place as possible. I don't care where you go, but the further away the better. Mexico, Costa Rica, South Africa, Brazil - go wherever, but you need to go quickly. The guys I'm used to dealing with don't like loose ends. They will come for you. I know you don't believe me now, but before long you will. Promise me. I don't have much time left. You need to do this for me."

Harper's face is so close to mine I can feel her breath against my lips. My insides tighten at even that ridiculously light contact. The chemistry between her and me has always been off the scales. I just have to look at her to want her, and right now I *need* her. I need to be all over her, inside her, and breathing her in. I want to get lost in that body, with my hands tangled in her chestnut mane of hair. I want to yank it, pull it, push her down to her knees and then use it to feed my cock inside her. God, her mouth. I want that mouth. Watching Gabriel take her a few minutes ago made me crazy. I thought I could stand there and watch, taking it all calmly in my stride. What was Harper to me? Nothing. She was the girl who put me inside a cage for five years. That all flew out the window the instant I saw her deep-throating him. It should have been me. I was the one who'd been wronged. She was my prisoner. She was mine. Those three words should have put the fear of God into me, because this was no longer about revenge. I'm not sure it ever had been.

"Kiss me," I whisper. I can't help myself. I'm asking her because I don't want to take this from her. I want it to be given freely. I want more than what Gabriel's just had. I want inside her head.

She looks at me and makes a constricted sound in her throat. She opens her lips, but nothing comes out. Whatever she wants to say is lost in the electric pull between us. I wait. She has to come to me on her own. All I would have to do is move a quarter of an inch in order to crush her lips to mine, but I'm not prepared to make this easy on her. She has to choose. Painful seconds tick by as we drown in the sight of each other, neither of us able to take our eyes away. Come on, I urge silently. I know this attraction is not one-sided.

With a final little grunt of annoyance, Harper closes the distance between us. She can't fight this any more than I can. Her body flops against mine and our mouths lock. Supporting her head with my free hand, her hands still tied behind her back, I bury it in her hair as I twist her face up towards mine. She has no idea how much I need this, but I'm about to show her. For the next minute or two I'm going to rob her of all the air she owns, but this time, she won't care. In fact, this time I'm betting she'll barely notice.

Sliding my tongue against hers, I press against her body so tightly she can feel my erection rubbing against her through my jeans. My body is hot, I swear I'll combust on the spot, and she feels so damn good pressed up against me. Maybe it's time to stop denying myself. Why should I fight this? Even if I can only have her for a day or two, at least it's something I'll be able to carry with me for the rest of my life. I'm done pretending. While thoughts of revenge featured highly in my thoughts while I rotted away in my cell, taking Harper's sweet body in every fucking position imaginable was also a daily occurrence. I have been obsessed with this woman for too long. It's time to do something about it.

Unfortunately I'm about to watch Gabriel take what's mine, unless I can convince him to take this cuff off me. I have a feeling that's unlikely. Once Gabriel gets something into his head there's no talking to him. He thinks he's doing me a favour, but the reverse is true. It's going to kill me if I have to watch this, and I have a feeling I'll never forgive him.

Chapter 18 - Gabriel

"Touching, oh so touching." My voice is mocking. When I march down the stairs to find Brandt and Harper locked in an embrace that looks like something out of *Gone With The Wind* I want to throw up all over them. What is Brandt doing? This is the woman who screwed up his life. He should be dissecting her, piece by fucking piece. I can only assume it's because she's the first woman he's laid eyes on since he's been out, and his hormones are running amok. He needs to get laid. That boy desperately needs to get his balls emptied, and I'd be happy to volunteer for the job, if he'd just get over himself.

"Back on the bed," I bark viciously at Harper, and she's lucky she's still of use to me, because if she wasn't I'd happily kill her now.

"Get me out of these cuffs," Brandt growls. As if. He's not going anywhere, and I'm about to make that abundantly clear.

"What, and spoil all your fun for the next hour or so? Come on, Brandt. You never used to be this boring. What happened to your adventurous side? If I remember correctly, you were quite the kinky bastard. A bit of exhibitionism should be right up your street."

"Get. Me. Out. Of. These. Cuffs." Brandt's voice has risen several decibels, but I treat it with the same amount of apathy. Ignoring him, I move over to my victim who is shuffling back towards the bed. It's taking her forever, but I didn't leave her a lot of room to move in the cuffs. That reminds me; I need to get rid of those.

Pulling a penknife out of the front of my jeans, I approach her slowly. Her eyes jump to the size of dinner plates and her face loses its colour instantly, not that it had much to begin with.

"What are you going to do?" she screeches, shuffling back until she hits the bedframe and tumbles on to it. Perfect. This is just how I like my females. Scared witless and unhinged. Today is turning into a very good day.

"It would probably be easier to ask me, 'what aren't you going to do?'. We don't have time for the other version. You'll just have to pay attention and I'll try to keep you updated as we go along." There. That'll give her plenty to think about.

Bringing one hand down to rest on her thigh, I use the other to sever the ties around her feet. I'll need her legs open for the next part.

"Ever had someone watch before?" I ask, as I spread her wide. She gasps in outrage, but there's little else she can do. There's no way I'm cutting the ties on her wrists. Those hands can stay behind her back for the foreseeable future.

She doesn't answer me, but then I didn't expect her to. The last thing I need is conversation right now. It will distract me.

"Don't do this," she eventually grinds out, her little plea music to my ears. I always love it when someone tells me 'no'. It's a sure-fire way to make me want to do something even more.

"You're in no position to be making demands," I say, not bothering to conceal my amusement. "In fact, you're not in a position to do much of anything bar obey, so let's take care of that annoying little mouth of yours." Dumping my duffel bag on the floor, I reach inside it for the ball-gag I brought. I knew it would come in useful.

As soon as it's in my hand Harper rears back as if I've struck her. "No," she whispers. "Please, I won't talk." It seems that her and gags are not friends. Too bad because I love them.

"Damn right you won't," I say. She fights me for a moment, but then I pinch her clit cruelly with my finger and thumb, and opening her mouth to wail, it's all the opportunity I need to push the thing in. Buckling it behind her head I take a moment to admire my handiwork, but Brandt has to spoil things, of course.

"If this exercise is about trying to get her to talk, doesn't that defeat the object somewhat?" He's glaring at my face as if he'd like to skewer me with a steel spike and then slowly roast my body over an open fire, but I don't take it personally. He'll come round.

"It is. You are quite correct. However, I don't want to hear idle chatter and she looks fucking fantastic with her mouth filled up with that. When she's ready to talk she can bang her foot three times on the floor." I smile at her evilly. "You'd better mean it, though. If you use it as a ruse to get me to stop, I'll drag you round this cell three times on your knees. Do we understand each other?" I don't bother looking to see if she nods because I'm back in my bag, searching for the next item I'll need.

Ta-da! When my fingers close around a long rectangular item encased in shiny plastic, I bite my lip in delightful anticipation. Pulling it out of the bag I stare at it happily as I wave it in front of Harper's face. It's a big, fat, juicy chocolate bar. I'm still not used to the joys of chocolate. In fact, my mouth is watering just looking at this baby, and that's nothing compared to what it'll be doing in a minute.

When her eyes try to zero in on my prize I put a finger under her chin to keep her head upright. "Eyes forward, sweetheart. Look at Brandt. In fact, keep those eyes trained on Brandt. I want him to see how much you're enjoying yourself in a few minutes' time. I don't think that will be a problem, will it? He's an attractive guy, isn't he?" Harper grunts, but she keeps her head high. Good girl.

Unwrapping the chocolate I put it to my nose. My God, the smell is divine. Although I had some money in prison, unlike Brandt, I didn't use it to buy chocolate. This is still a novelty to me.

Pulling the bar out of the wrapper, I insert a single finger into Harper's cunt. Sliding in easily, I replace it with two, and then three. The girl is raring to go. It seems the steamy kiss from earlier has really got her juices flowing. Either that or she's still turned on from my earlier ministrations. I wonder which one it is? Maybe it's a combination of the two. Maybe the girl is hot for both of us. Brandt and I could have so much fun if that were the case. I haven't had a threesome in forever. Well, not with a woman involved, anyway.

Crouching down, I slowly slide the bar into Harper's cunt. When she tries to look down I position my hand firmly beneath her chin so she can't. She lets out a little cry of distress as I put a little more pressure on the bar, but eventually it slips in. Beautiful. I push it further and further, until only an inch is showing. I'm going to savour this in sinful, decadent, and delicious bites.

Her legs twitch as I admire my handiwork, and when my breath catches her clit she tries to close her legs together.

"Nuh, uh, uh," I say. "Keep those legs wide open, or I'll make you watch as I bend Brandt over and fuck him sideways into next year. In case you were wondering, yes, that also means I'm going to hurt him. I like hurting things, but I think you know that." She can't say a lot to that statement, but she does manage to keep her legs open. Brandt, on the other hand, hasn't said a word. Is he even fucking watching this? Spinning my head around I find his eyes glued to the pair of us, and his face is a storm cloud of anger and rage. Well, at least that answered that question.

"Want to know what this is, Harper?" I ask, giving her clit a little flick. She mewls sweetly in response, and my cock rises to the occasion. I am going to have so much fun with this girl. "It's a chocolate bar, because even though you're a cold-hearted bitch with no conscience in sight, I like my cunts to taste sweet before I eat them." She visibly recoils, but it doesn't stop my mouth diving between her legs to taste some chocolate-covered pussy. With two hands around her waist to make sure she stays still, I clamp my jaws to her and prepare to get messy.

She fights me at first, which is almost laughable because I know how badly she wants this. She's already revved up to hell, and I'm willing to bet Brandt's not let her get off very often if at all since she's been here. She wants what I'm offering, she just doesn't want an audience. That's too bad.

The candy bar doesn't take long to melt. After a few minutes the thing begins to disintegrate, and damned if it doesn't taste all the better for it. My lips and tongue are coated in thick milk chocolate and gooey caramel, and the soft sweet scent of pussy. I have to confess I'm thoroughly enjoying myself.

Brandt doesn't say a word behind me. He already knows there's no point asking me to stop. Once I've set my mind on something there's little chance of changing it. I can feel his eyes boring into my back, though. Once this little stunt is over he's either going to kiss me or chop my balls off. At the moment, the latter is far more likely.

When Harper begins to strain towards me, actively looking for more of what I'm offering, I know the battle is almost won. All I have to do is find something to tip her over the edge. What would little Miss Wilkinson find morally reprehensible? What would cause her to spill her secrets and run screaming from the pair of us? I think I'll start off slow and work my way up to the good stuff. We've got all night, after all.

"Ever had two cocks inside you at once?" Let's see what the thought of a little two-on-one does to her. I'm not sure whether she's heard me because her head is rolling back on her shoulders in pleasure. Her eyes are flickering, but mostly closed, and the soft moans coming out of her mouth tell me she's close. Maybe I'll need to speak a little louder.

Raising my voice, I say, "Two cocks at once, Harper. Fancy it? Brandt's in your mouth, and mine in your ass? Think you could cope with that?" She hears me this time because her head snaps up, and she shakes her head. She's not up for a threesome, then. Excellent. Maybe we'll try that one first. It's gotta be worth a shot, but somehow I don't think it'll get the job done. I have a contingency plan, though. Right now, I just want to sink my cock as deep inside Brandt as it will go, but that will take a little time and planning. When I eventually bend the guy over I want him to be so desperate for my attention that the thought of saying 'no' never enters his head. That's going to take some work, due to our rather turbulent history, but I think we can make it past that with Harper's help. Once we've smashed through that barrier, I think there's hope for us. We'll see.

"If you even think of involving me in this shit, I swear I'm going to kill you when this is all over," Brandt growls. That's my boy. At least there's still some fire left inside him. I smile to myself.

"You mean you're going to try. I'm not that easy to kill, or so I've been told." Several people have taken a shot at it, most are now dead. The clang of metal on steel tells me what Brandt thinks of my little statement, but I don't give a fuck.

Swirling my finger in Harper's cunt one last time, satisfied that I've successfully devoured most of the chocolate, I slide it into my mouth and suck it clean. Harper looks shell-shocked. Her eyes are pleading, begging for the orgasm I've started but won't finish. Poor baby. I don't feel sorry for her. I've felt like that for months. There's no substitute for a decent lover. Once you've found one you like, nothing compares. Once you've lost one, it's basically the equivalent of hell on earth. The recovery process is long, unending, and pretty much unrecoverable.

Anyway, I digress; back to orgasms. I'm going to let Brandt do the honours, if he so desires. It will be a good way to discover just how much he hates her, or if he hates her at all. The kiss I witnessed earlier would seem to indicate otherwise.

Standing up, I move over towards my ex, approaching him slowly. If he's going to lash out at me I want to be able to anticipate his next move. Strangely enough he doesn't thump me, even though I move in close.

"If you play nicely I might let her suck your cock," I whisper. That should get a reaction. Sure enough, Brandt is quick to fire back a response.

"If you let me go, I might let you keep your testicles when this is all over." His hand whips out to grab me, but as I've been expecting them, I simply hop backwards.

"Aww, Brandt. Take a look at the poor girl. She's desperate. If she sucks your cock I might let you lick her. She still tastes like chocolate. There's nothing sweeter on this earth than a chocolate coated pussy. Trust me on this. Spread those legs wider, Harper. Show him what he's missing," I say. That really sends the poor boy nuts, but that's what I've been waiting for. When his hand reaches out to grab me but falls about five centimetres short of its target I reach out to snatch his instead, snaking the other cuff around his wrist. I then slam my fist into his solar plexus, winding him for a second, while I use the opportunity to make sure his other wrist is also securely fastened to a steel pole. Now we're getting somewhere.

"You bastard!" Brandt roars, kicking out with his legs. Thankfully I've already taken a few steps back, so there's no chance he'll hit anything important. Standing there quietly for a few moments, I let him get some anger off his chest. I know it's mostly directed at me, and I want to explain, but he won't listen just yet. Hopefully he'll hear me out later. When the room goes quiet once more I decide to air my next ultimatum. He's not going to like it, but I don't much care.

"Harper is going to suck you off, Brandt. I think that's the least she can do, considering, right? But if you object I'm going to fuck you instead, and I'll get you off. This is definitely going down one of two ways, and you get ten seconds to choose which. After that'll I'll pick." There's no question Brandt will choose option one because the thought of me anywhere near him will drive him nuts.

"You don't get to do this, Gabriel. Fuck off and get out of my house."

I don't bother gracing that with a reply. "Ten, nine, eight."

"We're past these games, Gabe. We're over. You can't do this." His voice is rough and scratchy. He's going to lose it in a minute.

"Seven, six, five." Is it wrong of me to hope he goes mute for the next four seconds? Probably, but I do anyway.

"I am seriously going to kill you. Don't think I'm playing games, Gabe." There's a little hysteria in his voice now. He knows this is going down.

"Four, three, two."

"Fine. Harper. I choose Harper, you asshole," he yells, just as I knew he would. Brandt is nothing if not predictable.

"There, there," I say patronisingly. "Was that so hard?" I can hear his breath hissing between his teeth, so I know damn well it was. He doesn't want to go near either of us. How interesting. Have I put him off sex for life?

Walking back to Harper, I unbuckle the gag and throw it on the bed. Sinking a hand into her hair, I then tip her head back and croon, "Are you going to be a good girl for me? Do you think you can shuffle over there and show my boy a good time?" Her chest is rising and falling rapidly. She's still not recovered from her 'almost' orgasm, and that's a good thing. She might even put a bit more effort in, seeing as how she's almost ready to pop.

Bending down, I whisper in her ear, "Do a good job and I might let you get off later. Would you like Brandt to suckle at that sweet little cunt of yours?"

"You're an animal," she spits, but she's not going to defy me. The time for that has passed. Pointing to the floor I watch as she shuffles forward. Brandt, to be an awkward sonofabitch, positions himself flat against the bars, making it impossible for her to obey me. Well, two can play at that game.

Positioning myself to the side of him, I reach for his leather belt and yank him sideways. There's little he can do to stop me. As he brings a leg up to kick me I say, "Hurt me, and I'll hurt her much worse." He doesn't have to look at me to know I'm not joking. I'll make mincemeat of the girl if he gives me trouble, and I'll enjoy it. Pulling the penknife back out of my pocket, I grab Harper who hasn't the sense to get out of the way fast enough and press it up against her jugular, to make sure Brandt knows I'm serious.

"Stop." His voice is seething with emotion, the bad kind, but he knows I'm not going to back down. "Don't." It takes a lot for him to get that second word out, so I know he cares about her.

"Then step back, Brandt." I tug on his belt again, and this time his feet follow me. I continue moving him backwards until his arms are stretched as far as they'll go out in front of him. I decide I like him like this, all tied up and helpless. Too bad we didn't have restraints in prison. They look good on him.

Moving close, I stand up against him and let my arms reach around to undo his belt.

"Gabriel," he threatens.

"I know," I purr, "you're going to kill me later. I'll deal with that then. Right now, you're wearing too many clothes and we need to do something about it." My fingers reach for his belt buckle and begin threading the leather tab through it.

"There is no chance of us ever being a couple again. You know that, Gabriel. I made myself clear." This is Brandt's way of retaliating, and sure enough, it hits where it hurts, but I'm not about to show weakness.

"I'm getting Harper to blow you, Brandt. Relax. As if I'd come near you." His body visibly relaxes. I wonder if he's still tormented by thoughts of us? I know I am. Maybe he protests too much. Pulling his belt from the loops, I roll the leather around my fist in a tight circle and then throw it on the bed. I might need it later if these two don't play nice. Then I begin unzipping his fly. I take my time on purpose. If I'm making the bastard nervous, that's just too bad. Brandt keeps quiet, though. I know if I could see him now, those eyes of his would be burning a path through my skull, so it's probably for the best. All the same, I make the most of this opportunity. Tormenting him with my fingertips, I run my hands over the delicious abs that I helped create. Without me he wouldn't be here. Without my help he'd be buried six foot under, and all his dreams of revenge would be dead. Maybe I'll remind him of that later.

"Don't," he growls again. Brandt doesn't want my hands on his body, but that's too bad. The man is far too delicious to resist, and I've been dreaming of this for a while. He'll come around to my way of thinking, eventually.

"Harper," I bark, "get in position." I think it's about time we distract Brandt, and what better way than with a naked woman in front of him with her mouth wide open. Oh, if he could see the look on my face right now I know he'd lump me - if he had the use of his arms, of course.

Grabbing his jeans I push them down to his ankles in one swift movement. I then trace a leisurely finger around the line of his boxer shorts, letting him know what I'm about to do next. Anticipation is a wonderful thing.

"Gabriel," comes his warning, but at the same time Harper is shuffling over on her knees, her head aligned perfectly with his crotch. I can hear his breath catch in his throat. I don't think he's going to be saying anything else for a while. Taking advantage of his momentary lapse, my hand dives into the front of his shorts and closes on his thickening cock. It swells further. Ah, how I've missed this.

"Beg him to let you suck, Harper. There's a good girl." Squeezing the tip gently in my fingers, Brandt makes a strangled sound. Poor baby. I bet he hasn't got laid since he got out of jail. The man is still punishing himself for something or other, no doubt.

Harper isn't backward in coming forward, though. She dives straight in.

"Please let me suck, Brandt. Please use my mouth for your pleasure. I want to feel the silky-smooth skin of your cock taking..."

The reason she's pausing there is because I've taken Brandt's cock out of his shorts and am now spreading the bead of pre-cum that resided on the tip all around her lips. Brandt is making these adorable little tormented noises in his throat, which is enough to create a fairly impressive party in my pants. We need to move this along.

"Oh God," Harper whimpers in a throaty little voice, and that's the best kind of dirty talk there is.

"Open wide, Harper." She does. I'm desperate to see Brandt's face, but equally afraid to. If he feels for her what he once felt for me, I am going to lose my shit.

"Fuck that throat, Brandt," I purr in his ear. "Take what you've been dreaming about these past five years." Harper gives head like a pro, so he's not going to be disappointed. I need her to make him a little more pliable. Then we can all get what we want.

Guiding Brandt's cock, I gently slide the tip of him inside her mouth. Keeping a tight grip of the base, I inch forward slowly, so she gets nothing more than a taste.

"Want to fuck her with me, Brandt? I bet between us we can ferret out the information you want." He doesn't answer me. He's trying to push his hips back, so he can avoid being anywhere near her mouth, but I'm standing right behind him, so he's going nowhere. Brandt needs to get with the programme. I am ninety-nine percent certain that I can get all the answers we need by using sex as a weapon, but if he doesn't cooperate, we get *nada*.

"Remember what I said about enthusiasm, Harper," I warn, when things go a little too quiet for comfort. If this doesn't work I'm fucked, which means I won't be fucked - which means I'll be pissed.

Feeding Harper another inch of his cock she suddenly seems to come to life, and when I lean over Brandt's shoulder, I see her eyes fluttering in appreciation of the beast that's coming her way. To make things a little more convincing, she's suddenly slurping and moaning in earnest. Actually, I'm not even sure the girl's acting. These two definitely have a 'thing' and I don't like it. Still, as soon as she tells all I'm pretty sure he'll hate her guts and I'll be more than happy to lend him my shoulder as he gets the little bitch out of his system.

Inch by slow and careful inch, I release more and more of Brandt's cock into her throat, until she can barely make a sound.

"There's a good girl," I say, patting her head as I take my hands away. By this time Brandt is rock hard, and he's so far gone I'm pretty sure he'll do whatever it takes to get what he wants. Just to make sure, I place my hands around his waist and piston him hard inside her mouth, knowing he'll be watching every little nuance on that pretty face as it gags and splutters around him.

My hands go between his legs, fondling his balls as I stroke his perineum. It normally drives him wild, and if his sudden violent thrust is anything to go by, nothing has changed. We're getting close.

"That's it," I croon. "Fuck that throat hard, Brandt. Make her feel you. Make her savour every inch of that delicious dick." He doesn't really need my encouragement because he's doing a pretty impressive job all on his own, but I figure it can't hurt.

Now that he's almost there I have a decision to make. What will get Harper to talk? I have a feeling it won't be a little two-on-one action. If anything, I suspect she'll enjoy that. She's hot for us both, whether she likes it or not. While she might like to think she can't stand the very air I breathe, I expect that might change if I show her a little attention. All girls love me if given enough time and Harper won't be the exception to the rule. So that leaves the other option. The one that's liable to get me into trouble. Still, it's no secret that I'm a deplorable member of the human race, so at least no one will think any less of me when this is all over. This is the right way forward. It will be quick, and I'm pretty sure Harper will cave at the first hurdle. Then she can vomit up her story, and we can get rid of her. Job done.

When Brandt throws his head back I know I'd better act quickly, or my chance will be lost.

"Enough." With my hand against her forehead I push her backwards firmly, until her body connects with the bars behind. Her eyes flutter open as she wonders what has just happened. Now I know I have her attention, I say, "Listen up, sweetheart. I'm now going to bend Brandt over and fuck him in the ass, unless you tell us what we've all been so desperately waiting to hear. Personally, I think you're going to let him suffer as you have all along because that's what you live for, isn't it? You've bent this guy over so many times he's lost count of the amount of atrocities you've committed. You were the one that did this to him in the first place, so why shouldn't I show you exactly what he suffered under my hands? I'm sure it'll make great viewing, sweetheart. There's going to be lots of yelling and screaming, take my word for it."

Harper's eyes fly open as she realises what's about to happen here. I'm pretty sure she expected some nasty shit from me, but I'm also fairly confident she didn't expect this. I've outdone myself. Fancy that. Brandt's reaction, on the other hand, is fairly predictable. He lashes out with everything he's got.

Chapter 19 - Harper

When Brandt barrels backwards so hard he nearly tears his wrists off, I make a dive to the side. Gabriel's already moved out of his way, so we both know he's about to go 'pop'. I'm fairly confident Gabriel is just testing me on this one, but I've been wrong before. He can't just... can he? Surely he wouldn't be that cruel? He must know what that would do to Brandt. They had an agreement.

"Get away from me!" Brandt screams. His hands are now ringed with red as he stretches his wrists to the limit. Telling Gabriel, at the top of his lungs, exactly what he thinks of him, I feel my ears begin to burn. Cowering in the corner I wait to see what happens next. No one will do anything. This is all a ruse to get me to talk. Stay strong. It's easier said than done. I can't watch that happen to Brandt. If Gabriel goes through with this I'll cave. I know I will. The trouble is, I'll save him from one disaster only to catapult him straight into the next. What do I do?

"Have you got anything you'd like to say, Harper?" I look up to find both men staring at me. Brandt, mostly because Gabriel has him in a headlock and he can't look anywhere else, and Gabriel because he's an evil fucker who wants to watch me squirm.

"Don't hurt him," I plead. I know I'm wasting my breath, but I can't help myself. My eyes are glued to Gabriel as he releases Brandt's head and moves lower, his hands slowly circling his waist. This is going to pan out like a horror movie, I just know it. Why oh why does this stuff have to happen to me?

"It's too late for that, Harper. The only person who can stop this is you. The only question is: will you? Or are you the type that can happily sit back and watch while bad shit happens to others? Actually, I think you've already proved that you are, so this should be a piece of cake, right?"

I'm only half-listening to what he's saying. My gaze is fascinated with the path Gabriel's fingers are taking. They are grazing Brandt's abs in long, sweeping caresses, but I'm fairly certain Brandt is taking no pleasure in the proceedings. His face looks an unpleasant shade of green, and I have a feeling he's trying hard to not vomit.

With his eyes on me, Gabriel make's a grab for Brandt's hair, and tugging it, twists his head to the side. The man looks like a vengeful vampire as he bites his neck. I can see Brandt's teeth slam together in pain while his body goes ramrod straight, but he doesn't let out a sound. I think the time for begging has passed. He also knows what he's up against. I'm willing to bet that words don't work on Gabriel. Being a mere mortal is bad enough when you're up against a God.

Finally, after a few tense seconds of silent pain, Gabriel releases him.

His eyes sparkle wickedly as he looks down at me and gives me a grin that has sharp, pointed icicles piercing nearly every pore of my body.

"You have no idea how much I'm going to enjoy this, Harper." Actually, I have a feeling I do, and it's far too much. That sick fuck is going to love every damn second of this showdown.

You need to stop this, I tell myself. That's all very well and good, but I can't actually get my mouth to work at the moment. My eyes are glued on the scene unfolding before me.

Gabriel isn't waiting around. His hand is already reaching for Brandt's cock, and he's all about playing to his audience.

"So good of you to get him ready for me," he scoffs. "In this state he'll pretty much do anything he's told." Gripping Brandt's cock tightly, he then begins to move it slowly up and down in his fist, so that just the head is revealed. It looks angry and red. When my gaze moves its way up to his face, I'm met with exactly the same colour. Brandt's eyes are blazing with anger and helpless defeat, and my heart goes out to him. I know that look so well. My eyes must reveal all, for Gabriel continues to taunt me.

"Want to watch him take my cock, Harper? Do you think he's a better cocksucker than you?" I can see Brandt's Adam's apple bounce as he realises what's coming his way. It's that moment when you know that all your worst nightmares are about to happen, and there's nothing you can do to stop them. I'm used to this crap. Brandt isn't. He managed to get himself out of his mess. I had to wait for someone to die on me, and I'm still not free of it.

Gabriel isn't bothered by my lack of response. "He is, Harper. He's one of the best damn cocksuckers I've ever had. Brandt's going to show you exactly how it's done. Isn't that right, darling?" With a hand on each of Brandt's shoulders, he pushes the poor bloke to his knees. The evil monster is stronger than he looks. Brandt's built like a brick shithouse but hits the deck hard. Gabriel might be the smaller of the two, but he's certainly no less powerful. I already know they are not evenly matched in a fight, and I'm pretty sure I know who calls the shots in the bedroom.

When Gabriel steps over Brandt's arms so his crotch is right in front of his face, I wince. Take a deep breath, I caution myself. After all, this isn't anything I haven't had to do myself in the last few minutes. The sound of Gabriel's zipper coming down again rings in my ears. The sound of my heart thudding in my chest accompanies it, as does the first taste of bile crawling rapidly up my throat.

"Let me do it," I say. "Leave Brandt alone." My voice is loud, clear, and firm. I mean exactly what I say. I don't mind them torturing me, but I can't watch somebody else take it. I never have been able to. We all have our weaknesses.

Brandt looks at me as if I've just grown two heads, and Gabriel gives me a puzzled look. He can't figure me out. Too bad. My request doesn't throw him for long, though.

"No can do, Harper. Been there, got the T-shirt. I have new fish to fry." I can see the bones of his tattooed ribcage peeking out at me and they move in a macabre dance as he positions himself for blowjob number two. What the hell is this guy on? If he popped a Viagra we could be at this for hours.

"You promised me you wouldn't do this," Brandt finally manages to spit, when he realises he's been backed into a corner on a one-way street to completely fucked up. His eyes are closed tightly shut, as if he's afraid of what he'll see when he opens them. The view isn't too awful, to be fair, but then, I'm not the man who had to put up with Gabriel's caveman shit for the last year or so.

Gabriel slides his hand along the side of Brandt's cheek, his thumb caressing the flesh softly. "Things change," he says, shrugging his shoulders. "Besides, you knew I'd come for you, eventually. What we had between us was too strong to let go of." That's a pained voice if I ever heard one. There's definitely some unfinished business between these two.

"I wasn't the one who let go of it." Brandt is still refusing to look at Gabriel, which is almost a crying shame as the man looks like an avenging God when he's half-naked. I'm pretty sure there aren't many who could resist that body, let alone face, and I'm not one of them. Perhaps that's why Brandt's keeping his eyes shut. I suspect Gabriel gets his own way far too often.

"It was a mistake and you need to let me explain." The words are curt and clipped. It seems there are more secrets in this room than just mine. I'm not the only one who has some explaining to do.

"Don't want to hear it. If you want to fuck me, go ahead. Just make sure you kill me afterwards, because if you let me live I'm coming for you, and I won't stop until there's a large hole bleeding out of your chest."

Brandt does open his eyes then, and the expression within them is dead. He's already preparing himself for what's ahead. It's a kind of emotional shut down. I've had to use the same technique no end of times with Mal.

It's just a blowjob; Gabriel won't actually fuck him. I'm trying to justify my lack of action in my head, but it's not working. I shouldn't be allowing this to happen. But if I talk everything becomes so much worse. Mind you, if Mal finds me with these two in tow he's liable to kill them anyway, so I might as well just tell all. I'll have no way to bargain for Brandt's life if the worst happens, but it was probably a long shot anyway.

"Harper, eyes on us, sweetheart, else there'll be trouble." That's Gabriel reminding me that this show is solely for my benefit. Actually, I suspect some of it is for his too, not that he'd admit it.

My eyes reluctantly refocus on the gruesome twosome. The evil monster is now tipping Brandt's head back, positioning him for penetration. How can I let something like this happen? How can I stand here and watch? But somehow I do, with the kind of sick fascination that is usually reserved for perverts and sex pests. Since when did male on male turn me on? I don't know the answer to that question, but the truth of the matter is that I am utterly entranced by this pairing. What is wrong with me?

"Harper go stand behind Brandt and fondle his balls, sweetheart. He likes that." Oh shit; now I'm going to have an active part in this?

"Wait, let me just get those ties off your wrists." The penknife comes out again, and with a quick slash my hands are free. "You even think of doing anything stupid and I'll take it out on poor old Brandt here, after I do some serious damage

115

to you. We clear?"

I nod. We are clear.

"Then what are you waiting for? Get on your knees and let those fingers get to work."

After a moment's hesitation, I obey. Gabriel will just start barking out more threats if I don't do as I'm told, and I have no wish to be hurt further, if I can possibly avoid it. My poor knees are still throbbing with pain, and my backside isn't faring much better.

Kneeling behind Brandt's prone body, I hiss as the flesh across my knees stretches. There's no other way to do this, though, so I bite through the pain until they connect with the concrete.

"Pain and arousal are such a wicked combination, aren't they?" Gabriel seems to know exactly what he's doing, every damn step of the way. In response, I grunt. I don't want to be aroused by this, but I am. Reaching under Brandt's naked body, my hand tentatively brushes against his thigh, and I can feel his legs tighten in response.

"I don't think Brandt's had sex in a while, Harper. While I'm pretty sure he's got himself off quite a few times in the last couple of days, I don't think self-service is anywhere near as good as the real thing. Let's make this good for him, shall we? How about we show him what he's been missing?"

When my hands gently cup his balls there's a soft, tormented gurgle from Brandt. It tells me that Gabriel's cock is already inside his mouth and my eyes flutter closed as I begin to imagine the two of them together. I suspect Brandt will never forgive me for putting him through this, and I'll have to live with that. It's just another thing in a long line of many fuck ups that my conscience will have to endure. I'm quite surprised that the weight of my misdeeds hasn't managed to crush me yet, but there's still time. If this goes the way I expect it to, I'll be ground into dust soon enough.

"That's it, Harper. Roll his balls in your fingertips and use your thumb to stroke his perineum. Let's make sure he has some fun." Brandt isn't on the same page as his friend. He's still very firmly in the 'I-want-to-murder-you' camp. Kicking back with his hips he sends me flying, and I'm guessing his teeth sink into Gabriel's cock because there is a moment's shocked silence, accompanied by a loud howl of pain.

"You fucking cunt!" Gabriel hisses, grabbing Brandt's hair while he gives him a vicious backhander. I swear I can feel the force of the blow from here and my eyes smart just thinking about it. He then bends down to whisper something in Brandt's ear, and though I strain my ears hard to hear what it is, I can't hear a thing. It's probably more threats. Whatever he's said, it seems to quiet Brandt down. One moment the man is trying to bust both hands off at the wrist and in the next, he's as placid as a meditating monk on marijuana. Something is most certainly up, but as per normal, I'll be the last to know about it.

"Harper, get your ass back here." Gabriel is back to shouting orders and I can't help but roll my eyes in frustration. Looking at the locked cell door with longing, I wonder if I'd have put more effort into my previous escape attempt had I know what was waiting for me. I have a feeling I could have given it an extra ten percent at the beginning, and that might have made all the difference.

"Grab his dick and work it, little lady, but don't let him come. Only I get to decide if he climaxes or not."

I can kinda see why Brandt split from the crazy control freak because he's probably more than your average nut job could handle. With this in mind, I do exactly as I'm told. I'm in a locked cell, with at least one crazy person who may or may not have murder on his mind. I'm taking no chances.

"Grabbing his dick," I confirm dryly, as my fingers close around the beautifully soft, silky skin of Brandt's cock, "and pumping it up and down." With any luck that should appease the beast or beasts. There's not one person in this room who's on my team, that's for sure.

After around two minutes Brandt is putty in my very capable hands, and I'm getting a perverse sense of satisfaction from making him suffer for a change. He's making cute little gurgling noises, some of which are due to Gabriel's cock trying to strangle him, but most are because my very talented fingers are milking the life out of him. I figure this is probably the least I owe him, and if he wants to come, I'm going to let him. Gabriel can take it out on my ass later. I'm not overly bothered if I can't sit on it next week because I probably won't be alive to worry about it.

Tightening my grip around Brandt's cock I give it a few more almost violent tugs, certain that he's about to come any second. Gabriel must think the same thing too, because he's suddenly yanking my hand away and pushing me backwards.

There's then a loud roar and Brandt's head snaps backwards as Gabriel has finally finished with him. Stepping under his victim's cuffed hands, Gabriel walks around the back of him, fastening his eyes on me. He's not come. I wondered if he'd just emptied himself in Brandt's mouth, but his cock is still straining proudly through the flies of his jeans. As he swaggers to me my gaze dips downwards, admiring the beauty of his body and trying to figure out how something so gorgeous can be so deadly at the same time.

"Want to watch me fuck your BFF, Harper?" I struggle to my feet, moving backwards in the hope the man can't get too close to me, but there is nowhere to run. Those incredible tattoos are moving with catlike grace towards me and I can't take my eyes off them. Before I know what's happening, he's got me pressed up against the wall and I can feel his cock trying to poke a hole in my belly. My breath hitches.

"Don't pin this on me," I hiss. "This is what you've wanted all along. Brandt is going to hate you if you go through with this, and he'll never forgive you. I don't give a shit either way." Gabriel's black eyes stare into mine before his lips trail a soft line of kisses down my cheek. I swear I lose half my brain cells in that instant. My body is officially uncontrollable.

"Ah, but we are going to pin this on you," Gabriel purrs. "If you want to stop it, all you have to do is talk. We're not asking for much, Harper. Just the honest truth. If you can give us that, then I'll stop all of this nastiness in its tracks. If not, I'll bend him over while you watch, and then, when I've finished with him, I'll start on you. I can be really creative when I set my mind to it. For a girl who likes pain, I think you'll appreciate just how devious I can be."

He picks me up, pushing me high against the wall as his cock slides underneath my pussy. He rubs it back and forth against my slit in long, slow movements. The friction has me gasping.

"I think I'm going to enjoy playing with my new toys, Harper. You're both locked inside this little cell with me until I've had enough of you, and I have a feeling it could take a month or more before I'm well and truly bored with you both. There are so many possibilities. I might even let you two fuck each other, when I need a rest. I wonder how many creative punishments I could come up with, before I broke you both? I suspect you'll fall faster than Brandt, but who knows? There's a chance you might surprise me."

He drops me without warning, and I land with a bone-jarring thud on the floor. My knees scream at the impact but I bottle the sound up, mainly because I know my tormentor would enjoy it.

"Okay, sweetheart. It's time to finish what I've started. You can go sit over there on the bed and watch. When we're done I'll see about punishing you for your earlier behaviour. Off you go now."

When I lurch forward, trying my best to follow his instructions, Gabriel lands a hard swat to my ass as he strides past me. I suck in a heaving breath and clench my fingers into fists. I want to kill him, but I'm well aware that I don't have the skill set for that job, and I'm pretty sure Brandt doesn't either. We are royally fucked, and in more ways than one.

Settling myself gingerly down on the bed, I grab the sides of the thin mattress for support and wonder if this will all end if I talk; there's no guarantee Gabriel will release us if he gets what he wants. I don't trust him any further than I can throw him, and as there's no chance I can pick the guy up with my pathetic arms, that isn't far.

"Are you sitting comfortably, Harper?" Gabriel calls out, almost pleasantly, as he throws a look my way. He is now standing directly in front of Brandt's ass, and I instantly feel sick. He won't do this. I'm almost ninety-nine percent positive there's no chance this will happen. Mind you, I've always been overly optimistic.

Playing to the crowd (me), Gabriel brings his penknife back out of his pocket, and my heart dives down to my feet. What is he up to now? I swear if he starts slicing him open I'm going to run over there and tackle him to the floor. Okay, fine, try to tackle him to the floor. I can't watch any more nastiness. I had enough of that with Mal.

But Gabriel doesn't do what I expect. Instead, he begins slicing a line through the back of Brandt's T-shirt. When he's cut a big enough split he simply grips both ends and tears the fabric in two. I swear Brandt and I both wince at the same time. We both know what's coming and for all my earlier talk, I am nowhere near as convinced that this won't happen now. It is happening.

"I like my men naked, Harper. Don't you?" Gabriel turns around to grin at me, while his fingertips draw a meandering line down the expanse of Brandt's back. It is covered with bold black, twisting tats, and when matched with Gabriel's torso,

I think I nearly come on the spot.

Gabriel hasn't finished, though. "I like them even better when they're naked *and* helpless." He then fists his cock, aiming the beast towards me, and I watch in horror as he primes it for his target.

"If you love him you can't do this. It'll kill him," I whisper. My eyes don't leave his fist. It's making swift, jerky movements, and the beast is once again standing firmly to attention.

"It's because I love him that I am doing this," Gabriel says, far too quietly. The soft sound of that voice sends shards of ice up my spine.

Gabriel then walks over to the bag he brought and takes out a bottle of lubricant. Pumping three squirts into his right hand, he slowly covers himself in the viscous fluid, before pumping another two squirts onto his fingertips. Positioning himself back behind Brandt, he presses his fingers firmly between his ass cheeks and begins to prep him for what's ahead.

"There's no lube in prison, Harper. Who said romance was dead?" Those words cut a steely, unpleasant path down my spine, while I watch those fingers do their worst. For some sick reason, I can't tear my eyes away.

Brandt, who has been fairly quiet until now, finally panics. He goes crazy against the bars, howling for all he's worth - and I can take any more.

"Stop it!" I scream. "For God's sake, stop it!"

Gabriel is placing his cock against the entrance to Brandt's ass, and I nearly go into meltdown.

"I'll talk!" I yell. "I swear I'll talk! Please stop it. No more. I can't take any more." I begin screaming hysterically, and I don't stop until Gabriel claps a hand over my mouth.

Chapter 20 - Harper

"I've stopped. I'm not going to hurt him. Calm down." This is Gabriel trying to placate me after what's happened. Understandably, it's not having much of an effect. I'm still screaming through the hand he has plastered over my mouth, and I'm not planning on stopping. I need to. Tears are pouring from my eyes, and breathing is almost impossible because when I throw a fit, I do it in style. I'm on all fours on the floor and waving my arms around frantically, which is the same thing I was doing when begging him to stop five minutes ago.

"I'm okay, Harper. He's taken the cuffs off. He's not going to hurt me. Calm down." This is Brandt. His voice is oddly shaky, but his tone is soothing. There are too many tears for me to see a thing, but I can somehow tell that he's close. "Move out of the way. Let me hold her. You're just making it worse." Someone grabs my arms and presses them to my sides. Oddly, I do not fight them. I can tell instantly that it's not Gabriel. I'm not sure how I know this, but I do.

"Don't fight me. Relax. We're going to let you go, Harper. We just want to know your story. We want to know what happened. No one's going to hurt you now."

The voice beside my ear confirms that it is indeed Brandt, and he then picks me up and cradles me in his arms. Considering we've both been horribly wronged in the past hour or so, this is almost laughable, but I don't send him away. For one, I haven't the energy, and secondly, his arms feel too good wrapped around me. The cold that seems to have permeated every single cell of my body slowly begins to recede as he rocks me gently back and forward. Eventually the tears subside of their own accord, and I rub at my eyes with trembling, fluttering hands.

"Shh." Brandt's been making comforting noises in my ear for the past twenty minutes or so, while we've rested on the bed. Through this I've heard the clank of the cell door being opened, so I know Gabriel has left us to it.

"What now?" I whisper. I can barely see straight, and I think it's a combination of exhaustion and stress. I just want to collapse somewhere warm.

"Now we have a drink. It's been a stressful day. We deserve a drink, don't you think?" Brandt is standing up, moving through the door of the cell and up the stairs of the frigidly cold room that has been my prison for the past few days. I hope this is the last time I'm down here, because I certainly won't be sad to see the back of it. I think I'd rather die than go back to the boredom and concrete, and that's saying something.

For some reason I expect to be taken upstairs to Brandt's bedroom, but I'm not. Instead, I'm wrapped in a soft, wool blanket and propped up on a leather armchair next to a roaring fireplace. A massive Victorian mahogany bookcase adorns the far wall, and there are velvet-lined tables around us. Card tables, perhaps? There is so much history contained within these walls, and I bet it has its fair share of stories to tell. I almost laugh. None so odd as the one currently unfolding, I bet.

Brandt is busying himself with a large bottle of what must be Scotch. The amber liquid almost glistens in the firelight as he pours, and he decants it into two heavy crystal glasses. Passing one to me, he sits down beside me and waits for me to take a sip. Perhaps he's hoping alcohol will help loosen my tongue. He needn't worry. He asked for this sorry tale and he'll get it. Now that I've committed myself to talk, it's almost a relief to finally get it off my chest. I've been holding it inside for far too long. There might still be a way to save him after this is all over. If I tell him to run, there's a chance he'll listen after he's heard me out.

"Drink." Brandt clinks the side of his glass to mine, and tips it up to his lips. He takes a hefty swig and settles into the armchair opposite me. Grimacing, I do as I'm told. I know what whisky tastes like, and I'm not particularly looking forward to draining the glass - but I'm going to do it all the same. Hopefully it will make the rest of the evening slightly more palatable. This past week hasn't been one of my best.

The first sip burns like acid. The liquid takes up residence down my throat with a burning path of fire, and I almost choke in the wake of the fumes it leaves. How can anyone find this stuff pleasant? Ignoring the misery it's just imparted, I take a gulp now that the worst is out of the way, and then another, waiting for the amber magic to do its thing.

"Steady there. That stuff will have you on the floor before you know it." Brandt swirls the liquid around in his glass and brings it up to his nose as if appreciating the scent. I have no idea what he can smell because when I try to do the same the vapours make my eyes water.

"I think I deserve a glass or two of this after the day I've had. As do you." My lips soften in sympathy. Gabriel has made himself scarce for the time being, but I'm positive he'll be back shortly. I'm not sure what Brandt's reaction will be, but I suspect things will be tense for a while.

Brandt smiles, but it doesn't reach his eyes. He's thinking about the same things that I am.

"Are you hungry?" Holding the whisky in both hands, he looks over it to examine me. I'm not doing too badly, considering.

"No, I ate off the floor earlier," I say dryly. I have no desire to repeat the experience any time soon, either.

He snorts. "I'd forgotten about that. Gabriel is a complete bastard when someone ruffles his feathers. He's being an asshole because he's trying to protect me. The sentiment is misplaced. I can do my own dirty work."

I nod. I already knew that.

He rubs his knee, which is once again clad in jeans, and sighs. His top half is still worryingly naked, considering I find it hard to control myself around the man, but I'm sure I've been given enough ammunition from Alex to hate men for life, so I should be good. Not all men are the same, my inner voice says silkily. The trouble is, in my limited experience, I've found that most of them aren't that different.

Brandt clears his throat, snapping me out of my daydream. "I would apologise for him, but there'd be no point. Gabriel is a law unto himself. Ultimately he's looking out for me, though." He drains his glass and sets it down on the table next to him.

"Didn't look that way a few minutes ago," I remark wryly. "It looked a whole lot like something else."

Brandt doesn't respond but looks at me pointedly. He's waiting for me to start talking. He wants to know the answers to all the questions that have been running through his head for the last five years. He's right. He does deserve to know. I need a minute, though. I might even need two. Thankfully, the whisky is starting to grow on me. My throat is now anaesthetised to the lava-like fluid that is beginning to warm my whole body, and the taste is growing on me.

Preparing myself to reveal all, Gabriel then waltzes in. Grabbing the bottle of whisky he takes a swig directly from it and plonks himself down next to Brandt. Oh God. He's still shirtless, too. I think I need more alcohol.

"Fill her glass up," Brandt says, as if he can read my mind. Gabriel does as told and then settles back with his arm around Brandt. Interesting enough, Brandt doesn't push him away. What is the deal with these two? If I were Brandt I would be raving mad about now, unless... oh fuck. How stupid am I?

"You were in on this from the beginning, weren't you?" My face darkens as I realise I've been duped. How did I not see this earlier? Putting my head on my hand, I laugh to myself.

Neither of them denies it, and neither have the grace to look guilty about it.

Actually, Brandt's face looks slightly flushed as he turns to speak to me.

"You promised, Harper. Start talking. I'm done with the nastiness. I'm due to get married in a few days' time, so I want to figure this shit out and get the hell out of here as fast as I can."

"You're leaving the country?" If this is the case, at least my conscience can rest a little easier. I don't need any more deaths on my hands.

"Hell, yes. I'm not going to be anyone's bitch, least of all my parents. Did you know they wouldn't even speak to me to coerce me into this marriage of convenience? They left that up to their solicitor. Nice touch, I thought. Anyway, as soon as I hear your side of the story, I'm off to whichever country will have me. Preferably somewhere warm with a sea view."

It's my turn to smile for a change. This makes me feel a little better. If Brandt is doing a disappearing trick in the next few days to get away from his bride-to-be, then I don't have to worry about finding his entrails decorating my neck. Yes, it's a thing, and yes, it's happened before. The deeper you dive into my past, the messier it gets - trust me.

Now all I have to do is figure out where to start, and as with all good tales, it's usually best to go back to the beginning, so that's what I do.

With my hands cradling my glass of Scotch, I tell them about how Alex and I met, and how jealous he was of Brandt. I tell them about the threats, and what I had to do to make sure Brandt wasn't sold down the river.

"I didn't put you in jail because I wanted to, I did it because I was forced to. I know you don't believe me now, but I hope you will. Just listen to me for a few minutes, okay? That's all I ask."

Brandt nods and keeps his face neutral. At least he's going to give me a chance. Gabriel looks like he wants to murder someone, but he's worn that look for most of the short time I've known him, so I don't let it concern me overly much.

"Alex was always jealous of you, Brandt. He saw the way I looked at you. He knew I'd sell my soul to have a night with you, and he hated it. He was captain of the football team, the one all the girls drooled over, and he could have any female he wanted. The man was fawned upon by everyone bar me. It drove him crazy. To add insult to injury, the closer he got to me the further I pushed him away. I knew he was bad news. I'd seen the type before, and besides, I didn't need any distractions; I was on a scholarship and I needed to study. The trouble was, Alex didn't take no for an answer. The more I tried to avoid him the crazier he became, until the guy was stalking my every move."

Brandt looks sceptical, and Gabriel has a faintly bored look on his face. It's entirely possible they won't believe a word of this, but that's not my problem. They asked for my story, and that's what they're going to get. What happens after that is up to them. Continuing with my sorry tale, I pick up where I left off.

"Eventually he cornered me in my dorm. He'd waited until he was sure I'd be on my own, and then he basically forced his way in. Alex told me if I didn't date him he'd plant drugs in Brandt's room and then call the cops. Now I know you're rolling your eyes right now, Gabriel, but the man was more than capable of it. Back then he was a small-time dealer, and Brandt can confirm it. Alex wanted leverage over me. He knew I wouldn't risk ruining Brandt's life. He went to a great deal of trouble to tell me all the horrible things that could happen to Brandt while he was in there, so I dated the bastard. I figured it would only be a few weeks before he got bored with me and that it would be the easiest way to get rid of him."

Gabriel's been itching to interrupt, but he waits until I pause, before stating the obvious. "But you did send him to prison. You sold him down the river, without a fucking boat let alone a paddle. I hope this story is going somewhere, darling, because at the moment it sure feels like a heap of shit." He holds his hands up as if to say 'what-the-fuck?' and I understand where he's coming from, but if he'd just be patient I have the answers to all his questions.

"I didn't send him to jail back then. This was six years ago. He wouldn't go to prison for another year. Alex never got bored of dating me, and a few years later I would be forced to marry him. His jealousy of Brandt never disappeared, though, and it drove him crazy."

Brandt raises his head and looks me in the eye. "Alex mistreated you, didn't he? Was he the one starving you?" Brandt's teeth are tearing into his bottom lip and his forehead is buried in a deep furrow of concern. Gabriel is nowhere near as convinced, but then, I never expected him to be.

I nod my head. "Up to a point. He liked me to look good," I confirm. "Once I got above a certain weight he would lock me in a room or beat me until the scales were back in the black." I don't really want to share this stuff, but they'll figure out these details on their own before long. Brandt isn't stupid, and nor is Gabriel.

"Sonofabitch," hisses Brandt, but he doesn't say anything further. The onus is on me to finish my story, so I continue.

"Wilkinson liked kinky shit, much like you two do." I stare at them both, knowing that neither of them will deny it. I don't know if Brandt has always been into BDSM, but if not, I have a rough idea who introduced him to it. Gabriel shrugs, but Brandt's eyes are dark. I think he knows where this is going, and I think that look means he cares, though I don't want to speculate. I'm under no illusions that he'll want me around after this tale is out, and it's probably for the best.

Brandt waves his hand for me to continue. His movements are jerky, as if he's containing his temper. I hope the rage is directed at my ex-husband rather than me, but I have no way of knowing.

"Alex liked to hurt me. When I did something wrong, he enjoyed punishing me. At first this would be something simple, like a spanking, but he soon tired of those. Then we'd move on to the paddle, whip or cane. After a while, when I became used to those, he had to continually develop new ones in order to control me. That was where the starvation came in, but he liked to lock me up for days at a time, and he also came at me with his fists. There was never a dull moment with my monster." I pause, wondering where I should go next. There are so many pathways from this one, it's hard to know which one to take.

"Wait. You put up with all of that just to keep me out of jail? Are you crazy? Why didn't you come to me? Why didn't you tell someone? Family? The police?

The dean? Jesus Christ, Harper. There had to be someone." Brandt's voice catches as he realises what I've gone through. He knows I'm telling the truth. He's probably the only one who will believe me, and that really sucks after what I did to him.

"I couldn't. While I have no family much to speak of, I had friends I didn't want to see hurt and he knew who they were. He also had me watched. Back then he only had one guy, but that would grow over the years to several armed men who would always be on my tail. He also threatened to get me flung in jail. Said he could drop a little something in my dorm at any time and that would be it. No one would believe a word I said from then on in. Bye-bye, Harper - watch your life disappear in an instant." I click my fingers because that's how long it would have taken my ex to make a colossal mess of me. If there was one thing Alex was good at, it was reading people, and he knew exactly what to use against you. When that changed, it didn't take him long to find something else.

Brandt sits there, rigid in his chair, mouth open as he tries his best to digest what I'm saying. He looks sick to his stomach. Gabriel is now looking a little off colour, too. The trademark smug smile is missing, and his jaw has hardened. Oh, these guys haven't heard anything yet - and I can't even tell them the whole story. That would crack Brandt wide open, and he deserves to know, but while Mal's still alive there's no way I'm saying a word. I know first-hand how dangerous that man is.

"Continue." Brandt pours himself another glass of whisky, as he's just necked the last one. His fingers wrap themselves around the glass so tightly I fear the crystal will shatter, but thankfully it holds firm. Summoning up more courage than I have, I do my best to try and finish this sad tale.

"When I first knew him, Alex wasn't into the hard stuff. He dealt mainly marijuana, hash, coke, steroids and amphetamines to anyone who would have them. He used teenage girls for his mules, and that arrangement seemed to work very well for him. He wouldn't get into the hard stuff until a little later, but that didn't mean he couldn't get his hands on it if he wanted to. The threat was real, and he made sure I knew it. He'd have me deliver his 'product' occasionally, just to see if I could be trusted. He also had it filmed. Alex had so much dirt on me he could have sent me down for a lifetime, but he never needed to. I think he always figured I'd run away, but I knew better. I knew right from the beginning that there was no escape."

"You sucking all this up, Brando?" Gabriel doesn't want to believe my sob story. He desperately wants me to be the villain in the piece, and this isn't working out well for him.

"Shut up," Brandt growls, giving him a warning look. It appears he's still on my side for the time being. That's something, I guess.

"Anyway, back to my fun tale," I say, as I feel my body begin to relax. The effects of the alcohol are finally taking hold, and I have to admit it feels rather nice. My head feels a little lighter and considerably happier. It's almost as if someone's removed a ten-tonne weight from my body and is now suspending it above my head. I know it will be back, but for the time being I'm going to enjoy my reprieve. "Alex did get into the hard stuff. It didn't take him long. He was approached by one of London's bad boys and offered a lot of money to take things up a level. He didn't need much convincing. My role in his life suddenly changed from a fun-time playmate, to something more useful. He basically pimped me out and got me to run drugs for him. I'd later find out he'd often earn money for both services, and that would tickle him no end. He found it extremely funny that he'd managed to crush my proud and haughty demeanour in the short space of a few years, and that he could get me to do just about anything for him, including fuck other men. The trouble was, Alex, as I've mentioned before, was an extremely jealous man. He could tolerate me being with other men as a one off, but not much more. Brandt drove him absolutely crazy because he knew I had feelings for him." I wave my nearly empty glass in his direction. "Even though Brandt was no longer a figure in my life, and I never went near him through choice, Alex couldn't bear the fact that I'd previously had the hots for him. I think he wanted him removed from the scene, and he wanted me to have a hand in it. This was probably to torture me, because as I've mentioned, this was his second favourite pastime. And when he got in league with one of London's most notorious bad boys, Mal Adley, he had the resources to take him out of the picture for good, so that's exactly what he did." Just saying Mal's name out loud makes me shudder, because it holds so many terrible memories for me. That man made Alex look like a pussycat.

"Are you okay, Harper?" Brandt looks at me with concern in his eyes, but it won't be long before I'm not his problem any more. I bet he can't wait to get rid of me.

No. I'm not okay, and deep down, I'm not sure I ever will be. I don't voice my opinion, though, I just give him a nod. All he wants is his story, and that's what he's going to get.

"Alex got Mal to do his dirty work for him, of course. He knew that Mal would make far more of an impression on me than he would, and he also knew I'd be so scared of the asshole I wouldn't dream of crossing him. Mal's a bit like Gabriel," I add for effect.

"Explain," says Gabriel dryly, playing exactly into my hands.

I decide to let him have it. "He doesn't have a conscience, and he knows how to play people to his advantage. He lives in that in-between place between sociopath and psychopath, with a good edge toward the latter. In short - he's a fucking monster." Gabriel raises his eyebrows but doesn't correct me, so I continue. "People are his puppets, and he has the power to make them do whatever he wants. Mal was the same, but he had more power. He had lots of money and men behind him." Brandt bites his lip. He knows the kind of people I'm talking about. He's spent the last five years in close quarters with them.

"Did he do anything to you?" he asks. I immediately choke on my drink. What didn't the bastard do to me? But sharing all that right now isn't helpful, and I have my tenuous grip on sanity to think about.

"He did plenty of things to everyone. If you crossed him, you could expect to be tortured then killed. He was known as the Airfix King. He liked to superglue his victim's eyes together before he started to work on them. Sometimes he'd glue their nostrils together, and often their mouth too. He'd then insert a tiny little hole with a straw, or some such thing, and then watch them go blue and desperately wheeze for air until they died. Sometimes he'd chop off body parts and glue them elsewhere. He had a fondness for 'tails'. I don't go into detail. These guys are smart. They'll figure it out.

"What did he do to the women?" Brandt isn't going to let this go. I have no idea why he wants to know about my messed-up shit, but if that's what he wants he can have a little taste, I guess.

I smile weakly. "Mal was into dangerous, kinky shit. He had even more fun with women than he did with men. He liked to tie them up and choke them - more often than not with his cock, but he had other means. He also liked to scare them witless. He'd make them watch while he killed someone, and then he'd tie them up and blindfold them, watching while they went batshit crazy with fear. It turned him on. He knew he could ask them to do anything, and they'd obey instantly. That was why he made sure they watched him work. After you've had an hour or two of Mal maiming, stabbing and gluing, you give him anything he wants. Self-preservation is an interesting thing. I'm sure you guys learned it behind bars, but you're not the only one who got a hold on it."

Brandt's face looks haunted. "So you're the victim here as much as me. You might even have had it worse than me," he whispers. He looks appalled. He's just realised I'm not the monster in this story, but he's wrong. I am that monster because at the end of the day, there is always a way out. I just wasn't brave enough to take it.

"Don't feel sorry for me," I whisper. "I should have been braver. I could have run. I could have gone to the police. I could have taken my own life. I had options. Instead, I inflicted pain and misery on others because I was scared. I did what I was told because I was too frightened to do anything else. That makes me no better than either Alex or Mal. I've done plenty of horrible things in my life since meeting those two, and I'm not proud of the fact. You were right, Brandt. I should have spoken up. Instead, I let those two assholes ruin your life as well as mine. What a fucking mess." Burying my head in my hands, the tears come. I have so many sins to atone for I hardly know where to start, but it feels good to tell someone the truth. It's cathartic. While it doesn't purge me of my guilt, at least I'm on the right road. There is a way I can make this better; I just need the courage to see it through.

Chapter 21 - Brandt

"It wasn't your fault. Just about every human being on earth would have acted the same way, if they were in your position. Once you're dead you run out of options." I reach over the table to give her shoulder a squeeze. She looks heartbreakingly frail, and I don't like it one little bit. I can't believe that I'd never considered she might be a victim too in all of this. It never occurred to me. It was just too easy to hate her. I see now that all my anger and rage has been misplaced, and it needs to be redirected. While I can't do much about her late husband, there are plenty of things I wouldn't mind doing to that bastard Mal Adley, and I have a feeling I only know half the story.

When Harper's tears turn into giant, choking sobs, I go and pick her up, cradling her in my arms as I press my forehead to hers.

"It's going to be okay," I whisper, although I know no such thing. What I do know is that I'm going to do my best to get her out of this mess for good. There must be a way.

"It isn't," she whispers after a few minutes have passed. Reaching up to her eyes with the heel of her hand, she tries her best to brush the tears away.

"You know this could all be bullshit," Gabriel says, matter-of-factly. "This girl could be playing you." Poor old Gabriel. He's still jealous as hell, and he knows he can't compete with a woman. This situation is laughable. Where on earth do we go from here?

"Yeah, and I'm sure she starved herself for fun, too," I say acidly, looking at the livid bruises along her arm. There's a good chance I put those there, and yes, I feel guilty. Why didn't I insist on getting the story from her sooner? Now I feel like a complete shit, and I absolutely deserve to.

"Hey, she might be anorexic. Lots of chicks are into that these days." Gabriel's attempt at humour is not endearing him towards me.

"Shut up or get out!" I bark, flinging my thumb towards the door so he gets the message. "If you want to be here, stay quiet and listen. I'm not in the mood for your antics." While I know the guy is on my side, he's only there if it suits his own best interests. I've known Gabriel too long. I know how his mind works. Yes, he'd walk over water for me, but only as long as that allows him access to my pants. Cynical, *moi?* Absolutely.

Gabriel frowns, but grabs the bottle of whisky and takes another swig. He's not going anywhere. The man is one stubborn asshole, I'll give him that.

Folding his hands over his chest, he glares at me and says, "I'm staying. Someone here needs to be the voice of reason."

I resist the urge to roll my eyes. If Gabriel is the voice of reason amongst us then we are extremely fucked - even more so than we were already.

Ignoring him, I bend my head down towards Harper and say, "What did Mal want with me?" I've already got the gist of the story, but I want to make sure I haven't missed anything. I assume he was just getting me out of the way to keep Alex happy, but that might not be the case. There might be something I've missed.

She takes her time to answer me, and it makes me a little nervous. It's as if she's thinking too carefully about what she wants to say. That can't be a good thing. Am I reading too much into this? Maybe she's just tired. For fuck's sake, we're all exhausted. Maybe we need to get some sleep.

"He was doing a favour for Alex. Alex knew I wouldn't have dropped you in it if he'd asked me himself. He could slap me around and share me with every man on the damn planet, but there was no chance I'd ever see you hurt for his amusement." Her voice tails off, but I can fill in the blanks, so I continue for her.

127

"But Mal was a different matter. Alex didn't want to see you killed. Mal, on the other hand, didn't give a shit whether you lived or died." Harper grimaces, and at first I think I've offended her, but she smiles ruefully.

"Yes, and no. Mal wouldn't think twice about putting a bullet in my skull, but I'm not frightened of death. It's what would come before that. Mal likes to play with his victims before he kills them, and I wouldn't have been the exception to the rule. The thought of him..." Harper can't finish the sentence. I know she's thinking about what that bastard made her watch, and I want to kill him for it. Scrap that. I'm going to kill him. It's the least I can do for her. While I've been locked up with three square meals a day, she's been kicked around, starved, shared, choked for fun, and made to witness horrendous atrocities on a daily basis. I thought I'd had it bad, but now I'm not so sure. I know she has barely glossed over the details of what has happened to her, and the further I dig the more shit I'll find - I'm sure of it.

Hugging her closer I whisper, "I think we've talked enough for one day. Want to call it a night?" She is shaking in my arms, and she looks ill. Her skin is so pale it could almost be translucent, and I'm partly responsible for that. I need to get her to eat something and put her to bed.

Harper nods and runs a hand through her hair. "Soup and a bath. Can we do that?"

A flood of guilt washes through me. I have behaved abominably. I've dislocated her arm, kept her naked and chained up, violated her in nearly every way imaginable, and left her alone with a complete monster - not that I'm much better, as I've just described. I have no idea if I can make this right, but I do know I will have to at least try.

"We can do that." I'm quite frankly amazed that she isn't demanding to be driven to the nearest hotel so she can get away from us. That just goes to show the amount of crazy the poor woman has had to put up with for the last few years. How did Alex Wilkinson turn out to be such a bastard? I always knew there was something off about the guy, but what I've just heard takes it to a whole new level. His life was clearly on the FUBAR scale, and he was doing his best to take everyone down with him.

Picking Harper up, I decide to carry her straight upstairs to the bathroom. Giving Gabriel a quick nod, I figure he can sort himself out. We can decide what we're going to do in the morning. It's been a long day.

Harper snuggles closer to my chest on the ride up the stairs, and I wonder, for the millionth time, just what it would feel like to sink into her. I've imagined doing so too many times to count, but I've always been focused on angry, violent sex. Things have changed. Now I no longer want to destroy her; I want to keep her safe. She seems to think her death is imminent, but I'm here to prove otherwise. Nothing is happening to her on my watch. I don't know what we're going to do about the situation, but it will come to me. Perhaps I just need to sleep on it.

Focusing my efforts on getting her bathed, I'm somewhat surprised when she doesn't protest. She has every right to chuck me out of the bathroom, but she is surprisingly quiet. Is this because Alex has brainwashed her into obedience? The thought is abhorrent.

"Do you want me to leave you to it?" I have to ask. I have no right to be here. My actions from the past few days mean we are little more than enemies until I can try my best to make amends.

"No. Stay with me, Brandt." She steps into the bath and smiles at me. She is not eyeing me with menace, the way I almost wish she would, and now I feel even more guilty. In fact, she's smiling at me with those soft doe eyes of hers, and my cock wants to spear her in two. Jesus. My head is all over the place. The almost-blowjob I received from her earlier nearly made me implode, and I can't think like that around her. Perhaps I should just walk out. I really shouldn't be here. In fact, I turn around to do just that, but she puts her arm out to capture my wrist.

"Stay," she whispers with heart-wrenching sincerity. "This situation is not your fault and I can't be left alone. I'm so damn tired I'll probably fall asleep in the bath. Help me, Brandt." Her eyes flutter closed as if to confirm her statement.

Her hand drags mine into the bath and she brings it up to her lips and kisses it. She hands me a flannel and I sigh. This will just make things harder, but what the hell. I concede to her wishes and wash her, doing so with infinite gentleness. After all we've been through together she should despise me. If I was in her position right now I'd be clawing my eyes out and hurling as much abuse as I could muster.

"Why don't you hate me?" I ask, while she takes a sip from the mug of chicken soup I've brought her. Combing a vat of conditioner through her hair, I admire the dark chocolate, glossy strands. When it's freshly washed it's just a mass of bouncy curls that almost beg me to bury my hands in them. It's been flat and straggly for most of her time here thanks to me, but that's about to change.

"I could never hate you," she whispers. "You were just trying to get your own back for what's been done to you, and I completely understand that. If it had been me mistakenly put inside for five years, I'm pretty sure I'd have been pissed, too." I don't get how Harper can be so calm about this situation. If I was in her shoes I wouldn't be. I'm sure I'd be screaming the house down right about now.

"Tomorrow we'll get you some clothes, and then we'll sort out what we're going to do about Mal," I say. Bringing the showerhead up to her head so I can rinse the conditioner off, I reach for the faucet. She immediately sits upright.

"No. You can't fight Mal. We had a deal. You're off somewhere hot, remember? You promised. Mal has too many men behind him, and his empire is one of total corruption. If he can bribe the local police to look in the other direction, you don't stand a chance against him. You'll get yourself killed. I'm putting all this behind me, and so should you. Get out while you can. I have no idea how long it will take him to find me, but it won't be too much longer. Tomorrow I'll be off. You'll get to start your own life, too. All of this will be over. We will never get the closure we deserve, but that's a small price to pay for keeping our heads attached to our bodies."

She gives me a long look. It's a hard one that says 'don't argue with me'. For now, I'm not going to. We'll save that argument for tomorrow, but there will be an argument. I'm not leaving her here like a sitting duck while she waits for that bastard to come and gut her.

"Why don't you come with me?" I say, holding up a towel for her. "We could both leave together and start afresh." Even if she doesn't want to be anywhere near me, I could still look out for her.

"You don't understand, Brandt. I won't be safe anywhere. Mal will come for me, and if you're anywhere near me you'll be next on his list. I've accepted the fact. The best thing you can do is get the hell away from me as quickly as is humanly possible. Go with Gabriel. He'll keep you safe. He's smart, and he's an effective killing machine. He'll get you out of a tight spot if necessary. If Mal does catch up with you, you don't know anything. Tell him you got your hands on me, but I ran away. Hopefully that will be enough to get you out of trouble, but I wouldn't count on it. You don't want to be anywhere near that guy. I wasn't exaggerating when I told you what he got up to. He has no concept of morality. He makes his own rules, and if you stand in the way, you're surplus to requirement. If he thinks you're a threat, he'll take you out. Avoid him at all costs. Promise me, Brandt. I've done enough damage. I couldn't cope if I thought your death was on my conscience too."

I grab her hand and clench it tightly. "If it makes you feel better, I promise." The promise is weak, though. I'm not leaving her to die. Whatever we do tomorrow, we'll sort out some sort of plan. I'm going to get her hidden away. Even if I have to marry Helena in order to have the cash to do so, that bastard Adley is not getting his hands on her. I can get divorced as quickly as I can get married, and I don't owe Helena anything. If she can deal with getting knocked up, she can deal with a quickie divorce. It's not my problem.

"What now, Harper? Shall I find you a spare guestroom? I won't put you anywhere near Gabriel. You can have one next door to me if you prefer. It's up to you. I'll get you a T-shirt for a pyjama top. Sorry I can't do any better than that today, but we'll get you sorted first thing tomorrow." I know it isn't much, but it's the best I can do.

She towels herself off quietly. "I don't want to be on my own," she whispers. "Can I stay with you this evening?" Her dark brown eyes look up to me pleadingly, and something inside me shrivels and dies. How can she still trust me after all that has happened? If I were her I'd want to put as much distance as I could between us.

"I don't think that's a good idea," I say, frowning. "If we're sharing a bed together I won't be able to keep my hands off you. You've had enough men take advantage of you in your life, Harper. You deserve better. You deserve so much more than this." I don't wait for a response but walk over to my bedroom to get the T-shirt I mentioned. The woman needs to cover up and get in a room with a lockable door. Then she'll be safe. Or safe from me, at any rate.

She follows close on my heels, and just as I'm reaching my hand in the drawer to pull out the top her hand presses down on my shoulder. "I don't want you to keep your hands off me. If I only have a short time left on this earth, I want to make the most of it. I..." Her voice tails off. She doesn't know how to ask for what she wants, and let's be frank, it's not the easiest question to ask. Damn, there are so many things I should do right now.

Giving her some clothes would probably be a good start. Opening the door to show her to the guestroom would also be a good idea. Gently saying no to her request should be next on my list. We're both fucked-up enough already, without adding anything else to the mix. This isn't a good idea, which also means it's nearly impossible to resist.

I try to tackle the problem as carefully as I can. "I don't think we..."

"Please, Brandt. Don't push me away. All I'm asking for is one night. You can give me that. Hell, you owe me that after what you've put me through today. I won't come crying to you in the morning. I'll get out of your life and you'll never see me again. I just want one night. The one I've been imagining all these years and thought I'd never get. I know you've thought about it. Don't tell me you haven't."

Her voice sounds a little desperate as she pleads with me. Damned if it doesn't turn me on even more than I am already, and considering I've had my eyes on her naked body for most of the day, that's quite a lot. Although the sensible thing to do would be to push her away, I'm not sure I have that much willpower. I've imagined this night so many times in my head for the past five years, every fibre of my being is clamouring to take her up on her offer. I know it's wrong, and I know I shouldn't, but if I don't do this I suspect I will regret it for the rest of my life, and I don't think I'll be able to live with myself. If I were a sensible person I'd wait until Harper and I had gotten to know each other a little better and she felt a little more comfortable in my presence, but I haven't had sex with a woman in over five years. My hormones are clamouring for this, and it doesn't help that I've been half in love with her for years. I don't just want this, I need this, and I'm not strong enough to deny myself, even though I know I should.

"Are you sure?" Now I'm not one to look a gift horse in the mouth, but I need reassurance here. Gabriel would laugh at me if he could see this, but I don't care. I want to do it right. I need to know she's thought it through.

She smiles at me, and it's a bright smile full of promise. For whatever reason it seems we're forgetting about our troubles. We're taking some time out and damned if we both don't deserve it.

A palm flattens gently above my waist, and I swear the heat coming through it burns. I want to run ten miles in the opposite direction to get away from this kind of intensity, and in the next moment I want to jump through the rings of fire in order to embrace it. Conflicting emotions chase and torment me, but I already know what I'm going to do.

"I'm sure. Please take me to bed, Brandt."

Harper's hand searches for mine, and I clutch it tightly. We're doing this. Tomorrow will be soon enough to hash out all our problems. Then I'll do my best to convince her that she doesn't have to leave. Gabriel and I are more than capable of taking care of her. If we can survive through the rigors of a high-security prison, taking on a drug dealer will be a piece of cake. If anyone can take him on, Gabriel can. He'll have some contacts.

Walking quietly to the bedroom, I open the door and turn on the light. I wince when I see there is still a pair of cuffs on the bedside table and cross my fingers that she won't notice them. Letting go of her hand for a second I reach to turn on the lamp. I want to see her skin cast in tones of amber and umber, and the soft glow will be much kinder on the eyes. Turning off the main light I sit on the bed and pat the space beside me. She comes slowly, with an apprehensive look on her face. I think she's worried I'm about to change my mind. That's almost laughable. I wish I had that much willpower, but this is a done deal.

Sitting down on the bed, her featherlight weight barely making an impression, she turns to me and says, "I'm sorry I hurt you. I never meant for any of this to happen. I know there's no way you'll ever be able to forgive me, but I just wanted you to know that I never thought you'd go to jail. I thought your parents would pull some strings, hire you a hot-shot lawyer and get you off with a couple of months community service. If I'd known you'd serve five years in a high-security prison, I think I'd rather have died." The tears glistening in her eyes confirm that she's telling the truth and all I want to do is hug her, so I do.

"Shh. Don't cry. I've already forgiven you and for what it's worth, if I'd have been in your position I'd have done the same thing. You were out of options." I let my fingers curl in the hair at the nape of her neck. It's still damp from her bath, and smells heavenly.

"That doesn't make it right." Her voice chokes on the sentence, and she doesn't say anything further. She's been through too much. We all have. I don't know what will make it right, but I do know that if I ever get my hands on Mal Adley, he won't be breathing by the time I'm finished with him.

Using my hands in her hair, I pull it until her head twists sideways. I then lower my lips to her neck and feast upon it. I could drown in this body for days. It's all I've been thinking about for the past five years. I've never obsessed about another woman the way I have with Harper. Knowing I'm finally about to sink inside her is a high that's better than any drug I've ever known. When I gently bite the skin there, she makes these little mewling noises that have my cock almost exploding in my pants. Shit. I'm going to last sixty seconds inside her, if I'm lucky. Way to impress a girl, Brandt.

"We'll make it right," I growl. Fuck my parents, fuck Helena, fuck Gabriel, and fuck Adley. Harper is mine and I'm never letting her go. I don't know why I ever thought I could. There has to be a way to make this work, and I'm going to find it.

"We can't," she wails as my fingers slide between her legs. She's still damp there, but it has nothing to do with the bath this time.

"Let's not worry about that now," I say, as my fingers slip slowly inside her. "Let's forget everything that's happened and just focus on the here and now. Think you can do that?" I growl softly. Releasing the fly of my jeans with the other hand because there's so much pressure there I fear I'm going to bust the zipper, I slide two fingers inside her and begin pumping. Thank God she's ready for me because I can't wait.

"Oh God, Brandt. I can't, I can't hold on for much..." her breath hisses out as my thumb caresses her clit and it's comforting to know she's almost as aroused as me. This has been a long time in the making. It seems like sacrilege to rush it, but the torture of postponing it for any length of time will be just as bad. We can take our time tomorrow morning. For now, I'm going to give in to the moment and let it take us where it will.

"Brandt, please, Brandt. Please." The last two words off Harper's tongue are staccato and urgent. I can feel her clit pulsing beneath my fingertips. She's so swollen she'd come with the flick of a fingernail, but I don't want it to end that way. I'm desperate to be inside her when that happens.

Withdrawing my fingers I slowly strip, pulling my jeans and boxers down in one fell swoop, and then I lie down on the bed. Beckoning her over, I decide we'll play this round a little differently.

"Want to be in charge for a change?" After what I've done to her, this is the least I can give her; I just hope I can hold out until she's come. Once upon a time I used to be good at this shit, but that was a long time ago. I'm badly out of practise.

Harper looks unsure, and then I remember that all the guys she's probably been with have taken rather than given. She's not used to it.

"Go on, give it a go," I say encouragingly. "How hard can it be?" I give her a wink and she grins at me.

"Looks pretty hard to me," she says, trying her best to stifle a giggle. I wonder if I've ruined the moment, but in the next she's straddling my legs and lowering her hot little snatch down on my cock. Fuck. Fuck. FUCK. It feels exquisite. I twitch inside her as she sinks slowly down my length, and I can feel my fingers curling into fists. Don't come. Don't come. Do. Not. Come. By some miracle I control myself, but it won't be for long.

When her hands come down to rest on my abs and her fingertips run down them one by one, I groan out loud. Still, I have to admit this is the best kind of torture. I haven't felt anything like it in years.

"Does it feel good?" she whispers. It's heart-breaking that she's so unsure of herself. Wilkinson really did a number on her, and I need to change that.

"So good, I can't even begin to describe it," I murmur. "My imagination of the past five years has in no way prepared me for the real thing, and I'm pretty sure this is going to be over really quickly. It if is, I promise to make it up to you immediately afterwards."

"With more soup? Or is it possible I could have some chocolate this time?" She gives me a cheeky grin as she grinds up and down on me. My breath feels like it's being strangled in my throat. The little minx is playing with me, and fuck if I don't love her for it.

"Very funny. With my lips and tongue, and they cannot even begin to be compared to chocolate. I think I am horribly offended." I frown, but she bats her eyelashes playfully and pumps up and down again. Oh. God.

"You'll have to prove that to me later. Verbal assurances mean nothing to this girl." Her smile falters but then brightens. I can probably guess why. All the men she's ever been with have lied to her constantly. Her life has been filled with cruelty and deceit. She probably expects that I'll be exactly the same, and who can blame her? My rage has been uncontrollable these last few days.

"I'll take that as a challenge," I whisper, as my fingertips begin threading their way up her thighs. Her skin is so soft. One moment I want to crush her to me, and in the next I want to place her in a glass box so no harm can come to her. She is so delicate and fragile. I'm afraid that if I got the chance to do what I really wanted she'd shatter and break.

Harper continues to pump lightly up and down on my cock for the next few minutes until both of us are breathing in laboured pants. I can't take much more of this.

"Go faster, Harper. Let yourself go."

She brings my hands up to her tits that I've been ogling since we started and says, "I don't want this to end."

"I don't want it to end either," I say, pinching a nipple lightly, "but I'm afraid my balls might drop off if it doesn't. They've been pining for this sweet body for quite a few years now."

"Then take it, Brandt. Show me what you've got." Bending down to flatten her body against mine, she rolls us over until I'm on top. This isn't what I had planned.

"I don't want to hurt you," I growl, but the feel of her underneath me is messing with my head. Her tits are now mashed into my chest, her hair is flickering gently around my face, and my thighs are itching to see how much this amazing girl can take.

Harper rolls her eyes at me. When this is finished we need to have words. If she wants to be on top she can be boss. If I'm on top, I'm going to be the one wearing the trousers.

"You can't hurt me, I won't break, and I like pain. Fuck me like you mean it, Brandt."

That's really all the encouragement I need, and I take her at her word because I can't hold back any longer. Bending my head down to take her lips with mine, I decide to show her what we've been missing all these years. One night with me and she'll change her mind about running away tomorrow - I guarantee it.

"You'd better brace yourself then, darling." My hips are already pushing forward, increasing in speed and intensity. It's as if they have a will of their own and I'm not going to interfere.

"Thank fuck," comes her reply and less than thirty seconds later, she screams out loud.

I join her a mere two seconds later, but hey, I fulfilled my part of the bargain and am feeling quite proud of myself. We lay there panting like idiots for what seems like an age before either of us can summon up enough energy to speak.

"Oh fuck, that was incredible," Harper finally growls, when she can manage to get a word out.

"That? Oh, you've not seen anything yet, sweetheart. Now I'm taking you up on the chocolate challenge."

Chapter 22 - Harper

I wake up the next morning with the biggest smile on my face. I'd lost count of the number of orgasms I received after five, but I can safely say that was the best night of my life to date. Oh. My. God. The things that man can do with his tongue. It kind of helped that I'd been fantasising about the interlude for forever, but the real thing surpassed all my expectations. Which is fucking fantastic, and incredibly awful, all at the same time. When I finally get the love of my life on the same wavelength as me, I have to leave him the very next day. As far as unfairness goes, this is up there with finding out about Santa Claus, but worse, because there's no loving parent around to give me a hug and whisper that everything is going to be all right. I already know it isn't. I know exactly what's going to happen, which is why I need to get out of here as quickly as possible.

Still, the moment doesn't have to end just yet. I'm pretty sure I can give myself another minute or two to ogle Brandt's sleeping form before the world around me collapses. I'm owed that much, surely?

Lying on my side with my head propped up on one arm, I sigh. The man looks adorable when he's sleeping. There's not a single worry line on his face, and he looks very content. Ah, what I wouldn't give for that look while I'm awake. I sincerely hope that Brandt manages to lead a very long life with a gorgeous wife, and that they'll be very happy together. He deserves at least that much. The thought of it makes me insanely jealous, but at least I won't be around long enough to worry about it. I've already accepted my lot in life and made peace with it. While it isn't the life I'd hoped for, if Brandt somehow manages to come out of this mess alive, I'll be happy.

Speaking of happiness, I'm itching to sneak a peek at naked, sleepy Brandt. His body is incredible, the stuff dreams are made of, and I figure I might as well get my fill while I can. It'll be a nice memory to have uppermost in my mind while Mal gets his glue out.

Peeling back the duvet a couple of inches, I suck in a breath as a vista of perfection greets me. God, the man is testosterone on legs. There isn't a pair of ovaries in the land that wouldn't explode at the thought of being up close and personal with that body. The tattoos just accentuate the picture of male beauty before me. My tongue wants to trace every line, pattern, and shape that adorns his wonderfully toned flesh. I'm going to give myself another hour to appreciate it, and then I'm getting the hell out of here. I'm only human, after all.

Fuck Mal. The thought of him getting his hands on me sends ten-foot steel spikes up my spine, forget about shivers. I know what he's capable of, and I know he'll want to have fun with me. He'll want to set an example. He always does. If I was a sensible girl I'd kill myself now. It'd be a lot less painful. The trouble is, I can't bring myself to do it. I've tried. Someone else is going to have to do it for me. Maybe if I run as soon as he sets eyes on me I'll get a bullet in the back. It says something that I find that an almost pleasant thought. Believe me it is, when you compare it to almost any other scenario that will probably pan out as soon as he catches up with me.

"Morning, gorgeous." Brandt's eyes flicker open and he rubs his hand across them, trying to propel himself in wakefulness. I bring my hand up to his face and caress his cheek gently.

"Morning," I reply, with a shit-eating grin on my face. It's hard to be depressed about your future after you've had so many orgasms you're almost too sore to move. I'm about to go for another one, too, if I have any say in the matter.

Brandt snakes his arm around my back and pulls me into him. His fingers once again tangle in my hair, and he growls. "Why didn't we do this sooner?" I can already feel his cock hardening against my belly, and I'm wondering the same thing.

I sigh. While my land of make believe is one thing, reality is quite another, and I can't afford to live in dreamland. "Because we both decided it wouldn't work - and it doesn't. We're from two different worlds, Brandt. Perhaps it's best this way. At least we've gotten a little taste of it. We can be thankful for that." Funnily enough, I realise I am thankful for this little interlude of paradise. For the first time in my life I've lived out my crush fantasy - and it was a whole lot better than I expected. Unlike many girls my age, I never wanted to sleep with celebrities or famous people. All I've done for the past ten years is obsess over Brandt Browning. It's nice to realise that I was right all along. He's awesome in the sack. I suspect he'd be a pretty good husband, too, if that was on the cards and I hadn't sent him to jail for five years.

"This is probably a really cheeky question, but is there any chance we can go one more time? Do you think you have enough energy left after last night? Say yes, Harper. Please say yes." Brandt looks adorable as his sapphire eyes gaze down at mine. I am total mush in the man's arms, and I love it. No other man on the face of this earth has ever had this effect on me bar Brandt. What is his secret?

"Hmm. Let me think about that one." I pretend to consider his offer, with my index finger pressed jauntily against my bottom lip, but my answer is a no-brainer.

"Don't torment me, Harper. I don't think I can bear it." To make his point clear he takes hold of my left nipple between index finger and thumb and squeezes it. I yelp, but it's the good kind of pain; the one I like. He repeats the move on my other nipple, and I'm even mushier mush than I was before.

"Yes," I squeal helplessly. "Yes. Please fuck me, Brandt."

"Jesus Christ, you're easy, Harper. Are you sure you don't have a headache or something? Where have you been all my life?"

I can't help but let out a laugh. "Nope, no headache, and even if I did have one it wouldn't stop me. Anyway, I think sex is supposed to get rid of a headache, isn't it? And great sex pretty much blows everything out of the window. Besides, I like pain. I think I've mentioned that before." I jab him in the ribs playfully, and he gets his own back instantly by tightening his fingertips around my nipples. The current that rips through me is high voltage and strips me of the power of speech. It's his turn to smile.

"So, you enjoy the kinky stuff?" He finally releases my poor little nubs, and they burn like twin orbs of fire. I still can't speak, so I simply nod in response. He drinks in the expression on my face and swears. "Fuck, you would be so perfect for me, Harper. We fit together in all the right ways." He's completely right and horribly wrong all at the same time. We're a paradox that was never meant to be together. This fledgling relationship will never see the light of day, and that's a shame because it could have been the start of something amazing.

"Cuff me to the bed," I whisper, when I can finally talk again. Brandt shakes his head.

"You're crazy," he whispers. He's not wrong. "Why do you trust me? After all that has happened with those other bastards, why?" I don't know, but I do. My gut instinct is rarely wrong. It was right about Alex, and it was certainly right about Mal.

"Just do it," I growl, eyeing the cold hard steel that winks at me from the bedside table. The temptation to use them is too great to resist. I want to be utterly helpless, and at the man's mercy. He's the first person who will respect what I'm offering him - my trust. Brandt has always held my heart in his hands. Normally he's kind, gentle and affectionate. He's the type of person that would give you the coat off his back if you needed it, walk you home, or stand up for you while the school bullies were trying to tear a strip off you. Brandt's done all this and more for me in the past. I haven't forgotten a single kindness, and I know that man is still in there; I just have to bring him back out into the light. But what am I thinking? I know I can't have this. I am getting a little carried away with my fairy tale.

Just as Brandt reaches for the cuffs my fairy tale takes on a whole new light, because there's a crash from downstairs. Later, I'll realise the noise was a pivotal moment in my life where everything that was good instantly turns to shit. One moment I had hold of something shiny and bright, and in the next the sky clouds over and hailstones the size of cricket balls begin to fall.

Don't panic, I tell myself. My immediate thought is that Gabriel's gone cuckoo and is smashing stuff up. Meanwhile, Brandt jumps out of bed and pulls his jeans on. Grabbing a shirt from his drawer, he drags it quickly over his head and moves towards the door. He stops just short of opening it. There's already the sound of footsteps on the stairs - and there are several pairs. This isn't Gabriel, and that can mean only one thing. My eyes close in horror and I can't move. Even my little finger is paralysed. Jesus Christ. Please let no one die.

The next ten seconds feel like the longest of my life. Doors are being flung open left, right and centre, and it is only a matter of time before they reach ours. Instead of heading out into the storm Brandt flattens himself against the wall on the other side of the door. It's a sensible move, but utterly futile. If it's who I think it is on the stairs, he's not going to fall for that. If Brandt had a weapon he might have stood a chance, but he's got nothing, and he's outnumbered. I wonder if Gabriel will fare any better.

Just as the thought enters my head I hear a crash from a room down the hall. There are loud grunts and moans, and the sound of banging and splintering wood. Gabriel isn't going down quietly. Good for him. There's then the sound of gunshots and both Brandt and I jump. Oh my God. What just happened?

We both give each other a look, but that's instantly shattered as the door is flung open wide. Four men burst in waving pistols about, and they immediately centre on me. As I predicted, though, they aren't stupid. They're scouring the room, and as the door closes they spy Brandt. He manages to get his arms around someone's neck, positioning himself so the man is in front of him. That would work if there were only two of them, but he's facing far too many to win this war, and more are on the way. I can hear them. Three more men barrel into the room, with two more behind them, one of whom has Gabriel walking in front of him with a gun pointed at his back.

Mal follows shortly after.

When my eyes connect with his I swear my soul shrivels up and dies. Why didn't I leave first thing this morning when I said I would? Mind you, these two would probably still have been killed in my wake, so perhaps it's best I'm still here as a bargaining chip. Maybe I can get them away with their lives intact. It's worth a shot.

Mal turns to Brandt and says, "Drop him," dangerously quietly.

"Do it!" I scream because I know full well Mal doesn't ask twice. Brandt doesn't though, and in the next instant Mal turns around and shoots Gabriel in the leg. While Gabriel let's out a yell and drops to the floor he points the gun at me, looking at Brandt inquiringly.

Brandt releases his choke hold around the guy in front of him and is pushed to the floor, where the man pistol-whips his face with the back of his gun. Brandt's face snaps backwards, and when it reappears there is blood pouring from his nose. It's probably broken.

"'Arper. Long time, no see. Did you miss me?" Mal takes a couple of long strides to the bed and whips the cover off me. His gaze drags its leisurely self over my naked body, and my skin scrawls under the intense scrutiny. Running a hand up my leg he digs his fingernails into my inner thighs so hard I can't help but yelp. Brandt tries to move towards me, but he's swiftly stopped with the butt of a gun in his back. Hopefully that will keep him quiet because trying to save me will almost definitely get him killed.

"I thought I told you to stay where you were?" Settling himself down on the side of the bed, Mal shakes his head and makes a few disapproving noises.

Deciding to play nicely, I say, "I was evicted. No one paid the rent on my flat after Alex died." It's the truth. He can go check if he likes.

"You coulda rung me, darlin'. Nice girls don't go runnin' out on their partner to shack up with two blokes, now do they?" Mal sounds pissed, and that's a really bad thing where he's concerned.

I try to keep the panic out of my voice. "I didn't. Brandt was the guy I put in prison for you. Remember? He kidnapped me and brought me here. He was trying to get me to talk." The truth - my version of it - just might save my ass for a change. Well, not my ass, but hopefully Brandt's and Gabriel's.

"Ahh. So it's not as bad as it seems, then. I was quite concerned for a moment, 'Arper. I don't take kindly to being disobeyed. You know that, sweetheart." Daggers bite through my flesh as Mal's fingers rise towards my sex and I know what he's about to do next.

"I would never disobey you willingly," I whisper, lying my ass off.

"So you didn't talk then? Believe me when I tell you I can find out rather quickly." Mal gets a little tube of glue out of his pocket and spins it in his fingers. My heart feels as heavy as lead, and my pulse rate could power space rockets.

"I didn't tell them anything. Why would I? They kept me penned up in a little cell downstairs, knocked me about a bit, didn't feed me, wouldn't let me sleep - that kind of shit." There's something I'm deliberately not telling him, but he won't let that slide for long.

"And did they fuck you, sweetheart? You know I'll be pissed if they fucked you. That's why Alex got one in the brain, wasn't it? We decided we wanted to be exclusive, didn't we darlin'?" No, he decided he wanted me to be a good girl. He still fucks anything and everything that moves. I sensibly don't voice this thought out loud.

"They had cuffs," I whisper miserably. "I had no choice. You know you're the man for me, Mal." This could all backfire on me massively if I'm not careful, but it's worth a shot.

"Fine. Shoot them both." Mal waves his hand behind me, as if he's asking his men to go have a cup of tea. This is boring shit as far as he's concerned. He's found a problem, and a bullet will take care of it.

"Don't kill them. They don't know anything. I put him away for five years. He had every right to be pissed. You'd have done a lot worse if I'd done that to you, and you'd found me." Sitting up, I cup my hand around Mal's face and caress it gently. "They're both ex-cons. Put them to work somewhere. Find a use for them. Preferably far, far away from me. For now, can't we just get out of here? I've had one hell of a ride for the past few days and I can't tell you how good it is to see a friendly face." Fuck, I hope my acting skills are up to par. All I want to do is break down and cry, but that will almost guarantee their deaths and I can't have that weighing me down.

Mal thinks my request over, snapping his gum loudly in his mouth. "So noble of you, wanting to save these fuckers. You're not still in love with that pretty boy, are you?" He points to Brandt. He knows exactly who he is. Alex was obsessed by him, and in the end, he and Mal were pretty close. Until he died, of course. Mal doesn't really get close to anyone. If Alex had been a little smarter he'd have figured that out.

"Tell you what, princess. If you let these two fuck you up a little, while everyone watches, I might find a use for them. I'm not promising them a long life or anything, but at least it'll give me a chance to get some plastic sheeting underneath them when I decide to finish 'em off. Does that work for you? You know I like to watch, 'Arper. Of course, if it doesn't we can go back to the original plan. What's it to be?" Mal has a little smile playing around the edge of his face and I want to slap it off him.

It's my turn to pretend to consider the offer just presented to me. In reality, there is no choice. I'm probably not extending their lifespan by more than a few hours or days, but that's their problem. They'll have to figure it out. If Brandt has Gabriel with him, he stands a chance.

"Oh, just kill them then," I say, shaking my head. This is purposely done. Brandt and Gabriel nearly choke on their tongues behind me, but I have my reasons. If I agree immediately Mal is likely to shoot them both on the spot. If he thinks I care for them he won't want them around. If he thinks the last thing I want to do is fuck them, however, it's an excellent way to torment me - and he just loves doing that. Watching me with other men is one of his favourite pastimes. As long as he picks the man, and it's a one off. He and Alex are so bloody similar it's almost scary. They love to control people. Maybe they were brothers in a past life?

I stand up, as if getting ready to go. I am naked as the day I was born, but you wouldn't know it to look at me. My posture is proud and regal. It won't be for long. This is reverse psychology at its finest. I hear a gun being cocked behind me and bite my tongue, hoping no one is about to die.

"Wait, wait." Mal stands up and shakes his head. "I liked my idea. I think we're going to need to play it through. As you said, you did put him away for five years. Perhaps we should let him and his friend have some fun with you. Hell, if they do a good job maybe I will let them live. You can tell a lot about a man by the way he fucks. If they're evil bastards, I'm pretty sure I can find something for them to do. Maybe I could even use them to keep you in check, darlin'." His smile is wide and feral, and my face looks horrified, which happens to be his favourite look on me. Great. Now we're out of the frying pan and into the fire. I just hope these two can somehow get out of here alive when they're finished with me. I'm a lost cause, but they stand a chance at making it. If they run far enough away, Mal will get bored of the hunt. He hasn't got a beef with them.

Unfortunately for me, I've seen too much. I'm living on borrowed time. He may keep me alive for a few more days, maybe even weeks, but he probably already has a tombstone with my name on it. The thought makes me laugh. Mal's far too tight for that. I'll be buried in concrete somewhere, never to be discovered again... if there's anything left to discover, that is. What a pleasant thought.

"'Arper, we're waiting. Get back on the bed, darling." Mal indicates that his men should let Brandt and Gabriel go, and they advance towards me warily. Gabriel is regarding me with malevolence, and that's unsurprising as he thinks I've just dropped him in it. I think Brandt has seen through the act, though. He looks worried. He'd better snap out of it. Mal wants a show, and he'd better deliver. His life is going to depend on it.

Thanks for reading!

Beautiful Tyrant
Harper

Brandt and Gabriel have me tied down on the bed. While Mal points a gun at them, they're going to mess with me a little. Gabriel looks almost gleeful at the prospect, Brandt not so much. It's too bad. He might as well get his kicks where he can.

After Mal's finished with them, hopefully he'll find something unpleasant for them to do. He always needs a patsy to murder someone or other. My fingers are crossed that the pair can find an opportunity to run and get out of this mess. That's what I'd do if I had the chance.

Unfortunately for me, my last few days are to be spent at Mal's warehouse. The Airfix King is about to take his superglue addiction out on me, before he chops me up into little pieces and leaves me for dead.
    This is probably not the time to wish I'd killed myself earlier, right?

Please help a starving author by leaving a review

Ok, so I lied about the starving part, but books need reviews on Amazon in order to sell. Without them, they wither and die, and so do the authors. Honest.

You don't have to say much, and you can stay anonymous - just set your Amazon reviewer name to something like 'Amazon Reviewer 3982.' Anyway, here are a few examples of what you could write if you were a truly wonderful person who didn't mind doing a good deed every now and again:

This book was so awesome I forgot to feed my kids. Thankfully they reminded me, over and over again, so I haven't managed to kill them yet. Phew.

This book sucked. It was even worse than a certain president's infamous hairdo, and that is saying something.

Gabriel and Brandt are so hot, I want a threesome with both of them. As long as I'm allowed a safe word - because Gabriel is a little bit on the seriously freaky crazy side.

I would rather read War and Peace than this ridiculous smutty drivel and nonsense. Seriously - all Mandara talks about is orgasms, sex, and hot blokes.

Who wants to read about that?

Ms Mandara does not write quickly enough. I need her to release a book every month at the very least, and she keeps me waiting for months, and worse - ends everything on a horrendous cliff-hanger. I have a love/hate relationship with this author. She should probably be spanked.

This is not a good book to read on the train. Especially when the hot guy sitting next to me kept trying to read it over my shoulder.

Don't ever read this book to your wife. She will demand sex for days on end and will suddenly become insatiable in bed. Seriously, I have been considering divorce...

Any of these will do (I'm more partial to the nice ones...) and it will give you extra karma points that will be returned to you in due course in the form of cookies, money, hugs, and wine. Honest.

Thank You!

I just need to say a big thank you to all my wonderful beta readers who always step up to the rather tricky task of reading my books before they've had a good edit. Without you, my books would probably be unreadable as you manage to figure out that my heroine can't see things when she's wearing a blindfold, and that it's tough for her to talk if she's gagged. You also help me to correct my numerous errors and give me your honest opinions, which are more valuable than pixie dust. (The stuff that makes you fly without wings). (That is what pixie dust does, right?) A special thank you to Nikki! You know who you are :)

Another big thank you to all of my readers and fans - you always manage to brighten my day and make me remember why I started this journey. Please drop by anytime via my Facebook, Twitter Page, or email if you want to contact me. I don't bite - honest!

So, for everyone who's helped me along the way, thank you, thank you, thank you!

Stay tuned for more Harper and Brandt in **Beautiful Tyrant**!

Love 'n hugs to all xxx

Bio

Christina Mandara is a USA TODAY bestselling author and tends to write dark romance with lashings of kinky naughtiness. Her favourite pastime is travelling, and if it involves sun, sea and... sand then it's all good.

In her spare time she's usually cuddled up with a good book, exploring the countryside or baking in the kitchen. In fact, she loves her kitchen so much she's one of few women who wouldn't mind being tied to it! Her first and foremost love is writing, however, and more often than not you'll find her on a laptop spinning tales of romance, erotica or dark, paranormal fantasies.

Be the first to know about Christina's new and upcoming releases and get notifications on freebies and discounts by following her social media channels below: